La Basquaise

Oruela lay in a semi-conscious world of half-waking dreams. A serpent slithered up the ancient bark of a tree and perfumed flowers opened like silken vaginas, dripping their golden pollen on the cool grass. A naked man beckoned to her and, as she went closer, she could see he held a fruit – a dark purple fig. He peeled it and offered the ruby flesh to her lips. She sucked at the sweet juice as if her life depended on it. But as she swallowed the scene changed and she was falling, falling . . .

Other books by the author:

The Big Class

La Basquaise
Angel Strand

BLACK LACE

Black Lace books contain sexual fantasies.
In real life, always practise safe sex.

This edition published in 2004 by
Black Lace
Thames Wharf Studios
Rainville Road
London W6 9HA

Originally published 1995

Printed and bound by Mackays of Chatham PLC

ISBN 0 352 32988 2

Prologue – Biarritz 1925

'*Attention, s'il vous plaît!*' Madame Rosa had a voice that was rich, throaty and created for talking dirty. She moved like a liner coming into port, her dress floating around her in a rosy pink wash.

The salon of La Maison Rose grew quiet. There were about fifteen well-heeled men in the room attended by beautiful, semi-naked women who came to rest like butterflies on laps, on cushions, on the thread-flowers of the whorehouse chintz.

A couple of young men sitting on the soft green velvet couch exchanged a conspiratorial smile. Jean Raffoler was twenty-four and in the peak of masculine health. He had long, dark, curly hair and light brown skin. His body was big and strong under expensively cut evening clothes. He had loosened his black tie and he sat with his legs apart, confidently.

Paul Phare was in his early thirties and had a rebellious lock of sandy blond hair that wandered into his smoky green eyes. He was in his shirt sleeves, his cravat was awry and a day's growth of beard showed on his fine chin. A young woman in a chemise sat on the floor at Paul's feet, resting her head on his long, lazily crossed legs. He stroked her curly ginger hair with a tender, masculine hand.

'The moment for which you have been waiting has come,' trilled Rosa. 'My dear Baron has returned from his travels at long last, from the far-flung corners of the world, and he has brought with him some very charming erotica.'

She sailed across the room, a pair of naked young males bobbing in her wake, and stopped in front of red velvet curtains. She nodded to the boys. They clasped the curtains and drew them back. In the small room beyond stood a squat male figure carved out of opaque yellow stone. Its *pièce de résistance* was a huge, erect phallus, the head of which gleamed softly in the light from two thick, long beeswax candles.

The Baron stepped out from the shadows. He was squat too and he glowed with perspiration. His smile was accentuated by a long scar on one pale cheek and seemed to spread to his ear. He flicked his pudgy fingers at the boys and they each lit a flame from the candles. They fired a pair of silver incense burners with movements graceful as swans. The room began to fill with plumes of heady scent.

'Gentlemen,' said the Baron. 'The following performance is based on a rite over five thousand years old. This figure was found in the tomb of a queen. Around the walls of the tomb paintings depicted the dance that you are about to witness. It is re-created faithfully and lovingly for your enjoyment by a descendant of this ancient and beautiful queen.'

The boys began a soft roll on little drums as a tall, black girl, her hair cropped closely to her head, writhed out from behind the curtains. She wore nothing but charms and shells and beautiful bells. Every graceful movement she made was accompanied by the music of trinkets. From her earlobes hung huge silver hoops bearing little bells in their centres. Round her neck and clicking between her handsome breasts were hundreds of glass beads. At her waist a thousand tiny sparkling gems made a fine girdle and around her left thigh some kind of reptile had given his skin for a thong.

2

She shimmied, rooted to the spot like a tree in a breeze, stretching her arms up as if to the goddess of the dance. The men in the room grew still. When she could feel the whole room in her power she began to move.

Slowly she gyrated her hips, in half-moon shapes, to the drums. Her hands cut through the air like the blades of knives. She parted them at her navel and rested them on her thighs and then suddenly, she thrust her hips forward, opened her legs and showed off her best jewel. The movement was like a magician who shows off the beautiful girl he is about to saw in half. Her sex was beautiful. A mature rose. Someone in the audience growled with desire.

She turned her back on them and mounted the dais, taking some oil on her fingertips from a silver tray as she went. Slowly she oiled the head of the huge phallus. As she worked she spoke in some unknown language and her words became a strange, lilting song that twisted around the room like a rope.

The men were spellbound as she violated the statue, her body glistening with the exertion, her strong thighs rippling as her movements up and down the phallus gathered momentum. She built up to a crescendo and climaxed with a wild call that silenced the catcalls of the loutish element in the crowd, piercing everyone to the core.

Paul Phare reached for a cloak that was behind him and with one adept movement he covered himself and the girl who rose from the floor into his arms.

Jean Raffoler sat still as a bird entranced by a cobra.

But the show was not over. The Baron was announcing in his thin weedy voice that the girl would tell them a story. Hardly two minutes passed before she re-entered the room and, sitting in a big red-plush wing chair, she began:

'My people,' she said in accented French, 'believe that if a marriage is not right then it will bring misfor-

3

tune on the whole people. So the ancient ritual of the lizard is always observed. On the Day of the Marriages a very special lizard is pressed into service by each couple who wants to be married. It will take the first juices from the man's penis and take them into the woman's vagina. If the lizard refuses at any stage in the ritual it is taken as a sign that the couple must not marry. No one has ever dared go against the rule because to do so would mean living as an outcast.

'To guard against the chances of a refusal, each spring the young women who want to, go with more experienced women to the high ground where this lizard has his habitat. Once there they set about capturing and training as many as they need.

'The young women are shown how to hunt down the creatures by way of calls and beautiful songs. They beat the ground, make thunder with their fists until the lizards are drawn, compulsively, to the camp. Then the women decorate their bodies. They paint circles around each others' nipples with the juice of many different and beautiful coloured berries, till the nipples seem so huge that they almost cover the whole breast. Then they plait soft hair from female animals into their own pubic hairs and bead it so that it falls around their thighs. They make the lips of their vulvae red with the leaves of a sacred plant and paint a great area around in beautiful colours, so that the whole sex seems to reach out across their thighs. Lastly, their eyes and their lips are adorned with the brightest colours in nature and they drench themselves in the perfumes of the orange flower, jonquil and jessamine.

'At length they dance. They dance morning, noon and night; wild, sensual dances that become more and more frenzied until it seems that the camp is filled with huge nipples and whirling vaginas.

'The lizards grow mad with what they see and smell and hear and many of them die in the rush into captivity. But the dances don't end until the women are exhausted. And then they sleep where they drop. Their

4

colours smear and run in a crazy mess and everyone revels in it.

'When enough lizards are captured we gather roots that are shaped like the male organ; mandrakes they're called in Europe. It's easy to train the lizard to lick the root because if his reward is to snuggle between the legs of a woman, this animal will do anything.

'Within seven or eight days each woman will have her own, trained lizard. She decorates him with precious stones and gems. She carves pieces out of his very thick skin and embeds her mother's own jewels that are handed down, right into it. The skin grows back to hold the gems in place. The lizards have short lives. They live while the marriage is young and produces children and then they die. We keep their skeletons and use them as charms to bring our lovers to our beds.'

'See,' said the Baron, stepping forward. He grinned as he held out his podgy palm. In the middle of it sat a tiny white skeleton. 'There were no more female children in this family and I was given it by an ancient who knew she was near to death. I paid handsomely for it.'

With the story at its end the dancer rose and, virtually unnoticed, she left the room. Virtually, but not completely. Jean rose and followed her.

Evidently he was not successful. He came back into the salon a moment later. He approached the group talking with the Baron and hovered. A butterfly, with straps falling off her rounded, peachy shoulders, came up to him and entwined her fingers lovingly in his long, curly hair. But he brushed her off gently. Finally he butted in.

'I'd like to talk to the dancer,' he said to the Baron.

The Baron performed an obsequious little bow. 'I'm sorry, monsieur, but she is mine.'

'I sincerely beg your pardon. But I really do just want to talk to her,' said Jean firmly.

The Baron touched him on the arm. 'But everything has its price, monsieur.'

A note of distaste crept into Jean's voice. 'Let me be clear. It is the lizard that interests me. Might I be able to buy one? A live one?'

The Baron drew in a breath between his teeth, making a hiss like a plumber. 'Well, I don't know,' he said. He stroked his chin.

'Everything has its price?' mocked Jean.

'It may be arranged,' smiled the Baron. 'Your name, monsieur. I should like to know with whom I am dealing.'

'An unusual request, monsieur, in such a place. If you want credentials, I suggest you speak to Rosa. She knows me well and knows that I have money enough.'

'No, monsieur, you don't understand. Your name would be, how shall I say, a gesture.' He grinned. 'I am very discreet.'

'Impossible. Either speak to Rosa or I'm afraid . . .' said Jean.

'Very well,' said the Baron.

When Jean returned to the green velvet couch Paul was stroking the chin of his girl.

'You have the jawline of a goddess,' Paul was saying.

'Oh, you!' she giggled. 'You bloody artists are all the same. Goddesses, mices.'

'Muses, darling, muses,' said Paul.

'Whatever they are, I'm a real woman and I want you upstairs where I can fuck you.'

Paul threw back his head and laughed. 'Sounds wonderful but you'd better not let Rosa hear that. I can't afford you.' He turned to Jean. 'Can he get it?'

Jean sneered. 'He's a cad. He tried to sell me his girl.'

But their conversation was cut short. Rosa was bearing down on them, observing Paul with open hostility. Paul rose from the couch. He was tall, slender. He picked up his cloak. He had pushed his luck by staying for the Baron's presentation. Rosa let him spend his afternoons taking photographs of the girls and didn't charge him for their time. At present he was experimenting with movement. The girls seemed to enjoy

6

themselves rolling around on the Persian rug while he captured them on film. He did it with love and, of all the people he knew, they were the only ones who seemed to believe there was something fine in what he was doing. They dreamed together that the pictures would hang in Paris galleries and capture the attention of the whole world. Besides, he always gave them proper portraits if they wanted them and some of these sold on the seafront as postcards. Perhaps Rosa resented the fact that this money all went to the girls, without a cut for her.

Jean asked him to stay, but he refused. 'I want to develop some work,' he said.

Rosa brushed the seat he had vacated before she sat on it. 'Now, Jean, tell me everything, dear,' she said.

'I want one of those lizards.'

'Well, you know the Baron's a crook, dear. I wouldn't trust him as far as I could throw him. But, as I always say, if you want something badly enough in this world, you have to take risks.'

'Rosa, come on. You know I can't get my family name mixed up in anything dubious.'

'I know, I know. What is it you have in mind? You want me to act as a go-between? For a small consideration, dear, I shall be pleased to. That will sort things out nicely, won't it? And then even if he cuts up rough I would deny any involvement on your part.'

'Thank you, Rosa!' said Jean eagerly.

'I can't guarantee your money, my love, but your reputation is safe, and that of whoever you want to share your little whim with.' Rosa's eyes twinkled and her gaze strayed to his well-formed thigh. 'Now let me send one of the girls over to soothe away your worries while I deal with the Baron. Can't have any of my gentlemen solitary now, can I?'

'Send me Annette,' said Jean, stretching his arms.

The Haberdasher's Upstairs Rooms

'Here you are, dear,' said the tiny, red-haired, haberdasher. She took a key from under the counter and gave it to Oruela Bruyere with a wistful little smile. 'You are a lovely girl, my dear. A lovely, sad girl.'

'I don't know what you mean. I'm not sad,' said Oruela. She was feeling wonderful. Every cell in her body was looking forward to the touch of love.

'Mmmm,' said the little woman, wistfully.

Oruela went up the concealed staircase that rose secretly from the midst of silks and stockings. What a funny woman, she thought. The haberdasher was the aunt of her maid, Michelle, who said she was as good as a mother. Oruela had opened up to her a bit once and ever since, the woman had seemed to pity her. It was ridiculous.

The stairs continued up past one landing and a long narrow window that looked out seawards across the rooftops opposite. She came to a halt at the very top in front of a door and put the key in the lock. The door opened into an apartment in the roof.

She dropped her green kidskin purse and a pair of driving goggles on a glass-topped side table. A small glass-fronted stove in the fireplace heated the room against the unusually chilly spring day. That was thoughtful, she thought.

Heavy velvet curtains were tied back from the face of the small window. The room was never particularly light, even in the afternoon. She turned on a single standard lamp in the corner.

She removed her green gloves and then, carefully, a cream leather hat. She had flawless olive skin and soft brown eyes. Her glossy crown of deep brown, almost black hair fell into place. It was shingled at the back and swept behind her ears. She smoothed it in the mirror. Her figure was slender and she was tall. Her stylish driving coat of pale cream raw silk was buttoned diagonally from hem to shoulder and trimmed with creamy fur. She bent down to the hem where the fur caressed her pale, stockinged legs and slipped the first button free. One by one she widened the aperture as if rehearsing a scene. Underneath, her dress was a sumptuous hand-made peach mousseline. She tossed the coat on a chair as if it were no more than a bath towel.

A single string of pearls hung at her neck and cascaded over her breast to her waist. Following the fashion, the bodice of her dress was cut to disguise the curve of her waist and it fell straight to her hips where a sash was loosely tied. Her thighs suggested themselves to the eye as long and shapely; certainly, if her calves were anything to go by, her legs were a real asset. Her shoes were creamy, with kitten heels and a satin strap at the front.

She left the mirror and walked into the bedroom. The room was windowless. The only light was from a small skylight. Its patch of blue was turning misty violet as the evening drew in. Beside the big bed was a lamp made from the carved figure of a naked, plump cupid, his hands reaching up to hold the bulb. She turned him on and the soft light that filtered through the fringed shade shed itself on the sea-green counterpane. A fire burned in the small grate. She warmed her hands by it

9

and the firelight leapt about her face and body. A secret smile danced in her eyes.

Back in the sitting-room, she took a bottle of cognac from a low cabinet next to the table. She poured herself one and, glass in hand, she nestled into the big sofa, her legs underneath her, a hint of lace peeking from under the hem of her dress. She seemed to survey the tall palm standing in a pot in the opposite corner of the room. The door of the bedroom behind her stood slightly ajar.

She was too young to marry. That was the excuse she was currently giving her guardian who acted like he was fending off suitors left, right and centre. There had been two, as far as she could gather. She found the whole business of them asking *him* ridiculous. For the moment at least the excuse seemed acceptable, but she was on shaky ground. Apart from the fact that she was pushing twenty-five and wasn't anything like too young, although she felt it, her girlfriends were marrying all around her. There was a whole rash of weddings to be attended this spring.

Her friends were very practical. Of course they would take lovers, they said. Marriage was the only freedom that a girl could get. This wasn't Paris and even though Biarritz had its fashionable visitors, a single girl just didn't have the chance to explore love. Marriage therefore was a business arrangement, best got over with so that fun could start.

The truth was that Oruela wanted something different, something more. She didn't exactly know what, but she wanted to explore life. If she married it would be for love. Her guardians' marriage was like that of two stuffed dummies. Horrible! She would have something better. Besides, she had another, secret ambition which had nothing to do with marriage. She wanted to go to Paris, to the Sorbonne.

She didn't really have an academic mind but she had a romantic one and she had a vision of herself at Henri Bergson's philosophical classes, being noticed by artists and intellectuals for her beauty and brilliance. She hadn't articulated her brilliance yet but it was there, in embryo. She had a kind of confidence in it, even if others only described her as wilful.

The sound of a key turning in the lock shook her from her reverie. In whirled Jean looking more decidedly handsome and more in love than ever.

He immediately rushed to Oruela's knees and covered her hands with kisses. She laughed and pushed his chilly outside clothes away. He jumped up and unbuttoned his overcoat, flinging it on the chair and his hat flying after it.

'Oruela, Oruela!' he moaned.

This time she made no attempt to push him away. She stroked his long glossy hair and kissed his nose.

He touched her face and sighed, he ran his finger down her neck and sighed, he cupped her lovely shoulder in his hand, sighing all the while. 'I have something for you, my darling! Something so special you will hardly believe it! I wanted you to have this as soon as I heard about it. It's taken a whole year to get!' He reached for a package wrapped in brown paper, placed it in Oruela's lap, and fixed his eyes on her face.

'How was Paris?' she asked, not quite nonchalantly.

'Paris? Open your present!'

'I shan't until you tell me at least one word about Paris,' she said.

Jean laughed. 'Paris was Paris! It was beautiful! It was busy! Open your present!'

'Did it come from Paris?'

'It came *via* Paris,' he said enigmatically.

'It's got little holes in it . . .' She began unwrapping the parcel, under Jean's adoring gaze.

The tiny, ornate silver cage that emerged contained a greenish lizard. She couldn't help but shriek. The lizard stilled itself completely, trying to merge into the grass that lined the floor of its dwelling. But the ruby embedded in its forehead, and the cluster of sapphires at its

11

neck shone and sparkled in the twin suns of the lamp and the firelight, preventing its camouflage tactics.

Jean laughed. 'Don't be frightened.' He got up and refilled her brandy glass, pouring a generous measure of the delicious amber liquid for himself.

Together they sat in the gathering twilight and he told her the story he had heard about the lizard's role in life at La Maison Rose.

Oruela found herself aroused by the thought of the women decorating their bodies, by the dancing. 'Do you mean you think we . . . What if he refuses? I haven't trained him!' she whispered, barely trusting herself to speak.

'Oruela, my darling, don't be silly. We don't need to bother with the meaning of the thing. It's an adventure. Besides, why should he? We're perfect for each other.'

'Should we . . . should we do it?' she asked again.

'Do you want to?' he asked.

She could only nod her head. Her voice was too heavy with wicked excitement to speak.

Jean kissed the rustling fabric at her breast and her skin responded to the touch of him, gradually pushing away thoughts that had no place in this moment. The silence was broken only by the crackle of the coals in the fire. The lizard moved and sent ripples into her lap.

'My darling!' crooned Jean. 'Nothing will part us, I swear,' and he raised her chin gently.

She looked at him. I could be happy with him, she thought, I could really . . .

'What do you say?' he whispered.

A wicked grin suddenly lit up her face. 'What the hell! If he refuses, he refuses! There are plenty more where you came from!'

'Minx!' cried Jean, gripping her arm.

She wriggled herself free, sending the little lizard's cage rolling on to the couch as she climbed on top of Jean. The lizard darted furiously about in his cage as she slid the delicate fabric of her dress up her thighs, showing off the tops of pale silk stockings. Jean grew hard as she pushed her sex at him. He laughed, a little nervously.

She straightened her back, pushing out her breasts. They ached for kisses and the feel of his lips was heaven. His hands were strong and his touch a little rough. She pulled his hair gently as he slid her dress further up her body. Her knickers were mere wisps of silk that were tied on the inner leg with tiny ribbons. His fingers searched her sex through the fabric, rolling her swollen labia. She covered his face and hair with soft crooning kisses.

Jean rose, carrying her with him. He kicked open the bedroom door. The lamp sent wriggling shadows dancing over their bodies as they fell into the soft pillows.

'Turn over,' begged Jean. 'Let me undo your buttons.'

She rolled slowly over and lay still, sinking into the darkness as his hands discovered the lovely shape of her back, button by button, tie by tie. When she felt it bare, she raised her arse and slid out from her chrysalis and turned to him. Her bare breasts were beautiful, with lustrous dark nipples, her belly a little rounded, her dark triangle of hair waiting to be discovered.

'You're a work of art,' groaned Jean and he took her breasts once more in his mouth to suck. She loved the sight of his head bent at her breasts, his shoulders bowed at her service. A suggestion of expensive hair oil rose from his head. She wanted to see his body. She pulled at the shoulder of his shirt, reached for his waistband. 'Undress,' she said. 'Undress.' And he was forced to leave his worship of her to undress.

He hadn't an ounce of fat on him. He moved around the room, folding his clothes, like a young lion. His skin was just a touch paler than her own, the kind that goes honey-coloured in the sun. Even in his nakedness everything about him suggested wealth and the confidence that goes with it. He had just the right amount of hair on his chest. It trickled down darkly to his thick straight prick.

13

'Wait!' he cried and sprang out of the room. His arse was a delight to behold.

'As if I wouldn't,' she breathed.

He returned with the little silver cage and lay down next to her, resting on one elbow.

He lifted the latch.

The lizard darted out and stopped still on the counterpane. It stayed absolutely still for half a minute. Oruela watched it with a mixture of mounting apprehension and excitement.

It moved so suddenly it made her shudder.

It scampered on to his long thigh and jumped lightly from there into his lush pubic hair. It stopped, then it darted on to his cock and he groaned, falling back into the pillows helplessly. The lizard ran around his cock, up, down, across his balls. It ran into the crevice underneath and his legs fell apart. It ran under him to his arsehole and back up again. It circled his hard sex. With an effort Jean raised his head to watch.

Oruela suddenly thought, Hickory Dickory Dock, the lizard ran round his cock, and she began to giggle. But then it jumped. It was on her hand. It ran fast up her arm, over her shoulder and down across one breast, flicking its tail at her hard nipple as it went. The sensation made her serious. Her whole body tensed. The lizard ran across the smooth plain of her belly, its jewels gleaming. It dived into her soft pubic hair. She bit her fist.

The little green animal slid down into the folds of her vulva and pitter-pattered around at the opening, relaxing her, like adept fingers, gently. She began to open. She began to want it inside. She wanted it so much. Yes. She could feel the little animal begin to squeeze itself inside her.

At that precise moment Jean's fascination turned to rabid jealousy. He tore the little creature away from her and claimed her as his own. Yes, this was what she really wanted. His prick replaced the animal and he moved with a passion so complete it was

14

everything. His hair in her face, his breath on her hair. She ground against him, massaging her clitoris. There was no return from here. He was hers. The power of him made her gasp. Everything else was irrelevant. He gave one long moan as he came and she was taken along with him, into the best of all possible worlds.

Sometime later she opened her eyes and he was lying close.

She said his name.

'Let's get married,' he said, raising himself on one arm. The way his torso curved into his hip was lovely. It was perfect.

'What!' she said.

'Let's get married soon?'

'Oh!' she said.

'What does that mean?' he asked, sounding a little peeved.

She raised herself. 'I'm surprised, that's all.'

'I want you. I want you to be mine for ever,' he said, and kissed her bruised nipple.

'But I've told everyone I don't believe in it!' she said. 'Besides – don't laugh at me – but I want to go to Paris. I want to go to the Sorbonne and meet bohemians and intellectuals and go to salons and live outrageously!' There! It was out.

Jean smiled and kissed her lips lightly. 'As my wife you can do all the things you want to. Of course you'll go to Paris and meet the people I like.'

'Will I like them too?'

'Of course. And they will love you. Nothing you could do would displease me, Oruela. I love you so much.'

She reached for him and kissed his mouth, lovingly. There was a whole world in his kiss.

'Apparently, people are beginning to talk about us, did you know?' she asked after a moment.

'What? Who? How? I haven't heard anything,' said Jean.

'People meaning my father really. He says you won't suffer. It's me that's supposedly in the wrong.' She hadn't told Jean she was an orphan, looked after by guardians. She didn't know why.

'There isn't any wrong,' he cried. 'Oh, Oruela, what does this mean? Why are you telling me this. Is it an excuse for not getting married. Don't . . .'

'Perhaps it's an excuse *for* getting married!' she said.

'Yes. Yes. Yes!' cried Jean and leaped up as if he'd just scored a winning goal. 'Oh, my darling. Come here.' And he came back to her and before the first sex had grown cold they were making more. The stars began to peek through the patch of indigo sky in the skylight above them.

The streets outside had a touch of timelessness, the quiescence of aristocracy, of old money, even monarchy, enthroned or otherwise. On the wide, sweeping seafront the buildings of another age stood, barrack-like, pondering the great Atlantic. A stone's throw from Oruela and Jean's love-nest was one street where the houses had been turned into clinics. Each one offered a modern, specialist treatment in the galaxy of ailments that beset Biarritz's fabulously rich. Brass plaques announced the wonders of these therapies and some even had the new neon signs. About halfway up the street, above one such sign, an electric light was shining out from a first-floor window through the gaps in the shutters.

Inside this room Norbert Bruyere, Oruela's guardian, was sitting on the edge of a leather armchair in his underwear. His outer clothes hung neatly over a clothes-horse. A cup of coffee and a piece of cake stood untouched on an occasional table.

Norbert Bruyere looked tired. He stared blankly in the direction of the plain, white wall in front of him. He was a big man, yet everything seemed to droop from his bent shoulders.

A soft knock sounded at the door and the therapist, Dr von Streibnitz, entered. The doctor was a small, bespectacled man with lily-white hands that fluttered as he spoke.

'My dear Norbert. I'm so sorry to keep you waiting like this. Important phone call. Now. How are you feeling?'

'Not good, Helmut, not good.'

'Well, you know you always feel a little dazed after the treatment. I trust Nurse took good care of you. How long were you in the Hat?'

'An hour, as usual. But, Helmut, it isn't just that, it's my whole life. I have no energy, no zest any more. Sometimes I feel so tired.'

'Let me look at you,' said the doctor and he investigated Norbert's eyes, his ears, his throat and, with the aid of a stethoscope, his chest. 'I don't think there's much wrong with you except a touch of the spring sniffles. Change of season and all that, we're not getting any younger.' Finishing off, he washed his hands in the little sink. 'I'll give you more of the bathing salts you had this time last year. Do you the power of good. Get dressed now and come into my office for a chat.'

Norbert sluggishly did as he was told.

The pretty young nurse at her desk in the next room gave him a big smile but he didn't return it, or even appear to notice. She shrugged and went back to the study of her textbook.

'On here, my friend,' said the doctor, patting the big leather couch. 'Lie down and talk to me. What did you think of my new little nurse by the way?'

'I didn't notice.'

'Didn't notice! Norbert! Good grief, man. Didn't you notice her . . .' The doctor held his hands under imaginary breasts and juggled them.

'But that's my problem, Doctor! I've lost interest.'

'Now, Norbert, I've told you before. You came to me over a year ago in this same frame of mind and I told you that the physical treatment won't work without a

17

change of attitude. We perked up a little bit, did't we? Now, inertia is self-destructive, you have to think positive. Do you still have that mistress of yours?'

'Well, I was exaggerating when I called her a mistress. She's an old, um, friend who does me a service. I still see her, yes, once a month or so, but I've told you what that's all about. It's not enough. I wish I were young again, Doctor. I couldn't get enough women when I was young.' A tear slid down Norbert's cheek.

'Why not get yourself a nice young whore this evening, Norbert. You've got to think positive. Think of it, old boy, a nice young bit of stuff with bouncy tits all firm and pert.' The doctor's eyes were shining. A little bit of dribble squeezed out of the corner of his mouth.

'But I can't!' whined Norbert. And he continued to whine, for nearly an hour, at the end of which he paid handsomely.

'Think positive! *Think young*, Norbert!' boomed Dr von Streibnitz as they parted at the door.

Norbert plodded down the stairs and out into the street. He turned left and left again and halted at the door of the haberdashery. The sign on the door said 'Fermé', but a light was on in the back of the shop. Norbert rapped on the door sharply.

'Why, Monsieur Bruyere, come in.' The haberdasher let him in and locked the door behind him.

'Are you well?' she said. 'You look peaky. Oh, you do look pale. Were you passing and taken ill? Oh, I'm glad you knocked.'

Norbert sat on a chair and waved her offer of water away with a dismissive, gloved hand. ' I'm perfectly all right, thank you. I want to send something to Paris.'

She smiled professionally. 'I have the very thing. Just in yesterday. Let me show you.'

'No. No,' said Norbert, heaving himself up. 'Just send it to the usual address. Tonight, you understand. It must go tonight.'

'But my girl's gone, sir. Can't it go in the morning?'

'I said *tonight!*' shouted Norbert.

'Very well,' she said between gritted teeth. She showed Norbert the door.

And with plenty of cursing, a flimsy piece of lingerie, the colour of a summer sky, was wrapped, boxed and dispatched on the night train to Paris.

Don't You Lie to Me

The sun was rising as Oruela left Biarritz the next morning in her open Peugeot. The lizard's cage was wrapped in brown paper to protect him against the chill in the early spring breeze, and the whole package was placed carefully and lovingly on the soft red leather of the front seat.

Oruela handled the car confidently. She loved driving. But she felt a little dazed this morning. Was it the right thing, to marry Jean? The glow from their night together was still with her. At the thought of his body in the firelight, her womb seemed to thud inside.

'It will get me out of the morgue,' she said to the little cage beside her. About two kilometres before the town of Bayonne she turned down a lane and brought the car to a halt in front of the immense, decorative iron gates of her home. As she sprang out of the car her coat whirled open in the breeze. She shivered as she opened the heavy gates.

Three newly built garages stood at the side of the house, which in fact looked nothing like a morgue. Its cheerful white walls and lemony green paintwork in the sunlight was very fresh. Oruela cut the engine of the car and allowed it to coast in slowly through the open doors of the first garage.

'We're home, *mon chéri*,' she whispered as she wriggled out of the car. The garage was cold. Oruela shivered again; she was very tired. She carefully picked up the cage. 'There,' she whispered. 'Time for sleep.'

'Where have you been?' Norbert Bruyere stood in the doorway. He was in his dressing-robe which had been fastened, hurriedly, underneath his substantial paunch. Most of his nightshirt was hanging out of the front of it. His legs were bare, right down to the crocodile-skin slippers on his long, thin feet.

Oruela didn't answer immediately. She tried to gather her thoughts in a hurry.

'Where have you been, Oruela?' repeated Norbert.

'I've been with Marie,' she blurted. 'We were tired and fell asleep. I thought it was better than driving home.'

'Now, that's not the truth, my little girl,' he menaced.

Oruela pursed her lips.

'My dear,' he said, changing his tune. And he reached out and touched her chin with his long finger.

Oruela backed away. She dropped the lizard on the seat of the car and stood there defiantly.

Norbert moved closer to her. 'Tell me the truth and I won't punish you, Oruela. Marie telephoned last night. You weren't with her.'

Oruela's teeth began to chatter. The engine-metal gave a groan as it cooled down.

Norbert gripped her wrist. His breath stirred the fur around her collar. 'You were with him, weren't you?' he urged.

'So what!' she said, looking him in the eye.

Norbert smiled. 'I love to hear that haughty tone in your voice,' he said. He moved so close that his body touched hers. 'Come on, my sweetie. Tell me all about your lover.'

And then she felt his prick against her leg, felt it move, harden a little bit. It kindled a feeling in her belly. She realised, with amazement, that the feeling was desire.

21

He raised his hand to her chin in a fatherly fashion and then, slowly, he let it fall to her bare neck. He traced the outline of her dress where it touched the soft skin at her breast. He smiled wistfully.

'Just tell me about him,' he said. 'Please, just tell me what he does to you!'

'No!' she said. 'No,' and she pushed past him. She stood on the gravel outside and yelled, 'Leave me alone, you dirty pig. You're supposed to act like a *father*!'

'Oh, my Oruela,' he whimpered. 'I do love you. Don't push me away. I need your comfort, let me . . .' He groped after her.

But she was out of reach. She turned towards the house.

'It's your own fault, girl,' he shouted. 'If you behave like a tart you ought to expect to be treated like one.'

She spun round. 'You hypocrite. Everyone knows you have a mistress, so why shouldn't I have a lover? Anyway, we're going to get married!'

Norbert snarled. 'Don't count on it. Your precious Jean has a hundred women as well as you!'

'I wish you'd drop dead,' she screamed. 'I wish you'd die. Right now. Right there.'

He crumpled against the sleek wing of the car as her footsteps died away.

Norbert dragged his tall, drooping frame wearily inside the house. The big sleepy mansion seemed to settle down as if, realising the day was too much to wake up to, it turned over and went back to sleep again.

But, just as the stillness began to seem complete, a figure emerged from the bushes where it had been hiding. It was a woman, moving so quietly that she barely disturbed the gravel. She was dressed from head to toe in long old-fashioned black. Her figure was slender and upright, very stiff. Her face was small and pale, her hair was raked up into a tight blonde knot at the back of her head. Her mouth was turned down at the corners, accentuating her jowls.

22

In her ill-humour Genevieve Bruyere looked older than her forty-five years and there was disturbance in her violet-blue eyes. A hint of unreality burned in their depths.

She walked in a straight line across the lawn towards a small rose tree. Its leaves were bright green and hardly unfurled. Virgin leaves. She pulled a branch close to her face and examined it for pests. Finding a tiny cluster of aphids near the shoot she enclosed it between finger and thumb and squashed it until her skin went white.

She marched to the garage to sniff around and her eye alighted on the small brown paper package on the front seat of the car. She picked it up and tore it open without hesitation. The lizard eyed her and turned sideways. He crouched, he switched his tail, he shortened it and elongated it, he hid his feet. He looked like a little green penis.

Genevieve's surprise wrote itself on her face in capitals. For one brief moment the expression made her look younger, almost better. She picked up the cage and closed the garage doors.

Upstairs Oruela locked the door of her room before she undressed and climbed into bed. She would stay in bed and she wouldn't get out again until Jean came to get her. That's what she would do.

Something was wrong with Norbert lately and now he'd gone mad. She began to cry. Dammit, he'd always been kind to her before, not like his wife. Now there was nobody except Jean. She suddenly remembered the lizard. 'You'll have to stay there. I'm sorry!' she sobbed. She pulled the covers up over her head.

She dreamt she was floating down a river with the current, a warm, pure current. Every so often a weed caressed her bare skin, its slimy tentacles slipping in between her toes or her thighs. On and on she floated, her breasts raised up out of the water to the sun and

23

the warm splashing water sprinkling droplets everywhere over her skin.

Then suddenly, a change, a bed in the river and the
current got faster. She was scared. But there was Daddy
on the river bank and he put out his hand and grabbed
her and pulled her to safety.

He was wearing a Roman toga. It flowed over his
belly towards his feet. But it was all wet and Oruela was
really sorry she'd made him all wet and she undressed
him. She clung to him, climbing up his belly, feeling
very small but her sex was huge and she wanted him.
She could feel his huge hard cock right up her back.
She willed him to touch her sex and at last he did. His
hands pulled apart her buttocks and he lowered her
onto his cock. It filled her up, there was no room for
anything else and all of her emptied all over him.

When Oruela awoke her mind was full of the dream.
She tried to shake herself awake but she felt strange, as
if she had crossed some line and could never go back.

She rose from the bed and asked down the tube for
Michelle to bring up some coffee. There was some sort
of kerfuffle going on in the kitchen. She had to repeat
herself. It ruffled her taut nerves. She would dress and
rescue the lizard. Then she would telephone Jean and
try not to go crazy in the meantime. Oruela worried
about going crazy.

A minute or two later a sharp rap at the door made
her jump. It wasn't Michelle's rap. Despite having
already put on her knickers, her stockings and a skirt,
Oruela pulled her nightdress down over them and
jumped back into the bed, pulling the covers right up
to her neck.

It was Genevieve, her stepmother. She put the breakfast tray on the table by the window and folded her
arms.

'Can I have it on the bed, please?' asked Oruela.
'Where is Michelle?'

Genevieve ignored her and sidled to the side of the bed.

'What is it?' said Oruela.

'Your father died last night,' she said, pursing her lips.

Oruela sank into the pillows with a whimper. Her stepmother's face seemed to grow larger and larger, its sneering mouth opening wider and wider.

Genevieve sniffed.

Oruela watched her back going out of the room until it was a pinprick and then the wardrobe swelled and lumbered towards her . . .

Michelle rushed into Oruela's room and, seeing the look on her mistress's face, she ran out again and returned with smelling salts. She put them under Oruela's nose. Michelle was a lovely, sunny-looking girl with a plump peach of an arse that even the drab maid's uniform could not entirely conceal. Michelle had been in the house since she was twelve years old. They had grown up together.

Oruela pushed the smelling salts away and mumbled, 'Is he really . . .?'

'What?' said Michelle. 'What are you saying?'

'Is he really dead, Michelle?'

'Yes, he is.'

'How?'

'They don't know. Doctor Simenon says there's to be an autopsy.'

'When did he die?'

'During the night.'

'Was it a ghost then?' Oruela murmured quietly.

'What? What is it? You look funny. Come on, drink your coffee,' said Michelle, briskly.

'Michelle, something's wrong with me. Everything is moving.'

'Smell this bottle.' Michelle raised Oruela's head in the crook of her arm and held the bottle firmly under her nose.

Oruela shook her head. 'Michelle! He wasn't dead when I came home this morning!'

'What time?'

'It was dawn, about five. I was with Jean all night. My father caught me in the garage . . .. Michelle, you mustn't ever tell anyone this, but he attacked me.'

'He what?'

'He put his prick on my leg and touched me.'

'Oh, the wicked man. *Mon dieu*!' said Michelle.

'Never tell anyone, Michelle. Swear!'

'I swear!'

'I wished him dead, Michelle. I . . .'

'Well, that's natural,' said Michelle sensibly.

'There was nothing natural about my dream.' Oruela felt her own voice fading away.

'Look, don't upset yourself. You know you're a bit delicate sometimes. It was only a dream whatever it was,' said Michelle.

'Supposing I had the power to kill him! Supposing just by wishing him dead I did it! It might be possible, Michelle!' Now she was shouting.

'Sssssh! Calm down. You don't want people to hear you saying that sort of thing. Control yourself!' Michelle was having trouble being calm herself.

'Oh God, Michelle, I'm frightened. What if – '

Michelle suddenly grew angry. 'Now stop it this minute,' she said. 'Sit up. Eat your breakfast. Here.' She put the tray in front of Oruela. 'I'm going to fetch the doctor from downstairs and get him to give you something.'

Dr Simenon, the handsome young locum, followed Michelle immediately she told him what was wrong. As they ascended the stairs Genevieve came out of her drawing-room and looked stonily at them.

'Hurry, Doctor,' said Michelle. 'She needs a sedative. Her stepmother will upset her if she comes up.'

'Shock,' pronounced Dr Simenon. Oruela could hear his voice as if through a door. 'Give her this and here's another one for later. She needs rest and comfort. Rest and comfort. Keep her warm and read her a book to keep her mind off things. Poor girl.' He stood up and was packing his instruments away when the door opened and Genevieve came in carrying the lizard in its cage.

'Keep that door shut please, madame. Your daughter needs warmth,' said the doctor.

'*This* is no daughter of mine!' shouted Genevieve. 'I found *this* by the side of my husband's bed today after Robert discovered him dead this morning!' Madame threw the lizard on to the bed. The little creature whirled around and around inside, out of his poor little mind.

'My little lizard!' cried Oruela. 'Oh, my baby!' and she reached for him, sending the bedclothes tumbling. All eyes registered the skirt she had on in bed.

'I wouldn't be surprised if we find out that a bite from that killed my darling husband!' wept Genevieve, tearlessly.

'Wait,' said the doctor. 'I don't remember this in the room.'

'Well, you weren't looking, were you, *Doctor*!' spat Genevieve. 'I heard her threaten him with it early this morning in the garage. She didn't know I was there. Did you!' she hissed at Oruela. 'She said she'd kill him, just because he reprimanded her for coming home at all hours!'

Oruela opened her mouth to speak. She saw Michelle trying to warn her with her eyes. She whispered, 'It's no use, Michelle! I must have done it! I did it in my sleep!'

Dr Simenon bellowed, '*Madame* Bruyere! Leave the room please. Now! I insist!'

Genevieve snorted and marched out. Oruela collapsed back on to the pillows. The sedative was taking effect. She closed her eyes. The last thing she heard was Michelle saying, 'I'm frightened, sir.'

* * *

Dr Simenon's calm control of the situation made Michelle feel safer. He chucked her cheek and left, closing the door behind him.

Genevieve started shouting hysterically outside and Michelle put her hands over her ears to muffle the worst of it. Then there were footsteps and the sound of the front door slamming. Downstairs Genevieve picked up the hall telephone. Michelle ran to the bedroom door.

'Mayor Derive,' Genevieve was saying. 'Hello, Jacques. No, I'm afraid I'm not very well at all. Norbert is dead. Yes, dead, and we think there has been a crime. Robert discovered him.' She paused and a slow, almost sexy smile spread on her face as she listened. 'We don't know. That stupid Doctor Simenon has been. He says there should be an autopsy. But I have discovered a poisonous lizard belonging to Oruela and when I confronted her with it she confessed . . . Yes. Will you come yourself, Jacques? . . . Oh, I see . . . but please come as soon as you can. Who shall I expect in the meantime – Peine?'

It was Michelle's turn to sneer. Hark at her turning on the soft voice for that old fat pig, the mayor. If Genevieve was capable of it, which Michelle doubted very much because Genevieve was a frigid old baggage if ever there was one, she was probably having it off with the old pig. But their sort didn't have it off. They just breathed heavily at dinner parties. She knew. She'd seen it.

She slipped quietly back into Oruela's room and looked at the sleeping form. Poor love. She hadn't had much of a happy life and it was going to get worse. This wasn't the first time she'd lost her senses. It wasn't surprising with those two as parents. There was no love in the house. A girl needed the sure ground of love.

She went to the window and pulled the curtains back into their ties. When she and Robert married their children would always be loved. It was a beautiful spring day outside. It was getting warmer. But none of

28

it penetrated the north-facing room. Michelle shivered and turned away from the window.

It was then she noticed the little lizard again, in his cage, sitting on the bed. She went up to it and bent down. 'Look at you then,' she said. 'Cor! Look at you. You're all covered in jewels. Aren't you smart. And a little collar. You're a pet. I bet you're a pet that Jean's bought, aren't you?' She lifted the cage up to her face. 'Look at your scales. You're like a little dinosaur! You're beautiful!'

The lizard turned around slowly and squatted. It seemed drowsy. Michelle laughed. 'You're trying to show off, aren't you? I would too if I was as beautiful as you.'

And then she heard Robert's voice in the echoing downstairs hall, answering the mistress.

Oruela was sleeping soundly and Michelle needed Robert right this minute. She locked the bedroom door behind her and, putting the key in her pocket, tiptoed down the stairs.

Robert looked up and grinned when he saw her. He wasn't a particularly handsome man, but he was sexy in his way. Probably because it was mostly what he thought about. He was in great shape. His real love was sport of any kind and he kept in shape with dumbbells and barbells. Michelle frequently spent her nights watching his muscles developing.

She flew down the stairs and straight into his arms.

'You all right?' he said. 'No, you're not, are you. Come in here. It's conference time.' He opened the broom-cupboard door under the stairs and shoved her in. Inside, he lit a stub of candle, bending down to put a large rag at the base of the door so the light wouldn't show in the hall.

'We ain't been in here for a while, have we?' he said, grabbing her pussy as he stood up.

'Have you heard what's going on in this house?' said Michelle impatiently.

29

'I've got the gist,' he said, and grabbed her arse with his other hand.

'They're screaming blue murder!' said Michelle.

'They're all nuts,' he said. He was inching up her skirt. 'He's not cold yet and she's just told me she wants all her stuff moved out of the back room into the front where it's sunny.'

'Oh God, Robert,' whispered Michelle. 'I bet she did it!'

'Did what?'

'Killed him.'

Robert finally stopped what he was doing. 'What? Killed the old man? What makes you think anyone killed him? He died in his bloody sleep, didn't he?'

'Robert, I thought you'd got the gist. She's accused Oruela of murder and it's her all along!'

'Eh?'

'Didn't you hear all . . . Never mind. Hold me, Robert.'

He put his arms around her and squeezed her tight, kissing her hair.

'I've got to be strong. Oruela hasn't got anybody that'll stick up for her but me.'

'She can stick up for herself for once, can't she?' His hands slithered down to her arse.

'No. She's gone all hysterical, like she used to when she was a kid.'

Robert let out a sigh of contempt and held her firmly by the shoulders. 'I told you they're all mad, the lot of them. You're soft on Oruela. I know she's a nice kid and that but she's always had funny turns. Maybe, if someone did kill him, it was her.'

'Oruela's not that kind of crazy!' she insisted a little too loudly.

'Ssshh!' he said, putting his hand over her mouth.

Michelle gently took his hand away and lowered her voice. She spoke very close to his face. 'She's not mad like that, she's just delicate sometimes . . .'

Robert stroked her neck with his finger and gently circled down on to her breast. It felt like feathers. 'While you're all worried about her, what about me? I haven't got a man to serve any more, have I? I could be out of a job,' he said.

'Oh, Robert, don't be daft. She needs a man around the house.' But it was a thought. Suddenly the world was crumbling to bits. 'Here, come on, put your hand back up there. I like it.'

Robert reached down and lifted the hem of her skirt, sliding his hand into her new underwear. She felt his cool fingers pushing into her vulva and suddenly she was hornier than hell. She pushed herself on to his fingers.

He took a sharp intake of breath. 'You want it, don't you,' he said. 'You're all wet.'

'On the floor,' she heard herself say.

'Get them mats out then,' he said.

She turned her back to him to get a couple of housework mats off a shelf at the back of the long low cupboard, and as she bent down to arrange them on the floor he had her skirt right up from behind and she felt the air on her buttocks and his fingers again.

'Stay like that,' she heard him say in that low voice she loved so much and then she felt his cock pressing at her pussy.

'You got that out quick,' she said. 'Oh!' She felt herself being lifted on to it like a coat on to a hook. But it was at an uncomfortable angle and anyway she didn't want it like that. He was too quick and he hadn't got the hang of keeping her happy with his hand around the front.

'Robert!' she hissed. 'I'm going to fall over!'

He took it out of her and she breathed a sigh of relief and turned over, settling herself on the mats.

He was smiling at her. 'You needn't have worried. I can last out long enough to do that and wait for you to come, little lady.'

'Oh yeah, since when?'

'Since I've been teaching myself a bit of technique, that's when,' he whispered

'I'll bet you five francs one night when we're comfortable in bed. But till then you just get down here and press on this,' she said.

He lowered himself towards her. His cock was beautiful, even if it was poking out of his shirt-tails like a gangster's pistol. She giggled and reached forward to lift up the shirt and get a glimpse of the way his muscled torso flowed down into that dense mass of dark brown hair.

It was at that moment that they heard the bell and the sound of the parlour-maid running up the back passage.

Michelle held her breath. The footsteps stopped outside the cupboard door. 'Where's my damn coffee?' hissed Genevieve.

Robert very slowly took down a doorstop from the small shelf by his head and slid it silently under the rag at the base of the door.

Michelle suddenly realised she was breathing hard and tried to control it but she was panting. Her breasts were rising and falling like crazy. Robert was smiling. He touched her. She was streaming.

'Where's Robert?' asked Genevieve.

The parlour-maid replied that she didn't know.

Robert rubbed the moisture from Michelle's pussy like he was feeling silk and then he smoothed it on to his cock. It glistened in the candlelight.

'Well, find him and tell him to come here at once,' barked Genevieve.

Robert held his cock and guided it towards Michelle's sex. He slipped inside.

Robert moved inside Michelle and sucked at her ear. She caressed the soft hair on his head and kissed it. He pushed into her slowly and silently.

Genevieve trotted up the stairs.

All sound drifted away and there was only Robert and his prick thrusting in and out. Michelle suddenly didn't care how much noise they made, she couldn't hear anything, she could only feel. His thighs on hers, his shirt against her breast. His head, his hair and his cock, slowly in and out. And yet they were quiet. There was no noise, even the slightest was willed away. He raised his head and kissed her, long and slow and kept his movements up. Michelle knew she felt love at that moment and she kissed him back and lay there, still as the earth, squeezing the walls of her vagina as hard as she could around his cock. She held it, held it, held it until it began like a sting inching its way to her belly and she knew it was going to burst. It started slowly receding into her, almost escaping; she was frightened it would stop. It was too good. She concentrated on squeezing again but her body had taken over and the sting burst into a million parts that filled her and settled her.

She gradually became aware of the sound of her own breath. She had no idea if Robert had come or not but he wasn't hard any more, so she assumed he must have. The candle had gone out.

'Are you all right?' he whispered.

She managed a noise,

'Is that a yes?'

'Aha,' she said.

'You were really gone there!' he whispered.

She wished he could've said something more romantic. But he smelt nice.

He moved away and lit a match. It was horrible to feel him go.

She felt self-conscious under even the tiny glare of the match-flame.

'Hold this!' he hissed.

She raised herself on her elbow and took the match. She watched him buttoning up. He smoothed his hair.

The flame touched her fingers and she blew it out.

He moved the rag from the door and reached for her to give her a kiss as he bent down.

'Take these,' he whispered, giving her the matches. 'Shuffle back there while I open the door.'

She pulled his head towards her and kissed him again. His lips were delicious.

'I love you,' he said.

She shuffled back into the corner and he opened the door. 'You get yourself together. Listen out. Unless you hear me saying something then assume the coast is clear. All right?' and he was gone.

She reassembled her uniform in the dark, feeling slightly surprised that her fingers still worked. Then she stepped out into the daylight. The key! She checked her pocket. It was still there, miraculously. She climbed the stairs, a little unsteadily.

Paris in the Springtime

The same morning, in a large apartment just south of St Germain des Prés, a woman turned her attention to the luxurious box that had arrived from Biarritz a little earlier. She opened it and unwrapped the sky-blue lingerie inside. She held it up briefly then dropped it back in the box and picked up a novel and her coffee.

Euska Onaldi was in her late thirties. She had dark brown curly hair clasped haphazardly in a clip at the back of her head. She had one of those faces that is lovely overall yet not composed of typically beautiful parts. Her nose was a little too long, her dark eyes were bewitching although a little too wide apart in her broad face. Her mouth was wide, her skin was clear and healthy and, after the new fashion, it was tanned.

Euska wore a robe with huge kimono-like sleeves cuffed with black. Its shawl collar was black while the loose body was a mass of big pale pink roses and emerald green leaves on a background of cream. It fell around her comfortably without obvious fastenings. On one big foot was a flat, black satin mule. The other mule had escaped.

She read for the duration of her coffee and then, retrieving the mule, she sauntered over to the gramophone and put the needle on a record. A moment later she began to move her luxurious body in a dance around the peach and green room, her silhouette crossing the long window. She danced slowly, stretching her legs, arms, loosening her hips, dropping her shoulders, letting her long backbone slip, vertebra by vertebra, into place.

An appearance in the bedroom door interrupted her. 'You're energetic,' said Ernesto. He had a towel around his waist.

Euska smiled. 'I'm exercising! It's good for the vitality.' The tune ended. 'Sit down, I'll make some more coffee,' she said.

'Never mind that, I want some of you.' He walked up to her and encircled her waist with one powerful arm, drawing her towards him like he was picking up a slice of featherweight pastry. He kissed her neck.

Ernesto was a man of medium build and Spanish features. His jet hair was a little grey at the temples. His back was broad and well-developed, his legs handsome below the towel, his waist only a little thickened with middle age.

'Come back to bed,' he said into her ear and he slipped the robe off her shoulders.

It fell to the floor, leaving her gloriously naked. She retaliated by pulling his towel and he laughed, holding out his hand.

She allowed him to lead her back into the bedroom. He lay back on the bed, his morning erection waiting for her. She crawled on to the bed and kissed him as he began to play with her sex, first with his hand, massaging the skin around her clitoris, and then with his tongue. All the while she stroked his back, his thigh, his balls. He surfaced and kissed her breasts for a little while.

'Come to me!' she whispered.

He manoeuvred himself on top of her and fucked her as only a mature man can. Euska reflected on the nature of her lover. The concentration of a man of fifty is better tuned, she thought. Like the muscle that attaches his

36

cock to the rest of his body he has relaxed with age and become more supple. He is ready to bend and turn and enjoy positions impossible for a younger man to accomplish without pain. Ernesto was a thoroughly sensual man. Unlike some men of whatever age who leave a woman feeling as if her mind has been fucked, he concentrated with his body.

His skin was brown and softly hairy. Even on his arse he had a light covering of down and his chest was the chest of a bear. Neither was Euska a hairless adolescent and her maturity was at peace with itself. She opened seriously, her strong brown belly and thighs huge with desire, matching him in strength.

As they gathered momentum together she held his arse in her hands, feeling the muscles working. She pulled him into her, using his strength to her own advantage. He loved this. The breath escaped from him in one long moan as it ended in a glistening heap of happy flesh.

'What's this?' he asked, as she came into the living-room with more coffee. He had picked the card out of the box that Euska hadn't looked at.

'You know what it is,' she said, simply.

'He's still around then.'

'He is.'

'I don't know how you can stand him.'

She shrugged her shoulders and sat close by him.

'What is it you actually do with him?' he asked.

'Ernesto!' She sat up.

'I know, I know. But I feel I have a right to ask. After all the time we've known each other, I want to know what the bastard has that stops you coming to Brazil with me.' He poured fresh coffee into big, dark blue, gold-edged cups.

'You know what he has. He has Oruela,' said Euska.

'It's not that you enjoy him, just a little?'

Euska shook her head. 'No. Not now. I used to get a certain pleasure from it.'

Ernesto kissed his teeth, a sign of exasperation.

'You don't understand how sweet revenge can be, do you? You haven't got a violent bone in your body,' said Euska.

'I don't see why you stay around even for Oruela. She doesn't even know you exist, does she?'

'She hasn't been told.' Euska paused. 'But I have a feeling about her, I always have, that I must be here for her.'

'Mmm. Your instincts are usually very good.' He sounded grumpy.

'Don't be angry with me, will you?'

'I'm not angry. Not at all. But I want you with me, in Rio. We could have such a life together there. Euska, you've never even seen my house!'

'You have a girlfriend, don't you?' said Euska, matter-of-factly.

'I haven't got a damn girlfriend, as you put it. I have several in fact. They're interchangeable. None of them mean anything to me. Good grief, I'm a man! What is this, you're trying to put me off the scent. I want to know what goes on between you and your paymaster!'

'I don't mind telling you. I don't have any conscience where he's concerned. I suppose that's it in a nutshell really, the complete suspension of my conscience.'

'Come on then.'

'You'll be shocked. I treat him very badly.'

'That's what he pays you for, isn't it?' said Ernesto.

'Well, he comes once a month,' she said. 'Regular as clockwork. He hasn't missed a visit in at least ten years. He begins with little notes and love letters and then he telephones and begs to be allowed to come. I tell him some variation on I'll crush him like a piece of shit on my shoe if he comes anywhere near me.

'Then he phones again and says he's coming and I warn him not to. He sends presents, like that there. Then usually the next day he appears at the door, which I slam in his face. He rings again and I open it and say

38

he can come in if he does exactly what I say. Usually, I get him to clean the house, from top to bottom.'

Ernesto roared with laughter.

'I've got it down to a fine art. I know exactly what I want done and how, and if he doesn't do it right I make him do it again. He likes me to stand behind him and nag him, but I get bored with that these days so I tell him he can like it or lump it. But I do nag him about the kitchen floor because he never gets that right, he's such a slob.

'He always takes his clothes off and begs for more. I made him redecorate the bathroom once, just for the hell of it. But the trouble was it took days and I got so angry having him around that I beat him up.

'He loved it but it disturbed me. I made sure he paid well for that. I make him give me the money half-way through. He's so turned on he'll give me anything and of course, once I've got it, I really can't stand him so he gets all the insults he wants.

'Once he's done it all I tell him to get out of my sight and he goes. Then a week or so later the phone calls start again and the presents, and so on.'

'He must be coming soon, then, if the present arrived this morning.'

'Tomorrow, without fail.'

'What about the sex? You haven't said anything about actual sex.' Ernesto was pouting like a little boy.

'There isn't any!' said Euska smiling.

'He must do it himself?'

'He used to. I mean he never actually wanted real sex but there used to be much more physical contact. He'd cut my toenails or something and in the beginning he used to want me undressed or just in high heels, but there hasn't been anything like that for months and months. I think he's finished with the physical side of sex. I think he still needs to feel the emotions but we never touch, ever.'

'I almost feel sorry for him!' said Ernesto, hugging her close.

'Don't. He enjoys it,' replied Euska. She kissed his chest.

'Well, until tomorrow comes you're all mine,' said Ernesto.

'I'm all yours anyway,' said Euska, softly.

The French Policeman's Whistle

*T*he investigating officer, Alix Peine, was a tall, blond and muscular young man, handsome in a pale sort of way. His square jaw and blue eyes gave him a decidedly Germanic look, indeed his father was an Alsatian. He stood upright in his black serge uniform on the doorstep of the Bruyere house. His buttons shone, his knee-length black leather boots gleamed, his burnished silver whistle-chain glowed between his buttonhole and his pocket. It was a watch chain, in fact, a family heirloom he had adapted to give something to the stupid uniform he was forced to wear.

He thrust the absurd hat that belonged to his low rank at Robert's stomach. Robert took it with inscrutable calm and showed him into the main salon.

Its owners had never heard of fashion, Alix supposed. It had been decorated sometime around the turn of the century. Were they hard up? Were they frozen in time? Were they ostracised by society?

He only wished the explanation was something as interesting. In his heart of hearts he knew that the truth would be much more dull. This room was no more or less fashionable than any other dull bourgeois salon in this dull, bourgeois town.

He caught sight of himself in the heavily framed

41

mirror above the mantelpiece and spent some time admiring what he saw. Bayonne was not his kind of town. He was much more interested in neighbouring Biarritz and its wealthy visitors. His milieu was the casino, the night clubs. But he didn't feel he was ever going to get the chance to break into the kind of society he craved. He sighed at his near-perfect reflection.

Until the previous summer he had been a rising star in Paris social life. Alix had been a special detective. Part of his job had entailed the execution of discreet services for the rich and famous and doors had opened for him that would normally have been closed. He had haunted Bricktops, Zelli's, Le Sphinx: fashionable clubs and whorehouses far beyond the means of an ordinary policeman. Not that Alix had been entirely a playboy, his heart wasn't in it. He had also frequented more respectable enclosures like the opera and the ballet. Indeed, just before his hurried departure he had begun to smell success; mothers had cast their eyes in his direction, asking the sort of questions that pertain to marriageable daughters.

Alix planned to choose a wife wisely. He didn't want to remain a policeman all his life. He imagined himself marrying the sweet, malleable daughter of someone influential who would ease his way into politics. But there was time enough. The world was at his feet. Unfortunately, though, the world also included the wife of the commissioner, and she was mad about him.

He found a certain charm in her mountain of quivering flesh and in Paris these things were tolerated so long as they were kept discreet. In fact the commissioner was quite happy to leave the physical happiness of his wife to one of his subordinates and get on with his own peccadilloes. The bad luck was that Madame the Commissioner's wife had twin eighteen-year-old daughters whose boudoir was just along the corridor from their mother's.

One hot and sultry night, when Alix was leaving his mountainous love, he was surprised by the return of the commissioner below. Not merely surprised, indeed he was almost petrified. His career flashed before him in a second; he saw the road back to his dreary little home town as clear as if it were to be trudged that very day. Coming to his senses he darted silently along the corridor and into the nearest room which of course was the daughters'.

He found them whispering together in bed. The covers were thrown back and they were naked as babes. Their twin bodies were plump and white and absolutely identical, right down to their pubes, which were as curled and silky-looking as the hair of cherubs. The arse of the one girl was exquisite and the belly and breasts of the other were classic in their beauty. What a vision! Both sides of the same coin at once!

They sat up together, their hair falling like angelic auras around their sweet shoulders. In the split second of their surprise they were still as statues, then the one nearest to Alix smiled languidly over her shoulder, while the other pulled the bedclothes up to her neck and stared.

Tearing his eyes from the lovely sight Alix dragged himself to the window and hid behind the heavy curtains. The sound of the commissioner's footsteps came closer and then died away down the hall. A door opened and closed.

Alix stayed where he was for another minute or two until he thought it was safe to leave. He mused on his discovery. Could he see himself married to one of the twins? Perhaps he could get them both to fall in love with him. Then through the heavy fabric he heard the sound of giggling.

He peeped out. Some urgent consultation was taking place between the identical girls. It seemed the one who had neglected to cover herself was trying to persuade the other to do something. The pair of them lay there, looking at him. Alix became aware of his erection at the same time as they did. How was he going to play this? He didn't feel quite sure what to do. He stood there,

43

feeling his prick heavy as stone and light as a feather all at the same time.

'What are you standing there for?' asked one of the girls. She was the more brazen one who hadn't deigned to cover herself in the first place. Something about her tone of voice compelled him to move. He left his hiding-place and approached the bed.

'Sit down,' she said. 'I am Angelique. This is Veronique. Tell us a story.'

For a moment he was surprised. He didn't have a story. He didn't have the kind of mind that thought in stories. 'I don't know any,' he said. 'I'm a man of action,' and he grinned a sly grin.

'Well, we like stories and if you don't tell us one then perhaps we will have to call Papa and then you'll have something to tell when someone asks you.'

Racking his brain quickly, Alix found something. 'I was in Bricktops earlier this week,' he said. 'They have a new show. Shall I tell you about it?'

'That will do for now,' said Angelique.

'There is a young girl and a young boy. They come on to the stage wearing animal skins, like cave people. They dance around the stage and have sex, right there on the stage.' Alix stopped.

'That's not much of a story,' said Veronique, turning to her sister. 'I don't think he has much of an imagination. Perhaps we had better call Papa.'

'*No!*' begged Alix. 'Please, let me please you in other ways. Have you experienced the delights of a man?'

The girls giggled. 'What have you to show us then?' said Angelique.

'This,' said Alix, opening his fly. He felt sure they'd never seen anything like it before.

'Well!' said Veronique and she reached for his swollen manhood, handling it with some expertise. She caressed it while Angelique rested back on her elbow and smiled.

Alix felt like a king. Their young bodies were just

waiting for him. Look how they admired him. 'Do you want it?' he said. 'I can give it to you both.'

'Can we use it, sister?' said Veronique.

'I think he should keep his boots on,' said Angelique.

'Oh yes, and his waistcoat,' said Veronique.

Alix felt a little bit silly but he realised he was in no position to do other than they asked. He put back on his long, shiny boots and his waistcoat. Something about being partly clothed made him feel more vulnerable than if he were completely undressed. He stood waiting.

Veronique rose and circled around him, looking him up and down critically. 'My sister needs relief,' she said. 'Lick her clitoris.'

Now this was more like it. He bent over Angelique and went to work on the pussy that offered itself to him. This was no toil. This was fantastic. He felt the other sister caressing his arse and ached for her to suck his cock. How delicious that would be. He surfaced and told her to do it.

'All in good time,' she said. 'Just get on with what you're told.'

On some unseen signal, the girls changed their positions, Angelique lay on her back and guided his cock between her breasts. Its length squeezed between them and dug into the little hollow of her neck as she pressed her breasts together. Their nipples strained towards him, two angry buttons of pink desire. Veronique, arranging herself behind her sister's head, spread her legs for him and forced his head on to her own sex.

Alix was so aroused that the first semen began to seep from him 'I'm going to come,' he whispered, 'I'm going to come!'

'Oh no you don't,' said the girls in unison. 'Not until we have.'

With a supreme effort he tore himself away and sat between them, his cock throbbing.

'You must understand, monsieur, that we are virgins

and we are not at liberty to lose our hymens to you. But we are not strangers to orgasm. You will have to make sure we get one each. Fair's fair. And then you can have your own,' said Angelique.

'Which one first?' croaked Alix.

'Both,' said the two of them and they lay back on the bed, legs parted in expectation.

Alix buried his face in Veronique's soft pubic hair and worked on her with his tongue, while with his hand, he sought its twin and massaged for all he was worth. He came up for air and swapped but this time Angelique leapt on his arse and rode him like a horse, working herself up on his buttocks that squashed underneath her.

Bored with that she decided to slap him, hard. It hurt. What's more it made a noise and it terrified him. He stopped what he was doing. Veronique raised herself.

'Now look what you've done. You've put her off!' said Angelique. 'Continue what you were doing. Now!'

Alix obeyed. He couldn't feel Angelique any more and he tried to concentrate on Veronique but the memory of the stinging slap was on his backside and he imagined there would be another soon.

She was watching, silently. She walked around the room. He caught a glimpse of her out of the corner of his eye, in one corner. Then she was gone. Where had she gone? There she was, on the other side of the room. He could almost see himself as she saw him, with his boots on, the waistcoat enclosing his back, leaving his arse and thighs exposed. Nothing like this had ever happened to him before. He felt humiliated but incredibly turned on. He wanted her; where was she?

Suddenly, Veronique, sensing his distraction, grabbed his hair and worked his face up and down on her. She was coming. He could feel it. She stiffened. His hair hurt where she pulled it. He hated the great groan of pleasure that came from her. As soon as she released his head he came up for air.

But before he knew it, Angelique was there. Angelique's face had nothing angelic about it: it was openly full of lust.

His cock was aching with the weight of jailed sperm. 'Touch me!' he begged Veronique. 'You've had your pleasure. Touch me.'

There was silence. In front of him another wet sex was waiting: Angelique's. She, who'd had the nerve to slap him. He raised himself. He must have her. He must give it to her. He was all cock. He got it almost there. It was just touching the opening of her delicious sex. But she grabbed it as it was about to go in and made it rub up and down on her clitoris instead. How dare she not want him! How dare these little girls refuse to give in to him! Her pubic hair was rough against him but the sensation strong and hot. She wouldn't be able to resist surely. Any minute now and he would slip it home, she wouldn't know what hit – and then he felt the shock of something cold at his arsehole.

He couldn't tell what it was but it wasn't human. It distracted him long enough for Angelique to come and then it was gone and he lay there, confused, as the girls lay back on the bed, smiling and satisfied.

They didn't give a damn. They really didn't. He was humiliated and desperate. He begged them but they merely turned over and yawned. He moved against the bed at their feet, trying to make himself come but it didn't work. So he rolled over and pumped himself. He – Alix! His sperm shot from him like champagne released from a corked bottle and he fell back on the bed, gasping.

Unfortunately he didn't hear the turning of the door handle, nor at first did he see the commissioner.

His demotion was swift as it was complete. The very next day found him on the platform at the train station in Bayonne in a hot August sun, angrily waiting for the sergeant at whose house he was to lodge. His heart was full of humiliation and revenge and for three weeks now he had fallen prey to fits of gloom. He was desperate.

But he was forming a plan. He was looking for a rich widow, no matter what she looked like or how old she was. With some money behind him he might be able to find something to do, even here. The clamour of neighbouring Biarritz beckoned him like the finger of a witch queen.

He was standing by the fireplace in the Bruyeres' front parlour, swaying slightly back and forth on the soles of his long black boots, pondering his plan, when the door opened and in came Genevieve. She had loosened her hair a little. Alix locked on to the target. The prey became the hunter.

'Monsieur Peine,' said Genevieve matter-of-factly and she seated herself in the straight-backed chair on one side of the large window.

He sat down on the couch. 'Monsieur the Mayor presents his compliments, madame, and apologises for not being here himself,' he said, all charm.

'Where is he?' said Genevieve.

'He sits on the Provincial Board of Health today, madame.'

'That's what he said on the telephone,' said Genevieve and she looked Alix up and down as if she was waiting for something.

'Madame, I understand that there has been a death?' said Alix. He fiddled with his whistle chain, curling it in his fingers and tugging at the buttonhole.

'Well, yes. My husband was found dead by his manservant at 8.30 this morning. I think you'll find the matter very simple. An autopsy will show that my husband has been poisoned by my daughter.'

Alix was fascinated by her. The way she sat demurely, her features showing barely a trace of emotion except perhaps impatience. Since his experience with the twins he found himself drawn to women who displayed even the slightest callousness. With a little business-like cluck she continued.

48

'She's feigning sickness upstairs in her bed. A local doctor saw her and give her a sedative. She admitted it all and then she passed out. It's all very simple!'

Alix asked to be taken first to see the corpse and second to see Oruela. Genevieve led him. She had a slim figure, he noted, and with excitement he felt *her* eyes travelling up the length of *his* legs as he bent over the body. It was unmistakable! There was an extra spring in his step as he ran downstairs to phone the coroner.

Michelle marched towards Alix as he entered Oruela's bedroom, barring his way. Oruela was lying dazed among the pillows. 'Monsieur! This is a lady's bedroom and the lady is asleep!' she said.

'I am a policeman,' said Alix, barging past her, 'and I am used to ladies' boudoirs.'

'Not this one you're not.' Michelle charged again and stood firm.

'Do stop it, girl,' sighed Genevieve. 'Get out of the way and allow this man to talk to your mistress.'

Michelle glared at Genevieve and was about to tell her she was a vicious old bag but some instinct told her to hold back. She had to be a bit clever here.

'What time did your mistress come in this morning?' asked Alix.

'I don't know, sir,' answered Michelle sulkily.

'Did you hear your mistress confess to killing Monsieur Norbert Bruyere?' he asked.

'I heard all sorts of things when she was delirious, sir, but I can't say I remember any of it.'

'Oh, this is ridiculous,' said Genevieve. 'Just wake the girl up and she'll confess.' And with a cluck of impatience, Genevieve got next to the bed and gave Oruela a shove. 'You killed your father, didn't you?' she said nicely.

Oruela roused herself. The question seemed to come from on high, booming down a tunnel of tranquillisers.

If she answered it with what they wanted to hear then perhaps this madness would stop.

'Don't answer!' she heard Michelle say. But what did Michelle know?

'Yes,' she said. 'I did.'

Alix Peine wrote something in his notebook.

'That is the poisonous animal she used,' said Genevieve, pointing to the lizard.

Alix went to the bedside table and picked up the cage. The lizard took one long look at the policeman, turned, lifted his tail and crapped. A terrible smell invaded the room. Michelle looked at Alix in disgust.

'I shall take this for examination,' said Alix and, holding the cage at arm's length, he walked out of the room.

Genevieve felt restless after the policeman had gone. She couldn't settle. Such was widowhood, she thought: a change in the routine. She made up her mind to go out and get some fresh air in the grounds, but then she spotted something shining on the sofa. It was his whistle! Fancy leaving it behind! Could it be a sign? Well, she would take good care of it for him.

She ran her fingers over the long shiny mouthpiece with its curling lip, over the bulge where the pea nestled, along the long, smooth stem, and into the slithery links of the chain. It was so deliciously cold. Cold, dead silver. She breathed on it to warm it a little and then she pulled out the neck of her dress and popped it into her shallow cleavage.

She went out into the garden and attempted her usual inspection of the budding flora but she couldn't rid herself of the image of Alix Peine's backside, his long legs. She paused in front of the tulip bed. The flowers were in full bloom. Suddenly they were a mass of dwarf red penises!

If it hadn't been for the servants, she would have run up the stairs to her bedroom. It was a dingy room, the scene of so much marital disappointment and frus-

50

tration. She drew the curtains and by a chink of light she undid the bodice of her dress in order to retrieve the whistle. Just when she thought she'd got it, it slipped away again into another part of her plentiful, old-fashioned, cotton underwear. In the end she was forced to undress almost completely. All she had left on were her knickers.

She looked at herself in the full-length mirror on the wardrobe door, shyly at first, but with increasing boldness. She raised her arms above her head and twisted this way and that. Her breasts were quite long and thin, as if everything they contained was in the tips. The nipples were the palest rose colour. Her heart beat fast. She grew bolder, slipping off her knickers now and posing coyly, like the paintings of Venus in Bayonne Town Hall that were her only knowledge of female nudity. How she hated her unsightly hair there . . .

She brought the whistle between her breasts and held it by its chain, letting it drift downwards towards her tangle of pale pubic hair. Suddenly she ran and jumped on the bed and clasped the whistle to her lips, whispering to it.

'I want to make love to your owner. Do you love me? Yes, he says, I've never known a woman like you . . .'

She rolled languidly on to her back and pressed the whistle to her clitoris. There it rubbed and tickled her and made her bold. She pressed it into service further down. She lolled back in a state approaching ecstasy. After all these years, to be doing this in the afternoon! How free she felt. Wonderful!

And then, as the silver pleasure began to pump in and out, a little bit of air that had whipped up Genevieve's vagina in the excitement took its chance to escape and PEEEEEP – the whistle was blown.

Friday's Girls Are Full Of . . .

Over the next twenty-four hours the Bruyere mansion imploded with strange passions. Michelle and Robert fucked till they bruised. Oruela lay in a semiconscious world of half-waking dreams. Such dreams they were! A serpent slithered up the ancient bark of a tree and perfumed flowers opened like silken vaginas, dripping their golden pollen on the cool grass. A naked man – it was Jean and not Jean at the same time – tried to talk but his lips were sealed. He beckoned to her and as she went closer she saw that it was Valentino, the great lover himself, and he was hers. He held a fruit, a dark, purple fig and he peeled it and offered the ruby flesh to her lips. She sucked at the sweet juice as if her life depended on it. But as she swallowed the scene changed and she was falling, falling. Before she hit the ground she awoke, sweating, and Michelle held her against her soft breasts and murmured soothing sounds until she slept again.

But it was Genevieve, her stepmother, whose sexuality was out and all over the place. Nothing could cool either her shame over the whistle or her need. They were twin peaks of emotion between which she rushed like a crazed eagle. Movement seemed to help. She had Robert move furniture for the rest of the day and

52

enjoyed the sight of his muscles straining under his clothes.

In the evening she sat down in the front room on a high-backed chair, shaking a cocktail of erotic images in her mind: a measure of black leather boots, shiny, slithering, enclosing shapely calves; a dash of long curving thighs . . . and a twist of pretty little jutting white arse, downy with soft hair and muscles flowing into the small of the back. She imagined how she would fling him on to the couch and he'd be helpless and then she'd lift up her severe black dress and underneath her little puss would open its little mouth and gorge itself on his helpless shank.

Her sex was so swollen and so hot that she had to touch it. She put two fingers through a little hole in her pocket and pressed the swelling. It felt so good and comforting. Little by little the rip enlarged and her hand got busier and busier and the feeling was tighter and tighter. It was lovely. She wondered what it smelled like. She shyly raised her fingers to her nose and held them there for the briefest moment. The smell was quite pleasant, she decided. Everything was pleasant.

This room had been Norbert's and it had more sun than the dingy back room he had assigned her. She felt a kind of liberation. Yes the bastard was really dead. And she could have sex with whom she liked.

Sex! Her thighs tensed of their own accord. It put a wonderful pressure in just the right place. Tense. Relax. Tense. Relax. It was a bit like riding a horse, she thought. There was absolutely no guilt either; her hands were perfectly innocent. She became hot around the waist and under her arms, her nipples scraped the fabric of her dress. She was very wet between the legs. She slid her fingers to touch herself and held on tightly as the tension built up with each squeeze of the rhythm: up and up, it was awesome! Up and up, irresistible! A shiver leapt up her back attacking her shoulders and her taste-buds at the same time. And then she fell forward and came face to face with the carpet. Well, she thought to herself a moment later, that must've been an orgasm!

In the morning, when she awoke, she was still panting on the edge of a sexual precipice and she retrieved her whistle from behind the bed. This time she watched herself in the mirror, lying on the end of her huge bed, her nightdress hitched up and fanned out behind her on the coverlets like the plumage of some proud bird. The silver whistle slithered around in the moist coral-pink of her cunt; it tangled in her hair and gently stroked her pale belly.

With her elegant, pointed fingertips she tantalised her clitoris and as the need became more urgent she rubbed hard. God, it was good! Was this what you were supposed to do? She had no way of finding out. There must be a book. She lifted herself up and again looked in the mirror. There were lines on her face. It wasn't fair that she was discovering all this so late. How she hated Norbert and his brat! She went into the bathroom and had a generous pee.

She left her knickers off for lunch. That felt nice. She couldn't eat much anyway. And when she took her customary drive afterwards she wanted very much to masturbate in public in the back of the Bentley that Norbert had imported from England. But she was too scared, so she contented herself with the thigh-clenching that she had learned earlier.

Madame Radotage, the wife of the prominent industrialist, who was also driving that afternoon, felt terribly sorry for Genevieve. 'I saw her,' she told Madame Derive, the mayor's wife, over coffee. 'She was terribly abstracted. She was literally rocking back and forth with grief. How dreadful it is to be struck so young . . .'

Genevieve was so frenzied when she got back from the drive that she told Robert to delay tea twenty minutes while she freshened up. She took her refresher, for the sake of variety, in the master bathroom. The cold white tiles, the bareness of the floor, the dried soap smell of the shaving brush, the deep blue bath salts bottle, all reminded her of Norbert. She never used it while he was alive. She had her own on the dark side of the house. The eeriest feeling that he was still there took hold of her. She raised her foot up on to the rim of the green enamel, hoisted up her skirt with a laugh like a gypsy girl and began to rub her clitoris again, up and down, up and down her fleshy sex, spreading it wide and screwing her lovely long-nailed finger into its wetness.

'Dead,' she whispered. 'He's fucking dead.' The words drove into her vagina and caused her a hot pulse of agony. 'Fuck him, he's dead,' she shouted, and suddenly everything hurt. She rubbed harder and harder till it really hurt so much that she had to force herself over the hill. She came in a burst of heat and tears and unsettling laughter.

The sun was dying. It slanted off the roof of the old stables and it came softly in the window. For the briefest of moments she felt its peace and well-being. But as the sun dropped behind the roof and the room was dull, white and antiseptic again, self-disgust and fear crept into her mind with the gloom. Unnatural woman! Turned on by his death! Coming at the sound of her own voice and loving it. Somewhere in the house she heard the bang of a careless door . . . She straightened her clothing and went downstairs.

It was comforting to find the large tray waiting for her as usual in the study. She was ravenous, suddenly, and she pounced on the pastries. Robert was a good servant, she thought. She wondered what it would be like to rip off his trousers . . . and then she sat down quickly. She chewed noisily on the pastry. Then, out of the corner of her eye she saw something move . . .

Alix Peine was hovering behind the oriental screen. He was studying the lacquerwork, it seemed.

'Oh,' gurgled Genevieve.

Alix spun round. 'Madame,' he said and clicked his heels as he bowed. 'I beg your pardon. I didn't mean to alarm you.'

'Well,' spluttered Genevieve, chewing furiously.

'Mayor Derive is with your servant-girl, madame.'

'I see. Please join me in some coffee and pastries,' she squeaked, getting another cup from the sideboard.

Alix sat down on the chair closest to her couch. He took the cup she gave him and his fingers touched hers in the process. Genevieve felt tingly again, all over.

But they were interrupted by the entrance of Mayor Derive. The mayor was about sixty, well-fed and wealthy looking. 'My *dear* Genevieve,' he said, 'I'm so sorry about all this.'

'Come and sit down, Jacques,' said Genevieve, leaping up again to get a cup from the sideboard.

He sat down next to her on the couch and took a cup of coffee.

'Excuse me, I think I'll ask some more questions of the servants,' said Alix and he hastily departed.

'Where's he gone?' said Genevieve.

'He's being discreet, my dear. Now, do you have someone to look after you?' As he spoke he put his hand on her knee.

'My servants take care of me.'

'Don't you have any relatives who could come and stay with you?' Derive lifted his hand from her knee and took a sip of his coffee.

'What do I want relatives for?' said Genevieve.

'To look after you,' he said, and patted her knee again. This time he allowed his hand to remain there.

She didn't move. 'You'll look after me, won't you, Jacques?' she asked.

'Of course my dear. I'd love to. I could really make you feel special again,' he said, pushing his hand up her thigh.

She didn't stop him. She didn't actually know what to do. His breath was a bit ripe and his skin was flaky, she noticed. She really didn't want him to do it but no one had ever done this to her before and she just didn't know what to do.

56

'What will happen to Oruela now, Jacques?' she squeaked.

'Whatever you like, my dear.'

'What are the choices?'

'Do you really want to talk about it now?' he gurgled.

'Jacques, don't think me ungrateful for your help or anything but I feel a bit strange at the moment.'

'Come to bed with me, my dear. Let me comfort you.'

'Oh, Jacques!' cried Genevieve, looking deep into his eyes. 'Give me a little time.' This seemed to satisfy him for the moment and she repeated her question about Oruela.

'Well, we could have her arrested and taken to prison to await trial,' he said. 'Or you could keep her here until a trial. You look perturbed, my dear?'

'Nothing, go on,' she said.

'The third option, and I must admit it's the one I advise, is that we don't go to all the trouble of a trial at all. We put her in a nursing home for the mentally insane. All that takes is a doctor's word and your consent. We don't need to make any of it public. I only need announce that she's taken her father's death badly and gone into hospital for a rest. Unfortunately the only local facilities for the insane are attached to the House of Correction at St Trou.'

'A House of Correction!' murmured Genevieve. She wriggled in her seat. 'How long would she stay there?'

'Oh, indefinitely, my dear,' he said, putting his hand right up her skirt and in between her legs. 'Does that please you?'

'Yes,' she whispered.

'I like to please you. Don't you worry your head about anything. I'll see to that bad little bitch for you.'

'Oh, Jacques!' said Genevieve. 'Oh, Jacques! I shall always remember how you took my side against Norbert. You are so good.'

Derive nuzzled into her breasts. 'I just don't like bad bitches. I like good women, like you. Genevieve, open my fly. Come on. Touch me.'

She obeyed him. It was the first cock she'd touched in twenty years! It was a long thin one, not hard exactly, a little bendy, like a carrot fit for soup, but it was growing harder.

'Oh,' he cried. 'Your hands are like little birds. Here. Get on top of me.'

'No. No!' she cried.

'Yes! Yes!' cried the mayor and he lifted her on to his lap. He hoisted his cock right out and pushed it into her. 'There,' he said. 'We'll put that girl away. We'll make sure she gets the bad blood beaten out of her.'

He was disgusting. His breath! But it was fantastic to have a cock inside her. She was just getting used to it when it was all over.

He slapped her arse before he left and she stood there a few moments, staring at the closed door. She heard the sound of raised voices out on the driveway, but they didn't really register. A few moments later a knock seemed to come from a distance.

'Come in!' she said, recovering.

It was the parlour-maid. 'Madame,' she said. 'I thought you should know that the doctor who came yesterday, Simenon, has just tried to get in the house but Mayor Derive sent him away very firmly.'

'Good.' said Genevieve. 'What's going on upstairs?'

'Oruela is still senseless. Michelle hasn't left her side.'

'Well, it will all be over soon,' said Genevieve, smiling. 'Thank you. That will be all.'

Genevieve sat back down on the couch. Things were looking up, she thought. Another knock came at the door. 'What is it?' she called impatiently.

Alix entered looking absolutely gorgeous. She could feel Derive in her knickers and she felt quite disgusting and bold. She held her breath.

'Madame, excuse me. Did I leave my whistle here yesterday?'

Genevieve swallowed. 'No,' she said.

'Thank you, madame,' he said, sounding puzzled. He bowed again.

58

'Before you go,' said Genevieve, 'would you come again tomorrow? I might need you. No need to tell the mayor though, if you don't mind.'

Alix beamed. 'Of course, madame,' he said.

Genevieve held her composure until she heard the front door close. Then she jumped in the air and, laughing hysterically, went to the window and fixed her eyes on Alix's long legs as he walked down the drive. The great knot of the curtain tie was just at crotch height and she leaned into it. Did Alix sense she was watching him? Did he know?

Oh, how she ached for him. She pulled the knot right between her legs. Alix turned. He had almost reached the gates and he was looking right at the house. Was he watching her? Surely he was. Yes! He knew what she was doing. She knew he knew. She murmured her thoughts on to the glass as he watched her. I'm going to come, she murmured. I'm going to come while he's watching me. She pulled the knot and pushed it and . . . what a feeling of freedom she had. It was so wonderful. So outrageous.

The curtain pole relinquished its hold under the strain and the lot, pole, curtains, knots and ten years' dust, fell down about her head.

Oh, Lonesome Me . . .

Jean sat in a large golden ear, drinking coffee that was hot, Algerian and strong enough to make a dead man shit. The ear was an expensive, handmade piece of furniture by the great Steingarnele who, as yet, was little known outside a tight and wealthy circle of collectors.

Jean would have, if he could, decorated his whole room à la mode. But Jean's mother absolutely refused to have him decorate anything else in his crazy modern style. The drapes on each side of his massive bed stood like heavy brocade sentinels guarding her son, while he slept, from complete modernity. The bed itself was swathed in oceans of white silk and frills and Jean felt like a girl when he was at home. Madame Raffoler had made a gesture towards his masculinity by hanging watercolours of famous battles by a long-dead and technically accomplished painter but she insisted on relentless gilt. The bases of lamps and the legs of tables were covered in it.

Jean took all of it in his stride. She was his mother and he liked to please her.

His silken, ruby-red dressing-gown hung loosely over one long leg, leaving the other bare. It hung open at his handsome chest. It was hardly worth him wearing anything really but he had made a stab at decency for the sake of his mother.

He leaned back into the auricle and opened his mail. It contained nothing interesting and he sighed. He was horny. Slowly the bulge under the ruby silk grew until his cock popped out. And then the door opened and in whirled his sister Hélène.

Unlike her brother she saw no need to stab at convention. What had it ever done to her? Hélène was at the age of absolute rebellion. Sweet seventeen and dangerous. What did she care if the men of the household lost their minds as she crossed the landing wearing only perfume? This morning she was wearing something but only because it had just arrived in the post from her favourite Paris shop. It was a black, fine, net affair with a fur collar that covered her ears and partially concealed her chin. Its hem, at knee length, was also trimmed with fur but between these two extremities every inch of her was visible through a charming, crisscross veil, like a precious gem behind a jeweller's counter. Her hair was copper-coloured and looked unnatural. But its tastelessness was somehow utterly alluring.

'Very practical,' said Jean, leering. He leaned towards her to touch one of her precious gems.

She stuck her tongue out at him. 'Maman's angry with you,' she said.

'Why?'

'Some servant girl came to the back door earlier, asking for you. Maman thinks you should stick to your own class,' she pouted.

'I do. Resolutely!' said Jean, covering himself. 'I haven't been making love to any servant girls. What was it about?'

'I don't know, but you could find out if you want. She's been standing outside on the street ever since. Look,' replied Hélène.

They both went to the window and looked over the

61

wall into the street beyond the villa. Michelle stood under a tree with new leaves, looking lost.

Jean withdrew from the window and pressed the bell on the wall by the fireplace.

'She's pretty,' said Hélène. 'Pass her on when you've finished,'

Jean tutted. 'I've never been able to fathom whether your lesbianism is serious or merely a fad. There does seem to be an awful lot of it about these days.'

'What do you care what it is?' said Hélène.

'Well, I'm not sure I really want my sister to become an embarrassment to me,' he said.

Hélène laughed. 'You really are the limit,' she said. She left the room without a backward glance.

As the servant came out of the gates of the sumptuous mansion to fetch her, Michelle was thinking about Robert and how he had been the night before when he'd walked her to the train station in Bayonne to catch the milk train at 2 a.m. They both had a sense that this was the end of something. She could never go back to the house. Genevieve Bruyere had allies in some of the other servants and she would know at first light that Michelle was gone.

Michelle had been happy in that house and it was sad leaving it. But the only hope for Oruela was to rouse Jean Raffoler to storm the house and rescue her.

A shower of rain had swept inland and shed itself on the dark road as they walked along. The gnarled trunks of ancient trees loomed in their path. Strange shapes glistened as the shower ceased and the moon appeared again. None of it frightened Michelle. She felt at one with the road and the darkness. What frightened her was the mayor and what he might do.

It was this fear that drove her hand to clutch at Robert's; this fear and the violence, perhaps, of the emotion she had been witness to that left her so raw that when, as they neared the outskirts of the town, he kissed her passionately in the middle of the road she was painfully aroused. If there hadn't been only minutes before the train departed they would have made love in the glistening, dark woods.

As the servant came towards her she was imagining how it would have been . . .

'Would you like to come in, m'selle?' asked the man. 'Monsieur Raffoler has instructed me to show you to his rooms.'

Michelle brushed her skirt front. She felt a little like a tramp after spending half the night at La Negresse railway station fending off revellers coming home from a night's drinking. Gentlemen! As far as Michelle was concerned you could keep gentlemen.

As she followed the servant into the house she decided she had rich tastes. The Raffolers were one of the richest families in Biarritz and she liked what she saw.

Jean still wore the ruby-red robe but fortunately for Michelle he had put trousers on underneath it and drawn the sash tight. He stood by the tall fireplace in his suite of rooms and listened to her story. 'Good God!' he said repeatedly. It gradually dawned on Michelle that he didn't believe her.

'Are you absolutely sure about all this?' he asked, more than once. Michelle's temper was rising.

'Of course I'm sure,' she said, rising from the chair he'd shown her into. 'D'you think I'd spend the night on a railway station if I wasn't?'

Jean was watching the way her breast rose and fell with quickened anger. He'd always fancied Michelle. That arse! There weren't many of those! But her eyes were flashing and it frightened him. 'All right,' he said. 'Calm down, Michelle. Sit down.' He started to pace the carpet. 'I just find it all so terribly hard to believe. It's like the plot of some dreadful novelette. As if something cheap has suddenly imposed itself on my world . . .' He stopped in front of the window and looked out on to the grounds of his home.

This time Michelle rose and stood her ground. 'I'm sure if it's any kind of imposition, I'll go and find Dr Simenon and see if he's gentleman enough to help Oruela before it's too late. Don't you understand they may be taking her away right this very minute!' God! Oruela might think that Jean was wonderful but he was acting like a *fou*! He looked like a man all right, pacing up and down in his dressing-gown. But what was the use of him?

'She didn't tell me there was anything wrong between herself and her mother,' continued Jean.

'Oh, there was plenty,' said Michelle. 'But look, there really isn't time to go into it.'

'And the mayor colluding in a plot to take her away? He's a friend of my father's, I . . .'

Michelle walked towards the door. She would have to do something else. Just as she reached it there was a knock and a servant entered.

'Telephone, sir, for the young woman,' said the man, and he gave Michelle a wink.

She took the receiver gingerly. It was Robert. It was the first chance he had had to use the phone. Oruela had been taken away an hour ago.

This finally galvanised Jean into action and he flew off into his dressing-room. Before Michelle could drink the coffee he had ordered her, he was back.

She rose.

'No, no. Please finish it at your leisure,' he said and he was gone.

Michelle decided to write him a note telling him she would be at her Aunt Violette's haberdashery shop if he wanted her. She was sure her aunt would take her in. It wasn't as if Jean and Oruela would be using the little apartment in the roof.

Michelle was putting the note on the mantelpiece when Hélène walked in the room. Michelle looked at the young woman's extraordinary outfit and her mouth dropped open.

'Has my brother gone off and left you? Oh, how could he?' crooned Hélène.

64

Michelle, in complete ignorance of the idea that two women could gain pleasure from each other's bodies, did not rise to this morsel of bait nor to any others. She left the mansion a little while later having come to the conclusion that the Raffolers, like so many rich people, were a touch mad.

Jean's open DeSoto screeched to a halt outside the massive locked prison gates with their spyhole that looked out but allowed no one to look in. He parked a little way up the road. The wall around the place was at least twenty feet high and the top of it was laced with barbed wire. He ran to the doors and pounded on them with his fists.

There was a loud shout from inside. 'Oi, Oi. Stop that!'

Jean suddenly realised he would get nowhere. Thinking fast he shouted, 'It's Dr Marchand! There's an emergency.'

'All right. All right,' came the reply.

Bolts were thrown back and a small door opened in the great gates. The guard behind it was a man, five foot nothing and grossly overweight. He bowed slightly to Jean, who had drawn himself up to a height appropriate to authority.

'You'll find the reception just as you go in,' grumbled the guard.

Jean thanked heaven for the stupidity of prison guards. He considered his next move. One or two inmates sat around on benches, obviously senseless. A young nurse walked across the garden . . .

The poor woman had just finished a novel in which a visiting psychiatrist bumps into a nurse and the encounter ends in marriage. Her eyes sparked with wonder as she looked up and saw Jean, who had set himself on a collision course. Two little red spots of embarrassment appeared on her cheeks. 'Monsieur!' she murmured. 'Can I help you? You look lost!'

'I am,' said Jean, seductively. 'I'm looking for a new

patient of mine. Her name is Bruyere. She will be with your Dr . . . er . . .' He fished in his pocket.

'Dr von Streibnitz,' said the woman, 'if she's new.'

'Of course,' said Jean, bringing an old receipt out of his pocket. He tapped it and smiled.

'Shall I take you?' she offered.

'No, no,' said Jean. 'Just tell me the way.'

Following her directions he bluffed his way into the cell block and climbed the spiral staircase at one end. The spring sunshine eked its way through a long window, where two figures sat playing cards in silhouette. He stood for a moment on the landing deciding which way to go.

'Excuse me, sir, can I help you?' A small, rat-faced female guard came from nowhere and sidled up to him.

Jean turned on his smile. But something told him his luck had run out. He could feel his blood chilling in his veins. 'I'm looking for Dr von Streibnitz,' he said.

'Who are you?' asked the rat-face.

'Dr Marchand,' said Jean. 'A colleague.'

'Why are you here?' she demanded.

'I was invited to see an inmate.' Jean tried to sound offended at the questioning.

'Where's your authorisation card?'

Jean grinned like a little boy. 'Mademoiselle, I must be honest with you,' he said. 'I had one last time I was here but I couldn't find it, and as they know me on the gate they let me through.'

'I'd better check up on this,' she said.

She made a move towards the telephone on the wall just behind Jean's shoulder. He caught her off-guard with a crack on the jaw that knocked her out in one. She slid down the wall.

He heaved her weight into a recess where he sat her on a toilet and used her stockings to tie her to the cistern. He stuffed the sleeve of her cardigan into her mouth and unhooked the bunch of keys from a chain around her waist.

* * *

Oruela's cell was about eight doors along the third landing. Jean opened the door with the keys. A big smile lit up Oruela's whole face when she saw who it was. But Jean had a job to disguise his reaction. Her eyes were glassy, she was as pale as death. He pulled the door to behind him and closed the spyhole. He took her in his arms. She smelt strange.

'Have you come to take me home?' she whispered.

'I wish I had. To tell you the truth I don't know what I'm doing. I just had to come but I don't know how to get you out,' he said gloomily.

They both instinctively looked at the high, barred square of the window.

He stroked her hair. 'Tell me what happened. Michelle said you told everyone you'd killed your father?'

Oruela started to cry. 'I don't know what happened. I don't think I killed him . . . I know I didn't. I just wished him dead. You can't kill someone by just wishing them dead, can you, Jean?' and she clung to him.

'Of course not!' said Jean, gently stroking her hair. It was not clean. 'But why did you think you had?'

'I don't know. I got so confused. I'm still confused. What am I doing here, Jean? This is a real prison.'

'Why were you so confused? Because he died?'

'I had a bad dream.'

'I can't believe you're here because of a bad dream. None of it makes any sense.' Jean was half talking to himself. 'Michelle said your mother put the idea in your head. Why should she do that?'

'Because she hates me,' came her little voice from his chest. 'She isn't really my mother. They fostered me. It was his idea, I know that. No one's supposed to know but I found out one night when I was ten years old. I heard them arguing about it. She hates me, Jean. She hates me.'

Jean looked down into the eyes whose clear depths he had loved. 'You never told me anything about this. Why? Who are your real parents? Do you know?'

'I don't know anything about my real parents at all,' she whispered.

Jean stroked her hand, her head, her shoulders. 'I would've understood. You should have told me. I would have taken you away from home months ago if I'd known you were so unhappy.'

'Oruela reached up to kiss him. But he didn't respond. 'What am I going to do now?' she mumbled.

'I'm going to go and see the mayor. There must be some bizarre mistake.'

'He doesn't like me,' said Oruela, looking at her lap.

Jean frowned. 'Has anyone told you how long you'll be here? Is there going to be a public trial or something?'

'No one's come near me.'

The sound of a guard walking along the landing outside filtered through the door.

'I must go,' whispered Jean, and he prised himself away from her gently. 'I won't be able to help you if I get caught. I must go and start asking questions. I'll get you out of here soon, don't worry. In the meantime you'll be a strong girl?'

'Yes, Jean,' she said and she lifted up her face for a kiss. It never came.

'Take this and hide it somewhere, you might need it,' he said, taking a hundred-franc note out of his wallet. And then he was gone.

She sat holding the money for a long time, unaware that it existed. She still felt really groggy from the drugs they had administered to her. She ached for Jean. If only he were there he would kiss her and things would be all right. She tried to collect her thoughts. At least she felt a bit better now that he knew where she was. She lay back on the mattress to soothe herself with thoughts of him and suddenly remembered the money.

The obvious thing was to stuff it in her mattress. But it would be found. She could put it in her vagina. She'd read a book once with that in it. But she baulked at the idea of money that had passed through a thousand hands going inside her. She settled for the mattress and lay down.

It was funny. She could picture him so vividly. There he was naked in the firelight in the room above the haberdasher's, his skin glowing and there she was, waiting on the bed with its soft sea-green counterpane. But this bed was hard. She opened her eyes and saw the pig-coloured door locking her away from the world. And then her tears came.

Eventually, when they were spent, she sat up and listened to the sounds of the prison around her. It was like being inside some animal, like Jonah in the whale, as its stomach rumbled and it clicked its teeth. Echoes of functions, small in themselves she guessed, were large and significant as they reverberated around the old building.

Someone had scratched a message on the cell door. '*C'est infernal*' – this is hell.

'Hey, new girl!'

She couldn't make out where the voice came from. Perhaps she was going mad again. But she got up and listened at the door. Again it came, but from another direction.

'New girl!'

It was somewhere between a shout and a whisper. She went to the window. 'Are you calling me?'

'So you *can* speak!' came the voice.

'Where are you?'

'Next door! The wind carried my voice to you to bring you comfort.'

'Thank you,' said Oruela. The voice was accented. She couldn't place it.

'Thank the wind,' said the voice.

'What's your name?' called Oruela.

'Kim Sun,' came the reply.

'Where are you from?'

The voice laughed. 'I am from everywhere and nowhere. I am the daughter of the god whose name I bear.'

A lunatic. Of course. 'Oh God, what am I going to do!' howled Oruela.

'I can't tell you what he says, only that he visits us early in the morning and it's wise to turn your face to him. Keeps you healthy.'

Oruela turned away from the window and sat again on the bed. She was scared. She might go really mad. 'Oh, Jean,' she whispered, 'Hurry, hurry.'

Suddenly a loud bell began to ring. The sound of crashing gates, of shouting, of heavy footsteps rushing, filled the whole prison. A rising panic threatened to take hold of her. It must be a fire, she thought, and they'll leave me here to roast alive in this metal box. She ran to the window. 'Neighbour! Can you hear me? What do we do? What is it?'

'They're searching for your boyfriend. Somebody found out!'

How the hell did she know? thought Oruela wildly. She must have overheard. 'You mustn't tell!' she called.

'Pisht!' came the disgusted reply.

Oruela waited fearfully, repeating over and over to herself: Don't tell. Don't tell. They don't know. They don't know who he was or they wouldn't be searching everyone. She stuffed the money further into the mattress.

At last the keys penetrated her own door and three female guards entered looking grim. One of them had newly been released from the toilet and she was red with anger. She ordered Oruela up off the bed and out of the cell and then she picked up the mattress and chucked it on the floor. Another one tapped the walls.

Oruela went out of the door and stood against the wall, her legs shaking. She looked to her left at her neighbour. What a surprise! The woman was as tall as herself, taller in fact and black. Oruela couldn't take her eyes off the woman's gorgeous skin. Her magnificent cheekbones looked like they had been sculpted, her neck long and sleek, her shoulders powerful. Her hair was cropped short on an exquisitely shaped head. She even produced a smile that lingered in amazing brown, almond-shaped eyes.

'*Eyes front!*' yelled a guard.

Both women looked in front of them.

The guards found nothing and two of them came out and ordered Oruela and Kim Sun back into their cells.

The angry, rat-faced one was still in Oruela's cell. She looked Oruela up and down with undisguised heat. She fixed Oruela's eyes like a man does when he means to have a woman. She walked slowly to the door without taking her eyes away.

That look stayed with Oruela behind the locked door. So that was what a lesbian was like, she thought. They looked like she had always imagined them, like the Bolshevik women that the Russian *émigrés* in Biarritz talked about. It was true then. No man would ever want a woman like that. She'd seen women like that but had always imagined they never thought about sex. How could they? Looking like that! But now the horrible truth dawned. They did. They thought about it with women and they worked in places like this. I'm a sitting duck, she thought. And she began to shake, uncontrollably.

Some Day My Prince Will Come

For a short while each evening the inmates were encouraged to mix with each other. There were only women housed on the wing. All three of the other wings of the prison were full of men.

Many of the women were in a state of decay but some were young and beautiful. Oruela came timidly out of her cell and leaned against the iron railing. She looked down on to the landing below hers. She wasn't surprised at what she saw, she was expecting it. But she was surprised at the strength with which the sight gripped her and held her in its spell.

Two women, both about her own age, were flirting together. They leaned against the wall between two cells talking. One was more slender than the other, too thin Oruela thought. Her face was sallow and unhealthy-looking. She was the one being seduced, Oruela imagined. The movements of her body, the coy little smiles, the way she laughed, everything about her was charged with an unmistakable sexual energy.

The other woman kept her distance to begin with but she moved closer until their two bodies, their faces, were very close, almost but not quite touching. It was an astonishing sight to Oruela. She wasn't sure she was enjoying being glued to it either. The thought of them together, naked, touching each other's sexes almost made her feel sick. But it was impossible not to be aroused by the sheer liberation of sexuality that was happening before her very eyes. The slender woman took the other by the hand and led her into a cell next to the staircase. They didn't even shut the door.

Oruela had to get a toothbrush. She made her way along the landing to the iron staircase and held the railings as she descended. Whether it was the after-effect of the drugs or the new culture that she had been thrown into that made her knees weak, she didn't know. As she passed the door, though, where the lesbians were making love, she looked firmly in front of her.

There were a lot of eyes on her as she went to the office of the guards to get her toothbrush. Some were friendly, some curious, some, she felt, overtly hostile. 'New girl,' they whispered and watched the movement of her hips underneath the ugly prison issue shift that passed for a dress. One thing she noticed was that the women all seemed to have adapted their own shift to make something different of it. It made her feel briefly optimistic to think that even in such appalling conditions women stamped their own individuality on their clothes.

She wasn't the only newcomer on the wing that day. The other one was getting much more attention than she was. He was the first male guard under fifty on the wing for many a month and he was a moving and vulnerable target for the heterosexual women's lust. He was about twenty, Oruela guessed. It was a wonder that such a young spawn was given the job. He had such a young face you wondered if he shaved.

The catcalls that followed him ranged from whistles to full-blown and loud descriptions of the women's fantasies. In fact it was unusual for any of the guards to patrol at the same time as the women were out of their cells *en masse*. The duty guards sat in their glass boxes like goldfish, mostly not even bothering to look out to see what was going on under their noses. The young guard had been asked especially to patrol by the senior woman officer . . .

He was trying, manfully, to carry out his duties, but he was overplaying his maleness perhaps to compensate for feeling as secure as a snail underfoot. He hoisted his trousers by the belt more than was necessary. He swaggered. He ignored their jokes, he even issued a stern command or two. The response to these were raspberries and worse.

Oruela happened to be behind him as he climbed the iron staircase to her landing. He had a shapely *derrière*, she noted. She took a discreet, sidelong peek into the cell where the lesbians were but all she could see was one pair of bare feet.

She and the young guard reached the landing at virtually the same moment. The women, at the end where the staircase was, were what Oruela would have called cheap and vulgar and outside she wouldn't have given them a second thought. But in here they were compatriots and suddenly more interesting. She watched as they formed a flock and began to devour the poor young guard.

'Move along,' he said bravely as he walked through them to the very end of the landing.

'Hark! I hear a little mouse squeaking,' said a brunette. She had a disfigurement that twisted her features. It was extraordinary: she was so ugly she was exquisite. She had commanded a high price on the streets.

'What does the little mouse say?' asked another woman.

'It says move along, move along,' said the scarred woman.

'Are you going to?' asked a tiny blonde woman.

'No,' said the brunette. 'I'm going to stay here and catch a little mouse,' and she made a wild noise like a big cat.

For a split second the young guard's face showed how terrified he really was. His back was pressed

74

against the wall and he looked as if he wished the bricks would open up and swallow him.

The scarred woman moved closer to him and he snapped out of his terror. 'What do you think you are doing?' he demanded. His tone was unsteady enough to portray his lingering anxiety.

'What do you want me to do?' she asked. 'Tell me in detail.'

At this the young man laughed, hoisted his trousers at the belt yet again and said, 'Well, ladies. If circumstances were different, I'd like you to suck my cock.'

There was silence. No one had expected it. He grinned cheekily, knowing he'd caught them off-guard. He took a couple of steps forward.

The flock of women closed ranks as one without an order. The young guard's face lost its grin. 'Now that's enough,' he said. He unhooked the truncheon from his belt and gestured with it.

The women stood their ground. 'Is this your cock?' said the scarred woman. 'It's a lovely big one. She touched it with her fingertips, lightly running them up and down the hard black surface.

'Perhaps that's what he wants sucked,' said the little blonde woman.

The brunette opened her red mouth wide, sending her disfigurement into a strange and beautiful pattern across her face. She wriggled her blood-red tongue at the tip of the black wood.

The guard was fascinated. It was plain he was no longer scared, but held, despite himself.

'I wonder if there's anything in his trousers or if he needs that big truncheon to make up for it,' someone called.

'There's more than any of you would know how to satisfy,' he said.

'He's an arrogant little mouse, isn't he?' cackled the scarred woman. 'Let's see,' and she grabbed his crotch.

His face was a mixture of astonishment, pleasure and dread all mixed up. Her hands were in his underwear.

'Help!' he squealed. It wasn't clear that he really wanted to be rescued.

'No one will come,' said the grinning brunette. 'It's a tradition. Someone has to keep a sense of tradition in this god-forsaken, modern world.'

The two main players in this game backed him into a cell and undressed him in front of a quite critical group of onlookers. He was willing, surprisingly enough. His penis stood out like a rod.

The beautiful, scarred woman pulled up her ugly prison dress to expose stately, milk-white thighs, and while the pale blonde woman held his arms, the dark woman took her pleasure from him.

Oruela peered over the shoulders of the crowd watching this symbolic deflowering and from her glimpse she decided he wasn't suffering although, surely, he must be humiliated by the calls of the women watching. They weren't vicious but they were low and lewd.

Oruela left the edge of the crowd. There was no doubt in her mind now about who ran this place.

Kim invited her for a smoke and took her into her cell. Inside there was a faded rug on the floor, some flowers in a vase, a few books. Kim lit a candle and closed the door.

Oruela took the tobacco tin she was offered and sat down on the straight-backed chair to roll herself a cigarette. It wasn't a very good one. It was too loose. But the tobacco went to her head and gave her a pleasant buzzy sensation.

'So tell me,' said Kim, lying lazily back on the bed. Her legs were long and slender and Oruela was stirred again by the other woman's beauty.

Oruela poured out the story of her arrest in a great tidal wave of relief. She only omitted the lizard, feeling nervous about that part.

Kim listened without saying much at all. She gave off a feeling of steadiness. She seemed to take everything

76

in but nothing affected her. Not even when Oruela said she thought she was really going mad.

'Everyone's crazy in here. You can join them if you want,' she said, finally sitting up and looking at Oruela directly.

Oruela began to cry.

Kim softened. 'Look, kid. It's your choice. If you want to be a pathetic deadbeat in their hands you can. But you can also keep some of yourself and survive. Let's face it. We're all mad. It's only those of us that give up that are destroyed.' The words made sense. Oruela felt overwhelming gratitude. She wanted to hug her but she pictured herself in her imagination, going over to the bed and bending over the black woman and a new fear gripped her. Perhaps Kim was a lesbian as well. She ached to ask her. But she daren't.

Instead, she asked, 'What's your story. Why are you here?'

Kim laughed. She had a lovely set of teeth. 'Guess,' she snorted.

Oruela blushed. She felt so naïve.

Kim turned over lazily and lay on her stomach. Her arse was well-rounded and high. She didn't look Oruela in the eye. 'I trusted the wrong man,' she said.

Oruela took that to mean she liked sex with men. She was relieved in a way. But a part of her had opened to an idea that wouldn't go away. She was horny. There was no doubt about it. Sitting here in this cell in the candlelight, she ached for love.

'I was illegal,' continued Kim. 'I hadn't got my papers sorted out and I hooked up with this character who called himself a baron. We invented this story, playing on the appetite of these Europeans for anything exotic. I used to do this dance with a statue. Like this.' She knelt up on the bed, making a thrusting movement with her hips. 'And I went round the brothels telling stories about a far-away erotic culture. It was all made up but they were good stories. We made a lot of money. But just my luck we had an African king in one of our

77

audiences and he made a fuss. Called it an insult and there was this terrible scene. My so-called baron played innocent. He made out I'd duped him and the whole thing was my fault. I was arrested for fraud. I couldn't believe how seriously they took it. Kurt, the baron, had gone too far though. He imported some lizards from Africa and got this taxidermist to embed stones in their skin so they were like the ones I talked about in my story. They were still alive, just, and he sold them for a small fortune. But I never felt right about that. The taxidermist turned up as a witness against me in court – '

'Oh, stop!' cried Oruela, 'stop.'

'Oh, I'm sorry. You're feeling wobbly and I'm going on,' said Kim.

'Owww,' cried Oruela. But it wasn't only tears. It was laughter.

'Hey, don't have hysterics on me,' said Kim Sun.

Oruela took some deep breaths and told her of her own experience with the lizard.

'Whoops!' said Kim.

Later, back in her cell, Oruela sifted through the tangle of her thoughts and stumbled on a kernel of truth about herself. She was going to give up giving up. Kim was right. You had a choice. She'd given up once too often and now she was in hell.

In the midst of these thoughts, a sound began next door. A strange, rhythmic sound, not quite singing, not quite speaking. A chant. She got up and stood by the window. The sky was beautiful. The sun was at last going down and the heavens were blushing. Soon there would be stars. The strange chant got slower as the sun dropped. The sound wound its way into her senses and stirred her.

The attraction to Kim had disappeared as they had talked further. It was as if the intimacy of friendship had filled the desperate need. What if it appeared again? The chant soothed her, like a mother's song. Now she lusted after the sky, after the stars. This was the kind of madness she could handle! She felt like dancing and began to move. The prison bars ceased to exist.

Suddenly a harsh voice rang out: 'Shut up, No. 7!'

Oruela lay down on her bed and watched the sky darken. Presently a new moon appeared.

The next morning was Sunday and it was shower time. She longed for a shower. She grabbed her soap and towel and rushed along the landing as soon as the doors were unlocked.

Women of all shapes and sizes stood naked in the steam under the hot jets of water pouring out from the walls. Steel poles that had once had shower curtains attached to them loomed in the light that filtered through the window and swirled with the mist. Oruela undressed and made her way to a vacant jet.

Some of the women turned to look at her. She felt their gazing eyes touch her and was thankful for the water that washed everything away. She closed her eyes.

Suddenly, she felt a hand on her bottom. She opened her eyes and saw a tiny, blonde girl grinning next to her.

'How dare you!' shouted Oruela.

Kim appeared from nowhere. 'You can handle yourself then!' she said.

'It looks as if I'll have to,' said Oruela.

Then at the end of the room a shout went up. 'La Grande Prix des Derrières!' and all at once there was a line of women forming at the wall by the door. They sat on the tiled floor with their feet on the wall. Women shouted their bets to each other.

'Stand back!' said Kim.

Oruela flattened herself against the wall as someone shouted: 'On your marks! Get set! Go!'

The racers pushed off from the wall with a yell and went skidding up the length of the floor on their bums, crashing into heaps of laughing flesh at the other end. The onlookers whooped and clapped.

Someone shouted, 'New girl! New girl!' and before

she could even think of protesting, Kim Sun had grabbed Oruela and she was on the floor waiting to push off.

'On your marks! Get set! Go!'

Oruela gave one almighty push against the wall with her strong thighs and she was off, yelling with the best of them, as the bump, bump, bump of the grouting thudded under her bum. She saw the steel pole coming up behind her and grabbed it. She spun round twice and hurtled off diagonally, crashing into a group of onlookers and laughing so much she thought she'd die.

'A stylist!' shouted Kim, coasting towards her. 'We could be a formation team!' Someone else took up the idea and someone else, until there were about six women sailing round the shower room on their arses, some with one leg in the air, Oruela with her arms up like a ballerina. All of them cracking up with laughter.

Inevitably the whistle blew and their game was stopped. Kim Sun and Oruela walked back to their cells dripping.

'Do you play cards?' said Kim.

'A little,' said Oruela.

'We usually have a game on Sundays, in the evenings.'

After breakfast everyone was called for church.

'No, thanks,' said Oruela bravely to the rat-faced guard. The last thing she felt she needed was the droning of a miserable priest. She was surprised, though, when everyone else seemed to go. She spent the hour alternately worrying and steeling herself should the rat-face come back and attack her. But nothing so predictable happened.

The evening's card game was in Kim Sun's cell. Three of them sat around on the floor. The third woman was about twenty, white, with luxurious rich brown hair. She had been a whore since she was thirteen. Her name was Marthe. She seemed to know everything there was to know about sex.

'Everyone wants to sleep with their father,' she told

80

Oruela. 'Even if they don't know it. Fathers are our first loves. But, naturally, societies build up rules about these things to protect their survival. Some of us are open enough to see through the rules, that's all. We wouldn't necessarily do it, but we admit it's possible. The fact is, that sexuality is a wild and roving animal. It doesn't move along straight paths.'

'I just wish I could be wild enough to make the first move,' said Kim Sun. 'Coming back from church today I got forgotten and I was locked in the ante-room with the fellow who fetches and carries for the priest down there. We stood there like dummies. I've been thinking about it ever since. We must have been there for ten minutes and I'm sure he had a hard-on. You could feel the sexual tension. But he didn't make a move. It's ridiculous. Me! I can dance in front of a whole room full of men but when it comes down to the real thing I just can't say it. I like a man to take *me*. Kurt was good for that. He was revolting but it used to turn me on when he ordered me to do things. It was that tone of voice he had. Commanding. Saying things like "Spread your legs, baby." Oh God I miss him.'

Marthe gestured with her finger to her temple. 'Mad as a hatter,' she said.

Oruela giggled.

'I don't have any problems with that,' said Marthe. 'I used to have one after the other like that. I had a different one each day. I had a couple of servants just to wash them first.'

It was Kim's turn to make the finger at her temple.

'And I'll have you know I'm going to have another one very soon,' continued Marthe.

'What? How? Who?' cried Kim Sun.

'Well, I found out that if you get married in here, you get a honeymoon.'

'No!' cried Kim. 'How long?'

'Forty-eight hours,' said Marthe smugly.

'Oh, think of it,' moaned Kim Sun.

'Exactly,' said Marthe. 'I've put the word out I'm

interested. I expect I shall be interviewing them next Sunday in church.'

'Nice and proper,' said Kim, sweetly.

Marthe laughed.

'We'll have a hen-night for you,' said Oruela, at last feeling able to offer something to the conversation.

'Yeah!' said Kim. 'What a great idea,' and she beamed at Oruela.

The conversation was interrupted at this point by the arrival of another woman who wanted to play cards. She was a short white girl with sandy, curly hair, rather heavy of feature and very curvy. She came in and they were half-way through a hand when Kim and Marthe were called out by the rat-faced guard. When they were gone, the girl suddenly took off her shift and sat there in only her pants.

'Whew!' she said. 'Freedom.'

Oruela felt the atmosphere change, as if they had suddenly begun to gamble with real money. The girl's breasts were magnificent.

'I can't understand how I put on so much weight on the meagre amount of food they give us,' said the girl, pinching her own belly.

Oruela looked at the girl's belly and breasts and felt an overpowering urge to touch. The tits really made her feel horny. Horrified, she rolled a cigarette from Kim's pouch. It was only a minute or two before the others came back but it seemed like an hour. Oruela played on, smoking resolutely until the bell rang for lock-up. The naked girl clothed herself again, gave Oruela a big, friendly smile and was gone.

Back in her cell Oruela repeated to herself, 'Sexuality is a wild and roving thing.' There was no need to worry, she told herself. Everything was OK. But she felt like crying.

'Psst,' came the voice from the window.

'Yes?' she called, shakily.

'You must go to church next week,' said Kim.

'That's all I need!' said Oruela, ruefully.

'The men are there!' said Kim.

'Men?' said Oruela.

'The inmates from the other wings,' said Kim.

'Hmph!' said Oruela and got down from the window. As if she could ever be interested in men again. She was probably a lesbian. That much was blatantly clear.

But Monday morning brought her a surprise.

She heard the jangle of keys at her door after breakfast and her stomach muscles tightened, a wall closing against intrusion. A male guard stood outside the door. He told her to come with him.

'What for?' she asked assertively.

'Doctor,' he barked. 'Get a move on.'

She prayed she wouldn't be interrogated and fixed a cooperative smile on her face. On the ground floor she was told to sit on a bench outside a cell. The guard disappeared into another door opposite and shut it behind him, leaving her alone in the cavernous pig-coloured space.

At least, she thought she was alone. And then she sensed a movement in the shadows. She turned around. It was a man. He emerged from the gloom backwards, sweeping. His back was broad and long and his arse was firm. Something about his movements was fascinating, even just sweeping.

He didn't seem to have noticed her. He was about six feet away before he turned. He made a brief, flickering but penetrating study of her body.

The look thrilled her to the bone. She found herself smoothing her hair, straightening her back to push her breasts out. Her eyelashes fluttered of their own accord and she looked right back at him. His body was truly magnificent. His shoulders and chest were massive under his striped prison shirt. The kind of shoulders that a woman would want to crush her cheek against when they were on top of her.

His face was not exactly handsome but it was rugged. He had the most sex-filled deep blue eyes she had ever encountered. His nose was magnificently hooked, like

83

an eagle. His dark hair curled into his neck. His shirt was only slightly open and the sight of his throat with his big Adam's apple intrigued her. What was his story, she wondered, looking again at his wonderful eyes. At that moment their eyes met. She looked at him steadily, thinking of sex.

Seeing his freedom, at least in her brown eyes, he smiled. It was an inmate's smile, so discreet as to be almost unnoticeable except to the person it was intended for. To Oruela it had the strength of an embrace.

Before she could formulate the word hello, the doctor's door opened and the man went back to his sweeping. It didn't suit him, sweeping, thought Oruela. He looked like a prince.

The doctor stood behind his desk not looking at her. He was searching through a pile of files on his desk. The nurse next to him pointed at one. He opened it and looked up, straight into Oruela's eyes.

Von Streibnitz appeared exactly the same as he did in his private practice. It would be gratifying to think that in this place he looked evil, but he didn't. Perhaps because it was Monday morning and the procession of lunatics had not yet eaten away at his calm, he was smiling, he was kindly. He bade her sit down.

'I'm glad we didn't have to inject you. I like my patients to be compos mentis if at all possible. Now, do you understand why you are here?'

'No,' said Oruela.

'Well, we have to find out the truth, because the truth is the best way. You're in here because you confessed to the police that you murdered your father.' Again he looked at her intensely. He was, in fact, trying to see a resemblance between her and her father. 'Did you kill your father?'

'No,' said Oruela. 'I was confused. I confessed because I thought I would be taken care of if I admitted it. I wished him dead because he attacked me. But I didn't kill him.'

84

'Aha,' said von Streibnitz. 'Very good. He attacked you. Yes.' He looked again at her file and then beamed at her. 'Tell me, what do you think? Is it right for a woman to have sex outside marriage?'

'I don't see the harm in it,' said Oruela.

'Have you had sex?'

'Do I have to answer that? It doesn't seem to me that it's any of your business,' she said.

Von Streibnitz merely smiled. 'Come with me,' he said. He opened the door and led her into the next cell. A guard in a white coat stood next to a surgical couch. Von Streibnitz opened a box on wheels and pulled out a huge hat-shaped contraption on runners. Oruela's bowels began to curdle.

'What is it? I don't need any electricity! I'm perfectly willing to stay here and cause no trouble to anyone at all,' she pleaded.

'It's not electricity. Look, there are no wires. This is a purely natural therapy, just to make you feel better. It's very exciting. You will benefit from the most advanced science known to man. Inside these compartments at the temple, see, we put curative crystals that come from the deepest recesses of mother earth. All you will experience is a deep feeling of peace, of oneness with nature.' He spoke down to her, like a father.

'I don't want it.'

The warder took hold of her arm and told her to lie down on the couch.

She didn't feel a mite different afterwards except for twinges around her head where the pressure pads had been. Back in her cell she massaged her temples and when the coast was, as far as she could tell, clear, she whistled out of the window to Kim.

She had heard of the hat. 'How do you feel?' she said.

'Absolutely no different,' said Oruela. 'It's nothing. I just lay there for twenty minutes and then he came back and asked me something about the modern woman.'

'Like what exactly?'

'Did I think the modern woman was somehow freer than her sisters down the ages? Something like that.'

'What did you say?'

'I said I wasn't sure. I guessed he was asking me the same question as he'd asked before, really.'

'Good girl!' said Kim. There came a strange noise. Oruela suddenly realised Kim was giggling.

'What are you laughing at? What if it brainwashes me?'

'Don't be a fool. Nothing can do that if you don't let it. You don't feel any different you said. Just fake it.'

'Oh, thank you, Doctor, I'm cured! I shall be chaste and virtuous from now on,' said Oruela in a silly voice. She suddenly laughed. She could do it too!

The pair of them were veritably snorting with laughter by the time the guard's footsteps came heavily down the corridor. Both of them leapt down from their windows.

The danger passed and Oruela went to the window again.

'I saw a gorgeous man,' she shouted softly.

'Oh yeah?' came a sceptical whisper on the wind.

'The cleaner down there.'

'Don't know him,' said Kim.

Oruela described him.

'Hang on a minute, that sounds like Cas,' said Kim. 'He's a bit of a bastard. Watch him.'

Oruela was more excited than she cared to admit. She was curious but pride stopped her asking further. Kim supplied the information without prompting.

'He had an affair with a woman along here so I heard. He kept telling her she was stupid all the time and then he dropped her. He just didn't show up one night. She really liked him and he just dumped her for no reason. The man is a goat. There was silence from the window for a moment. 'Mind you,' continued Kim. 'I know her and she is a bit stupid.'

'Wait a minute. You say they had an affair? What do

you mean? In here?' said Oruela. 'Marthe has to get married to do it.'

'Cas can pull strings,' said Kim.

'How?' asked Oruela.

'I don't know,' came the reply.

But Oruela had the feeling she might know more than she let on.

Alterations on a Theme

'Monsieur Raffoler!' trilled Madame Rosa. 'You're early today. Come in. Come in.'

The smell of washing soap hung in the air at La Maison Rose. It mingled with the cooking smells from a noisy lunch in progress in the back kitchen.

'Rosa, I want to see Annette,' said Jean.

Rosa squirmed. 'Annette is not available today, my dear monsieur. Let Diane see to your pleasure. She is very good.'

'OK. OK,' said Jean impatiently.

Rosa screeched kitchenwards, 'Diane!'

Through the half-open kitchen door Jean caught a glimpse of the girls in various states of morning undress. There were a round dozen of them, all Europeans. None of them wore make-up. Scrubbed faces shone and hair went every which way. They were charming in the raw. Their talk was of local politics and men. From among them the only redhead rose and came out into the hallway, closing the door behind her.

Diane led Jean up the pink and red stairway to the boudoir at the top. Inside the room the bed was on the floor with shimmering drapes hanging from a pole above it, desert-tent style. There were masses of cushions, a single lamp and on the dark red walls a number of drawings from a work of Persian erotica showing couples pleasuring each other in extraordinary positions.

Jean's movements were weary. He took off his jacket and shoes and flopped on to the pillows on the bed. Diane slipped off her camisole and knickers and joined him. She undid his shirt, button by button. She opened his trousers, sliding them off with the merest effort. There was a mountain in his underwear, a warm delicious, fertile mountain. She set it free. Jean closed his eyes as her hands enclosed him. In the darkness of his closed lids he felt both her hands but then he felt a third and he opened his eyes. There was Annette too. She was as graceful as a gazelle. Her body was boyish and she had small, honey-tipped breasts. The hair on her sex was little more than a wisp of straw, the same colour as her long, flowing hair.

For a moment Jean thought he was going to get a duo. But Annette shooed Diane away and set up her base camp at the foot of his mountain in a flurry of thighs.

She spread the lips of her sex and, taking his cock in her other hand, she pushed him inside her.

Jean cupped her arse in his hands as she moved up and down on him. He raised himself. The muscles of his stomach rippled as he caressed her thighs on the soft inner part that was stretched across him like a bridge to the next world.

She kept her hands on her own thighs, at the back, as if she was proud of her balancing. She made Jean wonder, briefly, what was going through this gentle whore's mind. But then she drove her clitoris into his belly and she fell forward on to him, her hands caressing his chest, his neck, her lips kissing every bit of his body they could reach.

This was why he liked her. She gave herself to him, unlike the others who did an expert professional job and indulged his every whim but saved their orgasms for someone else.

He sat up and took her with him. He seized her face in his hands and kissed her passionately, desperately. Her thighs slid around his back and squeezed him close.

'Annette,' he breathed her name. 'Annette.' His cry was full of pain.

Annette held him close, resting in the pleasure of being full of him. Oh, she was on dangerous ground. So dangerous she felt his pain and it stirred her. She began moving on him again and he responded with a thrust so powerful it jerked her body backwards. She let herself fall and lay stretched out before him, her sex enclosing his, the rest of her dreaming her private dream.

Jean climbed on top of her, pressing her slenderness into the bed. She was so tiny, underneath him, like a fragile child. His senses overpowered him and he drove into her hard again and again until she laughed with pleasure.

When it was over she lay in his arms until the sound of his breathing changed. He slept and she lay quietly, naked and alone, enclosed in his arms. Her eyes began to glisten with tears.

He slept for about half an hour. During that time Annette barely moved. When he began to stir she watched him come awake.

'I suppose I had better go,' he said, coming around. 'Where's my shirt?'

'Before you go, I have to tell you something,' she said.

'What?' he said.

'I've stumbled on some information that might help you and your . . . your girlfriend.'

'My girlfriend?'

'Oruela Bruyere,' she said.

'You mean my ex-girlfriend,' said Jean. 'I'm not . . . I can't consider her my girlfriend any longer. She lied to me, she's locked up and . . . I'm not interested.'

'That's because that old git Mayor Derive told you

what a whore she is. I wouldn't take his word for anything, he's such a creep.'

Just at that moment the door opened and someone coughed politely. Annette spun round with fear in her eyes.

'It's me,' whispered Paul.

Jean grinned. 'Come in, old boy.'

As Paul entered the room Jean began dressing but Annette made no attempt to cover herself. Paul looked at her body lovingly.

'Rosa's looking for you, Annette. She's in a bit of a temper,' said Paul.

'Christ,' said Annette. 'If she catches me here . . . Look, you two, I overheard Mayor Derive's cronies talking yesterday. They were talking about your friend Oruela.'

'Who were these men?' asked Paul, quick as a flash.

'Armand Pierreplat and Gaston Everard,' said Annette. The pair were known in Biarritz. One was a judge, the other the coroner.

'What were they saying?' asked Paul.

'I didn't catch everything but they seemed to be worried in case Jean caused a fuss. They were cursing Norbert Bruyere for being so softhearted. I didn't really understand it. I just listened. Rosa was trying to keep them sensible. She said that it was all in their imaginations and that the mayor had spoken to Jean so they should just sit tight and keep it to themselves.'

'Rosa was there?' Paul fired the question at her.

'Rosa knows them all from years ago.'

'I suppose she does,' said Paul.

'You haven't heard everything yet though. Earlier this morning a woman I've never seen before comes to visit Rosa and the old girl went white as a sheet when she walked in the kitchen. She hurried her off and I thought, it's the same business. So I listened at the door of Rosa's room where they were having their talk. They started having an argument. This woman was saying things like: "What do you expect me to do? How can I

91

let that bastard get away with it all over again?" And then suddenly Rosa rushed out of the room and bloody caught me! She's banned me from seeing Jean now.'

'Who was the woman, did you find out?' asked Paul.

'She had a Basque name. Rosa kept repeating it. "No Euska, no, Euska," she kept saying. She was really beautiful, the woman.'

'I wonder who she can be?' said Paul, looking at Jean. Jean had dressed himself during the conversation. 'Frankly,' he said, 'I really don't care. I don't want to know any of this. I'm trying to get over Oruela. I thought I was going to marry that girl and she's let me down. I really don't care.'

The three of them stood there momentarily in silence.

'But surely this information changes things, Jean,' said Paul. Then the door opened wide. Rosa stood before them.

'Go upstairs and pack your things, Annette. I warned you, and now you must go.' Her voice was soft but deadly. 'Now!'

'Oh come on, Rosa,' said Paul.

'Don't open your mouth, you leech. You get out too.'

'Don't call me a leech,' said Paul. 'You make your living out of other women's bodies, you're no one to talk.' His eyes were smouldering dangerously.

'If I just had shit like you to deal with I wouldn't make a living, would I!' shouted Rosa.

'I'll meet you outside,' said Paul, calmly, to Annette. He looked at Jean, a question in his eyes. But it was obvious that his friend was uncomfortable. He wasn't going to say anything at all. 'What's going on, Rosa,' continued Paul in a softer tone. 'What's the big secret? What does Oruela know? What has Derive got to be so scared of? Who was the woman who came here this morning looking for Oruela?'

The effect of his relentless questions on Rosa was marked. She seemed to crumble into an old woman. Her face sagged. 'Don't push me,' she said. 'I won't tell you anything.' She looked at Jean, who was staring at the carpet. 'I don't want anyone else hurt,' she said, 'so I won't discuss this conversation. But equally, I won't tell you anything either. Get Oruela out if you can. She's done nothing, poor child. But take the advice of an old whore who's been in this town, girl and woman for fifty years. There are people too powerful to mess with.' Her pale eyes seemed to wrestle with some unseen ghost.

'Are they frightening you into silence, Rosa?' said Paul.

'Just get out of here and take this bloody lovesick chit with you.' She turned to leave. 'And she's had her wages,' she said at the door.

'What do you make of that?' said Paul in wonder.

'She said Oruela's done nothing,' said Jean.

Paul looked at his friend hopefully.

'In fact, the whole tragic affair is causing me to feel quite unwell,' Jean continued, his eyes fixed on some distant horizon. 'I can't fathom this at all.' With that, he took his hands out of his pockets, picked up his hat, and went to the door. He left without saying anything more.

Annette watched him go and then began to cry.

'Come here,' said Paul, taking her in his arms gently. 'Don't worry. Get your things. You can come and stay with me until we figure this out.'

He went alone down the stairs. Rosa stood in the doorway of the salon. When she saw him coming she closed the door quietly in his face.

Outside, the fresh Atlantic wind rushed at Paul's face, soothing him. He walked right into it, as far as the promenade railing. A few early visitors walked on the beach. He was so angry he could have wrenched the railings from their concrete moorings and thrown them into the swelling sea.

So it had come to a head. Jean would never know the effect his turncoat behaviour towards Oruela had on his best friend. How could Jean believe that Oruela, the lovely girl he'd snatched up the minute Paul had pointed her out that night in the casino, was the monster that Mayor Derive had told them she was? The vitriol that Derive had poured on her when they went to see him was revolting. Paul had almost laughed in his face. That corrupt, no-good bastard who'd made his money selling cardboard shoes to the army during the war. As a rookie press photographer Paul had been sent to take photographs of the men at the front and he'd seen how they were dying as much from rotten equipment and bad food as enemy fire.

How could Jean believe it? When Oruela had chosen Jean, Paul had continued the relationship with Renée Salmacis that was still tearing him apart. Renée was hardly ever in Biarritz. She was a racing driver and she went all over the country. Their problems, she told him, stemmed from the fact that she was successful and he wasn't. Perhaps there was a spark of truth in it. A girl like Oruela went for Jean because they were of the same background.

But Oruela had been fooled by Jean. She thought he was a bohemian because he wore long hair and bought art in Paris. True, he was rich and he could do anything he wanted to whereas he, Paul, had nothing to show for years of stubborn addiction to his art.

And Renée was fundamentally wrong about their own affair. They fought because she was immature and attention-grabbing. They fought all the time and when they weren't fighting they were fucking. And there was his weakness. He loved to make love, and he loved to make love with someone he knew well. Even if he could have afforded it he couldn't have had any satisfaction out of making love to whores, not as a substitute for the real thing. He kept an ideal in his heart. The woman he would love for ever would be his best friend.

And what about poor Oruela now? Whatever she had come from it made her different. The one mistake she'd made with Jean had been not to tell him about her background before this happened. Jean didn't trust her any more. He'd retreated into his bourgeois fantasies about the evil nature of people from the wrong side of the tracks. He no longer cared. What a waste.

Paul looked out to sea and suddenly he knew he was going to do something. I'm from the wrong damn side of the tracks too, as far as these people are concerned, he thought. And I know how it feels. I don't know what I'm going to do but I will do something. Damn Jean. Damn the lot of them.

Annette was coming along the promenade, clutching a small cardboard suitcase in one hand. She kept close to the railing as if she was scared that the wind might blow her away.

'Come on,' he said, taking the suitcase from her. 'Let's go home and get drunk.'

Paul and Annette weren't the only ones to get drunk that afternoon. Genevieve had discovered the drinks cabinet and the effect was liberating. The words seemed to tumble out of her mouth like little things with a life of their own.

'Robert,' she asked, as he was moving furniture yet again. 'Would you make love to me?'

Robert stood up straight and said, 'Would I get extra wages for that, Madame?'

She thought she would die of embarrassment. 'Get out of my sight,' she screamed. When he was gone she slumped down on the sofa and cried. But the tears didn't last long. Oh, there was no need for tears she told herself. She was free! Robert was replaceable. Nothing could ever be as bad as it had been. Not now. Not now that dreadful brat Oruela was locked up and gone for ever. She pulled herself together and ran up the stairs and knocked on Robert's door.

'Come in,' he said.

She went in. He was packing his suitcase. He stopped when he saw who it was. In his hand was a photograph of Michelle. Genevieve had always suspected they were lovers. She felt an urge to be nasty but she held herself in check.

'I've come to apologise, Robert,' she said meekly. 'Don't go. I need you.'

Robert's chest was so broad and manly she found it irresistible, almost, especially as it was puffed up with pride. 'I am a servant, Madame,' he said.

'Oh look, I know, Robert. It was a momentary lapse. What I mean is, will you stay and be my servant? I need . . . I need some stability in this house, everything has changed so quickly.'

Her words seemed to affect him immediately. A look of pity crossed his face and he lowered his eyes.

'I'll give you an increase in wages,' she said.

'Then I'll stay, at least until things are more settled,' he said.

'Oh, thank you,' she said.

'I might remind you that you haven't done the accounts with cook for over a week, madame,' he said.

Genevieve sighed. What a bore. But she smiled, left him and rang for Cook. Within minutes the woman came to her sitting room and bored her even more with niggling little amounts of this and that. Genevieve found herself wondering, as the woman's ample bosom rose and fell, who Cook had sex with and what she looked like when she was doing it. Did she knead her man as she kneaded dough. No. Cook, she thought, would ride her lover like a horse, her breasts bouncing around, her great hips bearing down.

Thank God the accounts were soon finished. Alone again, Genevieve went to the drinks cabinet once more and poured herself a generous amount of Norbert's twenty-year-old whisky that he had sent especially from Scotland. The fire hit her loins and made her want to dance. Oh, how she and Alix, the lovely policeman, would dance. She jumped up and waltzed around the study with her invisible lover. She could feel his hands searching for her breasts, taking them in his mouth, sucking. And then her fantasies took another turn. He was begging her, 'Please, please'. She flopped down on the couch and passed out in a heap.

Literary Classics

*T*he next thing the prison authorities decided was that Oruela needed work to improve her. She wasn't the only one. Kim worked in the kitchen and wanted Oruela to try and get a job there. But as luck would have it, when the allocation came up, she got the library. So she began a new career.

Any woman who worked outside the wing where she might come into contact with men, was ordered to wear dungarees and a shirt – men's uniform, in other words. Oruela pulled on the shape-concealing baggy blue trousers and tucked in the shirt. She fastened the waistband with the big brown leather belt that came with the set. She had no mirror but imagined herself to look like a farm labourer. In fact there was something quite appealing about her slender frame swathed in all those clothes. No amount of disguise could hide the fact that she was a beautiful young woman. There was a certain androgynous quality about her now that was not displeasing.

The library was a small, dingy building. Its contents had been donated by a wealthy philanthropist for the improvement of the minds of the poor.

'There's bugger all left,' said the librarian guard, a fat hairy man who smoked stinking, cheap tobacco in a worn pipe. 'They use the pages as toilet paper, ignorant bastards.' Behind the guard stood his assistant, a one-eyed old inmate called, she found out later, Pierre. Pierre's job was to take the book trolley over to solitary confinement and the condemned cells.

The guard turned and spat over his shoulder. 'Where's the bloody coffee, that's what I want to know.'

Pierre shrugged his shoulders and shook his head and finally raised his one eye to heaven in a secret gesture to Oruela.

As the days passed, she found out why. The coffee was never on time and Gerard, the guard, said exactly the same thing every morning. The work was mainly humping books here and there according to where they were supposed to be and sometimes a whim would overtake Gerard and there would be a reorganisation. Apart from that, in between the hours when inmates were allowed to visit, there was plenty of time to pass among the dingy shelves and delve into the treasures she found there. Strange that she should have to come to this place to realise an ambition to read but here she was and she made the most of it. She moved, sylph-like in her boy's clothes, her mind a sponge, soaking up everything. She was almost content.

Two days a week she had to go to see the doctor and have her treatment in the hat. Every time she went the tall man with the hooked nose was there, sweeping the same piece of floor, over and over again. She was dying to find out if he was the cruel Cas that Kim thought.

One day, as soon as the guard who had escorted her went into the little office, he rested his broom against the wall and walked over to her quickly. He stood in front of her, a towering giant. For the briefest of moments she was scared.

'May I sit down?' he asked. His French was heavily accented and as he spoke his body seemed to beg her.

It was such a small gesture but it was beautiful, so

polite, so different from the crudeness she was coming to believe was normal. It turned her on. She felt the cream ooze into her knickers.

She nodded.

He sat his great body next to her, not too close, but she could feel him all the same.

'What's your name?' he asked.

She told him.

'That's very pretty,' he said. 'Is it Spanish?'

'Basque,' she replied.

'Aha!' he said, nodding sympathetically. 'Have you noticed how so many of us are political prisoners?'

It wasn't easy to concentrate on what he was saying. As he'd sat down she thought she'd seen a patch of skin on his hip, where the side opening of his work dungarees was not properly fastened. If she had, perhaps he had no underwear on. She could think of nothing else, but she dare not glance again. He held her in his gaze.

'Can I come and talk to you tomorrow?' he asked.

'Yes,' she said.

Immediately he had his answer he got up and walked back to his broom, taking it up again just as the nurse came out of von Streibnitz's office to call her in. It was uncanny. How had he timed it so perfectly? Oruela looked at the nurse as if she had come from Mars.

The next time she visited the doctor he was there and the same routine was repeated. This time as he sat, asking her questions and admiring her with his eyes as she talked – yes, she could talk at last – the strap of his dungarees slipped off one shoulder. Her eyes travelled over the expanse of muscle that was as good as bare to her heightened senses. Under his shirt his body moved. She could feel the heat of it. Looking at the fallen bib that had left his shirt bare and under that his chest, Oruela could only think of how it would be if she pulled it. She could hear it almost . . . rrrip! Underneath would be his underpants and in them . . . She adored the look of his skin. How would it be on his . . .

'Your mind is wandering,' he said. 'You're not listening to me.'

She apologised, searching her lust-drenched mind for something to say. With a smile that hovered on his red lips, he rose and was gone, just like before, with perfect timing. The doctor came out just as he took up his broom.

His name was Caspar, he told her eventually. He was Russian. 'Rossian,' he pronounced it, proudly. He was being held illegally. The bourgeois French were traitors and hypocrites and a conspiracy was afoot. One day the story would come out and the truth would shock many people. They held him for the killing of a Bolshevik pig.

Oruela never asked him if he had actually killed the man. It didn't seem the right thing to do. Besides, she had other things on her mind. That night she cut off the legs of her standard issue cotton bloomers and hemmed the edges the way Kim had done hers. She ended up with a pair of short wide-legged knickers that left her thighs air to breath. Even if she looked like a boy on the outside, she thought, she could feel womanly underneath . . .

The next time she saw him, he told her she was lovely and she felt lovely. He took two pieces of chocolate out of his pocket.

'Here,' he said. 'One's for you.'

'How did you get this?' she asked in wonder.

He looked at her with his deep blue eyes and they told her that in this place this gesture was equivalent to flying to Russia and back in a day to get her the best caviar in the world. He raised a finger to his magnificent nose and tapped it. Then he bit into the chocolate.

'You'd better eat yours,' he said, licking his lips.

She couldn't, her mouth was dry. She wanted him to bite her skin. He knew it. He smiled, taking her chocolate and breaking off a small piece. He fed it to her, touching her lips with his long, slender fingers.

* * *

So she worked in the library and thought of him. Other inmates came in and weren't oblivious to her charms by any means. They flirted with her like mad, men and women both. Pierre told her that the use of the library seemed to have risen considerably and word must be getting round. But none of them had the panache of Caspar. They all managed to get caught talking to her in the aisles.

Then one day Gerard the guard opened the doors and a queue shuffled in as usual. The daylight outside was white that day. The clouds were high and blanketing and the light hurt the eyes. All the same, the silhouette was unmistakable. The last one. Tall, black against the sky. She recognised him instantly. She felt him. He could pull strings all right, deep down in the secret recesses of her soul.

He made straight for her. His face was inscrutable but his eyes were hers and hers alone. She felt as if everyone around her must feel the sexual tension between them. But no. Gerard the guard was grumbling away at the hapless line in front of him as usual.

'Can you explain the system to me?' said Caspar. 'I want the literature section. I haven't been here before.'

One or two of the inmates noticed something. But they moved aside for him, without complaining.

Oruela came out from behind the counter, her knees trembling, and told him to follow her. They found an aisle that was deserted.

'I've found you,' he whispered. 'Now I can see you every day,' and he moved towards her and touched her face gently.

'Be careful!' she whispered.

'I know what I'm doing,' he replied. 'The secret is to do it right under their noses.'

She knew he was going to kiss her. She wanted it so much. He bent his head towards her and brushed her cheek with his lips. He smelled her hair. It was the desperate drinking of a man in the desert and it was

101

fast. There was no time for romance. It was his senses drinking her. She'd touched the boy in him and she felt it for the first time, the soft needing-her boy under the man carved of history and the rough stone of life. It was almost as if he'd come right there. She wanted to feel it but it was forbidden.

Every day that she wasn't at the doctor's he came to the library. She began searching for a nook, a cupboard, anywhere where they might slip beyond the public domain and be together. He had pressed his body against hers and she had felt the contours of it, the bulk of him in her arms.

Words became caresses. They talked to each other in whispers about the world, about the books they read and each word was loaded with passion. He taught her how to read one book following another so that her education had some direction and she didn't flounder. So he had her mind and her soul. Only her body was not yet his. One day, he promised, it would be.

Meanwhile, especially on Sundays, when everything closed down and she was stuck on the wing, she wondered why she hadn't heard from Jean. Not only Jean was silent. There was no news from the outside world at all. Not that she wanted to be free now without Caspar. But, as the hours ticked by and the gossamer thread that bound her to him dissolved, she lay on her bed in the belly of the whale, listening to the sounds around her and the boredom was excruciating. When evening came she could concentrate on her reading, which had become a habit. But the days were only punctuated by mealtimes.

The wing was a hothouse for whatever atmosphere was breeding that day. It seemed as if everyone was affected one way or another, by everyone else's mood. One Sunday, when she'd been there about three weeks, there was tension. Women were snappy with each other. Something was brewing. Kim appeared behind her in the lunch queue and whispered. 'Watch with eyes out of the back of your head.'

'What's going on?' asked Oruela.

'Watch those two,' said Kim. She nodded to a couple of big women further along and then she was gone.

Oruela missed Kim. Her work in the library and Kim's work in the kitchen kept them on different timetables and their intimacy had lapsed. There was only Sunday evenings and there was always, more often than not, a crowd playing cards.

Just as she was thinking this the queue suddenly erupted. Oruela was thrown back into the person behind her by the force of the disturbance.

The two women that Kim had pointed out were glaring at each other about two feet apart. Women were scattering. Oruela backed against a wall and from where she stood she could see that the shorter-haired of the two had pulled a knife. It gleamed with the fear of a hundred pairs of watching eyes. The other woman in the fight watched it closely.

Hovering like a wasp around the women was the small blonde who had grabbed Oruela's arse that first day in the shower. It was clear. She was the cause.

'Do it!' she screamed. 'Do it, Marielle.'

Marielle jabbed the knife point at the other woman. And then from nowhere there was a flash of body and Kim was there. She kicked Marielle's hand hard and the knife flew out of it. Marielle looked as if she would turn on Kim, but the intended victim saw her chance and she went for her assailant.

Marielle defended herself and the two women locked in combat. Oruela watched in fascination. They were like two rutting stags. Great grunts came from them as their arms gripped each other's and they wrestled each other to the ground. There was no pretence, it was life and death. Their shapeless prison dresses rode up on their thighs. Strong feet kicked and necks twisted in impossible ways.

After her valiant attack to stop bloodshed, Kim stood

back panting and watched intently, as did the whole wing. Thirty big burly guards swarmed in from different directions and pulled the women apart. One was kept on the ground, her head crushed to the floor in a mass of damp hair, her face twisted in pain. The other was frog-marched away first, screaming.

The whole wing was affected afterwards with a strange sense of the erotic. The way violence touched on a sexual nerve, the way fear twisted itself into the women's souls and made them jumpy. It was too much for everyone. They clubbed together and talked it to death.

Kim was treated like a brave warrior. Women showered her with praise and she walked tall, her face disturbed, back to her cell.

Next door, Oruela heard the chant begin. She wanted it to relax her but she was too filled with her own violence. She wanted to hit the damn walls. She cursed the damn cell and the damn daily routine. She cursed Jean and Michelle and everyone who had left her here to suffer. She was on the point of tears.

But then suddenly she saw the pad of prison-issue writing paper and she knew she had to get something down on paper.

Dear Michelle, she began. She wanted to write *Help me! help me!* on the page over and over but she couldn't. So she sat, listening to the sun chant for a while, staring at the square of moonless sky.

Dear Michelle, she began to write, I sit here thinking of nothing but sex. It has been so long since I felt the satisfaction of pleasuring a man sexually. You know what I mean, when they're surprised because you're ravenous. I have such fantasies about Jean and about a man I have met in here. In my fantasy, Michelle, I am no longer in this dreadful place. I am at a party at one of my friends' houses in Bayonne, it's Lauren's party I think. It's summer and the night is warm and glowing with stars. It's just like it used to be on her terrace with the torches burning in the trees. Beyond the garden is black as ink. I am with Jean and we have danced and danced, our bodies are tingling with the dance, small drops of perspiration trickle down my back. I know he wants me and I want him so badly that I cannot wait. I suggest to him that we walk away from the crowd into the dark garden. He is hesitant because our parents are in the ballroom but I manage to persuade him and we slip away. The darkness gathers on us until it's almost impossible to see our hands in front of us.

The night is drenched in the perfume of flowers and as soon as we can, we stop. He is still nervous, he wants to go further into the darkness so I allow him to lead me on. We come to the topiary garden and I pull him into a hedge made into the shape of a satyr. I pull at his clothes and he at mine. He has chilly hands and they touch my flesh like ice. He lifts me into him with my legs around his waist, my dress rustling against his clothes he takes me standing up.

He lifts me up and down on him, the cheeks of my arse spread wide apart and I am pushing into him; the hedge is springy and supports us. It prickles my arms as I cling to him.

And then I notice someone walking through the maze. It's just his head. His face is white in the darkness. I will him to see us and he turns. It is Caspar.

He is making his way towards us. Jean is unaware of him. Only I see him. He turns the last corner of the maze and comes to stand on the small lawn just beyond our statue, where I can see him. He is dressed in a flowing white shirt which he unbuttons and pulls out of his trousers. I'm still fucking Jean. His cock inside me is filling me up.

Caspar unbuttons his trousers and takes them off. He is naked from the waist down and he pulls up his flowing shirt to show me his body. He is performing for me. He starts to urinate on the ground. In the dark the only sound is of his golden stream hitting the floor.

I've never seen anything like this and it makes me

forget Jean. All I know of him is his cock and where I bang against his belly in the night.

Caspar goes to lay down on the stone bench. He lifts his shirt again and poses for me, like a model.

Then suddenly Jean gets wind of what is going on. He is angry but when he sees Caspar he is drawn to him himself. We both go to Caspar who comes up to meet us. Jean is behind me and Caspar in front. They sandwich me between their two cocks. I can feel both of them.

This time I climb on to Caspar and take him with Jean's body warm at my back.

Then we are on the floor and Caspar and Jean touch each other's pricks while I watch. They kiss each other and pump each other's sex.

Rescue Me

She went down to the doctor on Monday morning and waited as usual outside his office. But Caspar wasn't there. She spent the usual amount of time in the hat and as she lay on the wheeled couch she wondered where he was. She came out expecting to see him but he wasn't there.

The next day she went to work in the library and she was like a cat on hot bricks waiting for him but still he didn't come.

In the evening she whispered her agony out of the window to Kim.

'I'll put some feelers out,' said Kim.

Three almost intolerable days went by before Kim was able to find out the truth. Caspar had been taken to solitary confinement.

'What for?' asked Oruela out of the window.

'I wouldn't trouble about that,' said Kim mysteriously.

Oruela didn't. She had only one thought in her mind. To get to his cell. She began forming her plan.

All she would have to do was convince Gerard that she could do a good service if she swapped jobs with the old man. The next morning she asked old Pierre what he thought. She put it to him that she could save his old bones if she did it.

'You wouldn't be safe,' he said. 'I couldn't let you do it.'

'Oh, I'd be as safe as houses, all those guards around. Nothing would happen to me. Let me come with you.'

So they approached Gerard together. At first he was suspicious.

'So you finally got someone to believe your stories, did you, old man?' he sneered at Pierre.

Pierre didn't contradict him. He didn't say a word about how it was Oruela's idea. 'It wouldn't take such a long time. I'm sure she'd be back well before the lunch bell.'

'You'll have to show her the ropes,' said Gerard. 'She won't last!'

That evening in her cell, Oruela could barely breathe with excitement. She daren't even say anything to Kim during their nightly whisper, in case of being overheard. So the anticipation was hers alone. Her heart beat like a drum in the silent night. She put her trousers under her mattress to iron out the creases and slept fitfully.

The next morning she paid particular attention to her hair, to her nails. Gerard was in a bad mood because coffee arrived late as usual and they were late starting. They trundled the trolley out of the library and across the courtyard to the men's segregation block and rang the bell. There were three guards in the control room. The one that came to open the door was a giant, blond. Tattooed on his neck was the word 'Maman' like a scar.

'Haven't got authorisation for two of you,' he said, looking at Oruela suspiciously. 'Can't allow you in.'

Oruela thought quickly. 'Well, I can't stand out here on my own. I'm not authorised to move freely, only with Pierre.'

The guard snarled. 'That's not my problem,' he said, and he shoved the gate closed.

'Might I suggest,' said Pierre, with whining humility, 'that you telephone the library. It must be an oversight. Guard Gerard at the library was going to telephone you but the coffee arrived late and I expect it slipped his mind.'

'It's not for you to imagine what goes on in an officer's mind, you old lunatic.'

'I wouldn't presume,' said Pierre, he was wringing his hands in supplication.

The blond guard relented. 'Wait there.'

'You'll have to learn to lick their boots, my dear,' Pierre said, when the guard had gone. 'They think a lot of themselves, these ones here. It's a prison within a prison, you see. Rules of its own, it has.'

'Thank you,' said Oruela politely. She suspected she would do anything to get the man she wanted, who was buried within.

The guard returned and began opening the gate.

As they stepped into the doorway Oruela smelled for the first time the warm, human body smell that characterised the place. It wasn't pleasant. But neither was it totally unpleasant. It smelled like bedrooms in the morning. Human odours mixed with the inevitable prison cleaning fluid, an eggy smell.

There was only one landing and all the cell doors were shut. An energy filled the place. It was danger. Strange danger. As if the men enclosed in the steel cells were so huge that only this method could keep them small. They were dangerous beyond the normal run of damaged and impulsive men and women serving their time on the other wings. Captured danger. The dark side of humanity. But here they were tamed, kept behind thick steel. The doors were pig-pink as usual, but they had an extra bar on them that had to be lifted.

The guard asked for the first name on the list and, reading it, went to open the cell. The door opened inward. Oruela got the shakes. What would she find in there, what raging beast?

'Library visit,' said the guard, and stood back to let them in.

The man inside arose as a sick patient arises from a hospital bed, sluggishly, as if living with his own dreams, his own excavations, day and night, as if his self was his cell and it moved with him.

'Hello, Pierre,' he said. Then he saw Oruela.

He jumped up and threw a towel over a bucket in the corner and then sat down on the bed again. Pierre perched on the other end of the steel cot and Oruela made for the small chair that the man gestured to.

Pierre introduced her and the man held out his hand. Oruela looked into his eyes and saw something she hadn't expected to see. It wasn't lust, not sexual at all. It was gratitude. She felt acutely embarrassed.

They passed a few words.

They continued on down the wing, repeating the same process. Each door was locked behind them as they left. And Oruela began to feel the atmosphere changing in the place. A stir. It was as if the very walls spoke: 'Beauty is here. Beauty is here, even here, in the midst of all this warped humanity. There's hope.' Oruela carried the thrill of it in her body.

'What's the next name on the list?' said the guard, looking at it.

His words hit Oruela like a stone falling from her throat to her womb. 'Alexandrovich.' She had been expecting it but it still did it to her. Her feelings almost burst. It had been days.

Caspar sat, cowed, on the bed, in much the same attitude as any of the others they had visited. But there were his long legs, his broad shoulders, just as lovely as ever.

His eyes registered the joy he felt and his face broke into a great smile that, luckily, the guard didn't see. Pierre saw it though and quick as a flash the perceptive old man gave her the book, *Le Rouge et le Noir* by Stendhal, and asked if he could leave his helper to have a few words with the 'aristocrat'. The guard was of an age with Cas. He looked at him.

'He's no trouble,' he said.

The two men walked out of the cell leaving the door open wide.

'You're so good to see,' said Cas and he held out both hands as he leaned forward. She held out her hands to him and he took them, enclosing them. It was wonderful to touch him.

'I'm sorry you had to come to this disgusting place but I'm so glad . . .' he said.

'What are you doing here? What happened? I was so . . .' She couldn't speak.

'It's a mistake,' he said. 'I'll be out of here soon,' and he got up and pushed the cell door to so that it was almost closed. If she was not mistaken the bulge in his denims had grown. She did so ache to see it. It felt like another presence as he walked back and sat on the bed. Huge and powerful. The creases around the bulk of it were etched like rays from a warm sun. She could smell his sex. He moved with less agility than before, yet this spot was alive. Her entire soul went into her sex. It felt happy like a fruit waiting to be taken and eaten.

And so they were alone. They crammed a real conversation into five minutes and he laughed, saying he was going to get even more reading done. Then suddenly he held up his finger to stop her talking.

Perhaps he could hear something she couldn't distinguish.

'Stand up,' he whispered. 'Go to the door.'

She did as she was told, without question. She stood facing the tiny glass window, about three inches square. She could see the landing. He rose and stood next to her, very close.

The closeness of him was almost intolerable. She yearned for him to take her in his arms. She turned to look at him. He held his fingers to his lips and then put his fingers to her lips. A kiss that was not a kiss. But a kiss none the less. 'Keep look-out,' he said.

Then she felt his hand at her waist. She felt his strong hand push between her belt and her belly. She felt his fingers at the top of her knickers, then his palm on her pubic hair. Then his searching fingers at her sex, drenched in its moisture. His forearm, flat against her

111

belly, shoving down further, his fingers reaching, searching and yes, inside.

She reached for the bulge in his trousers and held it, just as the guard and Pierre came into view in the glass. They were about six feet away. Caspar wrenched his hand out of her pants and put both hands in his pockets. She spun around and assumed a stance natural to casual conversation. The first thing that came into her head was:

'Well, yes, but I think the Mercedes is a much easier car to drive . . .'

A glint of laughter shone in his eyes but he seemed to have lost the power of speech. She knew if the others came in with him like that they'd be able to smell something was up.

'Well, goodbye then,' she said and opened the door just as the guard came to the other side of it.

'Oh,' she said, surprised.

It wasn't easy to hold a conversation with Pierre on the way back across the courtyard. Her sex seemed to be yelling 'I've been touched! I've been touched!' in her pants.

All she could say was yes, she liked the job very much and thought she could do it.

And so it was hers. She became known as the library girl and all the men looked forward to the visit. Even von Streibnitz got to hear of the 'stimulating effects', as he said, that she was having on the solitary male population. She told him that literature was certainly improving their minds and rehabilitating even the most hardened criminals. He bought it. In fact the service became so popular that another woman was assigned to help her. A nun. And so Oruela and the nun went demurely twice a week.

Oruela managed to get Kim to steal some elastic from the workshop and made herself a hook and eye out of some lead wine tops that she purloined from the kitchen waste bins. This made Cas's explorations into her pants a great deal easier.

She gradually increased her time with him from five to ten, to fifteen minutes, leaving the nun to perform her mission with most of the other chaps. Despite the lack of time, Caspar somehow managed to observe the delicacies of courtship. Everything was just fast.

'How are you today?' he would ask and she always had the time to tell him. She learned to express herself exactly and succinctly.

But when words could say no more, they would stand by the door and he would ease his forearm into the elastic. He would press his prick into the softness of her arse, not urgently, just gently, while he worked on her sex with his hands.

She would lean back on him, stretching her belly a little, pushing her sex forward and he would work with his hand. At first she was scared to let herself come and then one day he whispered 'Trust me' and she closed her eyes to the jailers and let him keep watch, over her shoulder. She closed her eyes and concentrated on the sensation and let herself be taken away. In the dark the rub, rub of his fingertips, gently now, harder, massaging, compelling, took her to the brink of a precipice and held her there, terrified, in agony. Then came the ecstasy. She felt herself going and he felt her too and whispered, 'Go, my sweet, go,' and she went. He held her up as her body absorbed the first wave of release, and the second, the third and the soft aftershocks.

He still held her tight, kissing her neck. It was too much to bear, not kissing him back and she turned and pulled him down under the glass panel and kissed him full on the mouth. It was so brief it hurt.

The next time she entered the cell he wasted no time. Immediately he took her to one side of the door and kissed her again, drinking her in through his lips, throwing caution to the wind and just kissing, kissing, kissing. She decided it was his turn this time and at last

113

she reached down and undid his zip. His sex wasn't immediately hard. It was substantial enough though and warm and gorgeous. At last she had it in her hands after all this time. And as she handled it, it became hard, gradually, and wet at the tip.

He leaned back against the wall and she kept a look-out through the glass window. She moved her hand up and down, up and down, caressing his cock, smoothing its moisture over him and down, lubricating her hand.

He was helpless. His trousers pushed down off his hips and he crashed against the wall as if a tidal wave had washed him there. His eyes were closed, his mouth open in an 'O'.

'Come, Cas,' she breathed, 'come,' and she felt him responding. She went to him, and, lifting her shirt, she pressed his shaft against her belly. He opened his eyes, reached for her breast and gave a low groan. She felt his sperm shoot at her belly, his cock pumping in her hand and she held him.

Still she kept one eye on the little window.

The next day she went to the uniform issue hatch and persuaded the inmate working there to give her a much bigger shirt. She took it back to her cell and tried it on. Perfect. It covered her bottom and thighs. Then she took her trousers and undid the crotch seam. The wound in them was about six inches in all. She tried them on, leaving off her knickers. She opened her legs and *voila*! The fabric split to reveal her sex, easy to get to, displayed in all its glory. She undressed and folded the set neatly.

For some reason, the next time she visited, the nun told her to spend the whole time with Caspar and she would do the rest. Oruela didn't question it, nor the fact that the guard was gentle with Cas as he opened the door.

She sat down with him in the cell. She sat opposite him on the little chair and he asked her how she was.

114

She told him, thinking all the while of the split in her trousers. They talked for quite some time. And then he said, touching her chin, 'You're so beautiful.'

'Well,' she replied, 'this beautiful woman has got something very beautiful to show you.' Her own voice excited her. He cocked his head on one side, wondering.

Slowly she uncrossed her legs and pulled the fabric apart at her thighs. He caught his breath as he looked at her sex. He looked right into it, studying. She reached for his bowed head and stroked the curls at his neck. Then he put his fingers inside her and jabbed in and out.

'We must do it,' she said. 'Come and sit on this chair and I'll sit on top of you.'

'They'll see us,' said Caspar. 'Here, bring the chair up to the door.'

He sat with his back to the door and pulled his prick out. It was hard, standing there in the folds of his clothes at the crotch.

As she lowered herself on to him she could feel his clothes on her inner thigh. But oh, his cock was so wonderful. She clasped her legs together around the chair and pushed on to him. He held her arse and helped her up and down. It was fantastic. She suddenly thought of where they were and began to laugh. Her body felt so wonderful as he gripped her waist, his big hands almost reaching right round her. She kissed his head and lifted his face up to look at it. She smiled at his eyes and he responded. They laughed together. The feeling of fucking in this mad place while the guards walked up and down outside, while all the locks and bolts in this world tried to pin the wings of sex and hold it, was wonderful. Yes they had done it. Yes. Yes. Yes.

She came like she had never come before, while his cock throbbed inside her with his own orgasm.

It was even delicious afterwards to sit and smile and

come down. They sat apart again, very properly, each wordless for a while. And then he said something she would always remember afterwards. He said, 'Whatever you do, Oruela, be true to yourself. You're a wonderful woman. You're beautiful inside and out.'

The Anonymous Benefactor

The next day, Kim whispered across the food counter, 'They took Caspar last night,'

Oruela felt her legs go numb. She looked at Kim. Her friend's face was deadly serious.

'Why?' asked Oruela. But the queue was pressing behind her and there was no time for further conversation.

Oruela ate her breakfast still in a state of hope. They had probably taken him to another part of the prison, she thought. But as the eggs hit her stomach she knew it was impossible. The idea that she would never see him again was too hard to bear. She waited resolutely.

When it was time for work, instead of going to the queue for the gate, Oruela went along the landing to Kim's cell.

'Where have they taken him? she asked.

'Back to Russia,' said Kim, 'They've traded him for someone from the other side, a Frenchman the Bolsheviks were holding in one of their prisons for trying to stir up counter-revolutionary sentiment.'

Oruela's knees went completely. She sank on to the small chair.

'Don't go to work,' said Kim. 'I'll look after you. Just sit there and when I bring the guard, act it up a bit.'

Oruela didn't have to. She was feeling the old strangeness again. She didn't say a word to anyone as the guard and Kim helped her to bed.

'If she doesn't get any better, I'll have her taken to hospital,' said the guard.

'Let me bring her some hot tisane,' said Kim.

The guard agreed.

Kim wasn't long. The tisane smelt of blackcurrants. It also had a liberal quantity of cognac in it.

She slept for a while after that but when she awoke the reality hit her again like a hammer blow to the head. It was actual physical pain. Kim was there again, with lunch and another, miraculous tisane. Oruela drunk it and stared at the blank wall.

Kim reached across the bed and took her in her arms gently. 'I need to see some tears at this point, otherwise I'll be worried,' she said.

It was all Oruela needed. She let out a wail of total grief that turned into huge racking sobs that went on and on. Kim stayed with her until they were ebbing and then she left, to cook dinner.

Come evening Oruela felt less pain but she was still shaky. The thought of poor Caspar made her weep again. His own people would surely execute him. She felt the touch of his death. His last words to her came back. No! He was still alive now, surely. There hadn't been time to get him back to Russia.

He was out there, somewhere, in some lonely train carriage, only enemies for company. She would remain beautiful for him. She got out of bed, changed her clothes, putting on the drab black prison skirt and blouse. She took up her brush and ran it through her hair.

There was tons of hair on the brush! The sight of it shocked her. She felt her head. There was still plenty there.

She needed company. Her cell door was open and the sky was dark outside. She reckoned it to be about 9

118

in the evening. She crept out, feeling like a new chicken just out of the egg, and went along to Kim's cell.

There was no one in it. Then she noticed that the rug on Kim's floor was missing. A sword of sheer terror stabbed her heart. Not Kim too!! But no. Her other things were there. She backed out of the cell. Something else was strange. The place seemed empty. Then she realised what it was. There were no guards about. She made her way along the landing to Marthe's cell. That was empty too. The little wind chime that Marthe had made from bits of tin tinkled on a breeze that came in through the open window.

And then she heard another sound. The sound of soft laughter. It was coming from the communal room at the end of the landing. This was a tatty dump that no one ever went in. But someone was in there tonight. She crept slowly along the landing to the door.

The sight that met her eyes was fantastic. The room was lit with candles. It was full of women. They were laughing, lounging around on rugs, even cushions. It was luxurious, almost another world. She opened the door and all eyes turned her way. There was a strange sweet smell in the room. The air was heavy with smoke. A group of women in the corner passed a hookah between them.

'Oruela! Oh, I'm so glad!' Marthe raised her luxurious body from the group and, stepping over the legs outstretched on the floor, she came towards her.

Of course! It was the hen night! Marthe was dressed in a real dress. It was beautiful, a black silky affair, beaded and tied at the hip with a jet scarf. Around her forehead was a black headband and she had a feather poked in the side of it. Earrings made of heavy silver adorned her ears and her lips were red as strawberries. Her eyes were cloudy, the pupils dilated, giving her a sleepy look.

'Here, have a glass of wine,' she said, gently leading Oruela to one corner of the room where a low table held

119

several opened bottles and glasses. She poured a glass of the blood-coloured wine and handed it to her.

'There's hashish too,' she said, her eyes twinkling. 'I bet you've never smoked hashish.'

'No, I haven't,' said Oruela. She wasn't sure she wanted to.

'Come with me,' said Marthe.

Oruela followed her to the other corner of the room, stepping over the lounging women like Marthe did. Their bare legs gleamed in the candlelight.

Marthe beckoned to her to sit in the circle of women who were passing the hookah. Oruela sat next to a big-thighed black woman whom she recognised as one of Kim's co-workers in the kitchen. The woman smiled at her and adjusted her sitting position.

The hookah was coming round the circle and was passed to the black woman who settled it in front of her and took the mouthpiece between her lips. She drew on it, taking a big hit and withdrawing the mouthpiece. Her eyes closed as she held her breath, taking the smoke down deep into her lungs. She took three hits and passed it on to Oruela.

Oruela looked across at Marthe, who had fallen into conversation. Perhaps it would make her feel better. She copied what she'd seen the woman next to her do. She raised the metal mouthpiece to her lips and drew. Her heart began to beat faster as the perfumed smoke hit her lungs and a spot in the middle of her forehead seemed to open like a window. At the same time she began to feel everything. Her fingertips glowed. She could feel the muscles in her shoulders loosen and relax. Within, her bowel began to feel anxious and then relax soon after. But the main sensation was between her kneeling thighs. Her sex began to swell.

The old fear of her attraction to other female bodies surfaced at the same time.

'Take another hit,' whispered Marthe, just as Oruela was about to pass the thing on in alarm.

It worked. The fear gradually dissipated. So what?

Sexuality is a wild, untameable thing, she said to herself. She could feel the thigh of the woman beside her resting on her own. One long warm sliver of thigh. But she didn't move. It was human. It was nice.

There were conversations going on either side of her, intimate conversations. She didn't feel as if she had the resources to interrupt or join. So she relaxed into a sitting position, her legs tucked to the side of her.

It disturbed the woman on her left. She turned. She was a large-boned, blonde creature. Her smile was threatening but brief. Oruela caved in on herself, on her own thoughts. The introspection seemed to last a long time, whereas in reality it was probably brief.

She thought of Caspar, not with fear for his safety or with pain at the loss of him, but how he was. How they were together, that last time, laughing their heads off in joy at getting away with what they were doing. She was so proud of herself!

Was this the woman who went mad because the policeman came and accused her of murdering her father? No, it was not. Damn them all. She had come a long way. She would always hold Caspar, and Kim and Marthe in her heart. They'd changed her. They'd set her free. One day she would be out of here, too. She would be truly free and then there'd be no stopping her.

And then it hit her. The letter. She'd sent it to Michelle. Good God! Von Streibnitz would have her in the hat for ever if he read it. But he must have read it by now if he was going to and nothing had changed. Perhaps she'd got away with that too.

She wondered what Michelle would think of it. Perhaps Michelle would think she was a bit mad. But it wasn't a mad woman that wrote that letter, it was a free one. Oruela smiled to herself.

Here was the hooka again. Its body was made of glass that bulged at the bottom. It was passed on a wooden base. Inside there was a long black shaft that

121

air bubbled out from into the water. The long pipe slithered like a snake.

She took a deep hit, just as the door opened behind her. She saw through the smoke the way Marthe smiled with delight. She passed the hookah and turned round.

There was Kim, closing the door behind her. She was wearing dancing clothes. A long, flowing skirt fell from her bare hips. It was held up by a scarf, knotted at the side. Her midriff was bare. Bare and shapely, deep brown and beautiful. Covering her breasts was another scarf. Her neck was bare and her slender, beautifully rounded head moved like a black swan's.

Her ears, her wrists and her ankles were decked in bracelets that clicked as she moved.

A space parted for her, like the Red Sea parting for the Jews of Israel, and Marthe leapt to the gramophone in the corner of the room and cranked it up.

Marthe put the needle-head on the spinning disc and the sounds of a trumpet with a mute wound around the room. Slow, lazy notes as if through a fog.

Kim began to move to the tune, gyrating her hips on a single vertical plane. Up and down went her hips, her navel a dark centre of her body, mysteriously still.

She began to move her bare feet, treading a circle close to the women at the edges of her designated dance floor. Strong steps, proud and firm, marking the boundaries. Women shuffled back against the walls. Kim's feet beat on the carpet in time to the music.

She lifted her skirt, showing off her legs, long and thin calves, pale heels.

With the circle beat out to her satisfaction she moved into the centre of the rug again and gyrated her hips in half-moons, raising and lowering her arms alternately, caressing the air. Then the music changed and she brought them together over her head and sliced them through the air into the centre of her bare stomach.

She changed the position of her legs. Bending one knee, she rocked her hips. She held her ankles above

122

the higher hip. They seemed to say 'look at this'. One long thigh moving up and down as a woman's thigh moves up and down when her man is between her legs.

In the dimness of the room the dance churned the women's senses. Someone began to clap. Others took up the rhythm. Oruela found her palms clapping out encouragement to the dance. The music in the background came to a stop and the needle took up the rhythm as it rasped on the centre of the record. Oruela longed to sing but she was inhibited. And then someone came to her rescue. A girl on the other side of the room began the song. It was wordless, some kind of peasant tune that Oruela knew in the deep recesses of her unconscious. Others took it up and Oruela heard her own voice joining in, weaving around the others, now with, now against.

The power that seemed to generate in the room was intense, as if the breath of a great, strong-thighed goddess had blown in from the south. The excitement charged the air.

Someone began to beat on an improvised drum giving a deep bass undertone to the symphony of sound that mingled with the darkness of the room and the heat of the women's bodies.

On Kim danced, whirling and shimmying, swooping to the ground and up again, swaying. She seemed lost on the wave of sound. Her eyes closed and she raised her skirt further up her thighs. Her gleaming bare skin flashed around the room. She shook her shoulders so that her breasts moved voluptuously under the flimsy scarf. She shook and shook and stepped backwards and forwards. The scarf began to inch its way down until her breasts were bare. The scarf cascaded to her hips and rustled there, spinning around her like gossamer cloud.

And then the woman singing the lead in the song began to slow it. The rest of the room followed her like a flock of birds follows its leader, without any obvious signal. Kim began to slow. People's voices dropped away. And then it was just the lone singer and the drum, thudding.

Kim stilled her body gradually. The song ceased. The drum beat quickened and grew softer at the same time and Kim sank into a sultry heap, raising her head. It settled gracefully on her neck. The drum stopped and she lowered her eyes.

The applause was deafening. Women thundered their appreciation and Kim sat, smiling, her breasts heaving with the exertion.

Marthe got up and wound up the gramophone again, putting on the other side of the record. Women began their own dances and Kim crawled across the room to where Oruela sat, flopping against a cushion by the wall.

'That,' said Oruela, her words seeming to have a resonance, 'was fantastic.'

'Pass the smoke,' said Kim. 'I'm dying for a hit.'

Marthe refilled the bowl quickly and gave it to her friend with a smile. 'Thank you,' she whispered.

Soon after the dance, couples began to disappear off into other, private worlds. The sight made Oruela a little nervous but she was easily distracted. There was a group of five women in her corner of the room. Herself, Kim, Marthe and two other white older women of about forty or so. They sat on either side of Marthe and the talk was of men, of marriage and sex.

One of them had been a prostitute and she told Marthe stories, of nights in Paris under the glow of street lamps. Of men who nuzzled her breasts and pulled out their cocks before she'd got her skirt up so the push of it on her thigh felt like an attack. She liked the men who wanted her to wear clothing of some description while they fucked her. She liked, especially, something around her waist, tightening, or her ankles.

She liked to be bound. The feeling of being tied to the bed with her stockings, hand and foot, helpless was, she said, such a stimulant that she would come almost immediately. And she liked to watch the men come for her. She wanted to scream, get into the fear, terrify herself so that the coming would be intensified.

Oruela listened with mounting lust. She wanted to experience that. Then the other woman began to tell her stories. She told of working in the fields one day alongside a big labourer from outside her village, how the sun beating down on their bodies had warmed them until their blood boiled. She had finished a basket of strawberries and had taken it to the edge of the field where the baskets were stacked and empty ones waited to be filled. The stackers had driven away loaded full and there was no one else there. She had bent down to pick up an empty basket when she felt him behind her. He wrenched up her long, thick working skirt and felt her sex, just like that. She was wet and she wanted him. She spread her legs and he took her hips in his hands and held her tight as he slid his cock inside her and fucked her.

'I never could figure out how he did that,' she giggled. 'I was thinking: Look! No hands. But it was wonderful. It was over in a few minutes and I didn't even come. But I went back to work with renewed strength. We worked together all day and at the end of it he took up his bundle, collected his money and with a nod he was gone.'

Kim Sun had laid back on some pillows in the corner and seemed to be sleeping. The sight of her suggested sleep to Oruela's hashish-laden brain and she grabbed a blanket and some of the cushions lying around on the floor and settled herself. But then Marthe said, 'Loving a woman is a different experience,' and all Oruela's senses came awake. She opened her eyes a crack as one of the other women said, 'We ought to give you a perfect send-off you know.' And as she spoke she caressed Marthe's shoulder.

'I've never loved a woman,' whispered Marthe.

'Well, you should then,' said the third woman. 'Just once, before you become a respectable married woman.'

Marthe turned from one to the other, silently, and each of them smiled mysteriously.

'Me first,' said one and she gently kissed Marthe's cheek and her hair. She took her breast in her hand and fondled it.

The other one gently pushed Marthe down so they were lying among the rugs and went to Marthe's feet and stroked her legs. Slowly, as Marthe was being kissed at one end, the woman slid her hands to the hem of her dress and pushed it up. The other woman pushed down the top over Marthe's shoulders, exposing her.

Together they pulled the dress right away from the body of the bride-to-be. She lay naked, warm, living, theirs. Her legs flopped. Her sex, cherry red and swollen, glistened. Her triangle of wet hair spread luxuriously over her belly.

They kissed and they caressed the pale body. The bride's legs opened wider. They attended to her from the direction of four hands, here and there, every crevice delved, stimulated, every dark secret spot touched, invaded by a womanly need.

The bride responded with an arching of the back, her sex pushing on to her attendant's fingers, her strong arms supporting her body on its elbows, her luxurious hair falling to the rug in a cascade.

Then it was sixfold. Two mouths joined four hands in their work. Sex lips pushed. The gash in the face said 'Yeah.' Red, soft sex met a tongue, tastebuds crashed. Strawberry mouth travelled to a nipple and sucked it till it was wet and passed on to another and made the skin wet there too. A blonde head nuzzled at one pair of breasts, snuggling, crooning and then moved to another pair. Breasts pressed together like crescent moons.

The three bodies rolled and the pace quickened. Three full arses rose and fell, one in a face, one in the air, one sunk to the floor. Their hair was wet all over, their faces gleamed with sweat.

Three sexes were touched with white fingers, with lips again. But it was the bride who got most of the attention. The bride's sex had one of the finest nights of its life.

126

'She's going to make it. Look at her!' said one of her attendants.

The other one grinned. 'There's no way she's going to be a faithful wife now she's discovered this.'

The bride merely moaned.

'I always wanted to be a bridesmaid,'said the first woman.

The bride's legs closed together and she went rigid. Suddenly she collapsed and rolled and writhed as her orgasm was complete.

The bridesmaids had their own pleasure over the murmuring body of the satiated bride and then they slept, one enfolding the other's back with her arm in a gentle gesture of possession.

Oruela was fried! She was the only one left awake, as far as she knew. When she was sure that the others were asleep she rose and went to the door, intending to go back to her own bed and relieve herself of the wave of sex that had taken her over as she watched the other women.

The door was locked. She stepped back over the sleeping women and lay back among the cushions. Did she dare do it here? Not in public surely.

But her question was answered for her.

She felt the hand on her thigh, moving upward slowly and she almost cried out. She opened her eyes a crack but all she could see through her lashes was a covered body down by her thighs moving closer. She shut her eyes again and pressed against the fingers that massaged her sex.

Then they disappeared and she was left in agony for what seemed like an age before the mouth touched her. Oruela slid her hands under the blanket and felt the soft head of hair that moved between her legs. The tongue circled her clitoris again and again. It drove into her, hard and wet. Oruela pushed herself on to it, taking it inside her as her orgasm came.

* * *

127

For a few days, inevitably, she looked about her, trying to figure out who it could have been. At the wedding, she saw the little blonde wasp looking at her. When Oruela stared at her, she smiled secretively. But even that didn't faze Oruela. So what? She was hardening off.

And then, one morning, the letter came. It was on her bed when she came home at lunchtime from the library. It was from Michelle.

'Dear Oruela,' it began. *'Mon dieu!* Although I'm not sure I should write his name in the same breath as what I'm thinking. Your letter was terrific. It's started off all kinds of thoughts with me. Robert's wondering what's hit him. But I'll tell you about that later. There's news. Good and bad.

'I've had a job to stop Paul Phare, you know, Jean's mate, tearing the letter out of my hand. He's been fantastic. I haven't seen hide nor hair of Jean bloody Raffoler and I'm not sure I should tell you this in a letter but I don't think that man's worth a light compared to Paul. Paul says he's in a state of shock and you can't rely on him doing anything. Jean I mean. But I reckon you can rely on Paul. He's going to do some detective work. There's something very funny gone on. I mean we all know that but even funnier than we thought.

'Paul says he's going to come and see you sometime soon. So you can look forward to that. He is a nice man. I would've come myself but you have to get papers and that and, to tell you the truth, Oruela, I'm scared. That Paris policeman came and questioned me at Aunt Violette's (I had to leave the house to go and try and get Jean to do something the night before you were taken away). I was scared they were going to make me an accomplice and put me in there. But that's dropped, it looks like, and Paul said I should write whatever I want to you and he would bribe someone to get the letter in. I just hope it works. Anyway, don't worry, Oruela. Robert sends you his love too.

'So I must tell you what I did with him the other

night. We went down on the beach. He said he had to pee. It was that imaginary bloke in your letter that did it. The one that peed. It's got me really excited about that kind of thing. I made him let me hold his prick while he peed at the sea. It goes a long way, you know. I pointed it, like it was mine and it was all warm and lovely.

'I was so horny with it that I got him to make love to me right there on the beach in the dark with the waves crashing around our ears and not giving a damn about who was in the shadows.

'Well, I'd better sign off now before I wet my own knickers writing it! I'll seal this tight and send it with lots of love. Keep hoping, my love. We're doing our best.'

Oh, how it did Oruela's heart good to read that. She gobbled down her lunch with real hunger and lay down on the bed for a rest with a smile on her face.

Why she could still feel so happy if Jean had deserted her, as Michelle seemed to be saying, she didn't know. Perhaps she'd always known he might. It really just seemed expected, somehow. Had she grown immune in this place? Or had Caspar cured her of some wound for ever?

And then her thoughts turned to Paul Phare. How wonderful of him to find the motivation to help her. Why?

The thought hit her right in the womb. That time when the three of them had met. She remembered it and remembered that initially it had been Paul that she'd been attracted to. What had changed? Jean had come to her first and flirted. She'd known he was flirting and hadn't taken him entirely seriously. She'd been funny and he liked her sense of humour. He'd asked her out.

It had begun from there. But now she saw again something that she'd forgotten. She saw Paul at that first meeting, over Jean's shoulder, brooding, glancing their way. She saw him walking away to talk to someone else and coming back later, looking somehow more closed, smaller than he'd been a half hour before. She could hardly remember him after that. It dawned on her why. There had been something unmistakably there, but it had fled in the competition that he'd lost.

Dare she think that? It gave her a future if she did. That was something she couldn't think about. She wrenched her mind back to the sensual, to the brooding looks, to the first time she saw him and scuppered her sensible intentions. He was there. She could feel him. And for the first time in weeks she felt safe.

Summertime (and the Living Is Easy)

'There aren't many professions,' said Paul, 'where you are likely to ask another man if you can borrow his naked girlfriend.'

Paul and Robert, Michelle's lover, were taking a morning walk along the sands. The heat of the early summer sun had not yet begun to burn. The sea was blue and glistening and the sand was cool beneath their bare feet. Robert picked up a flat stone and skimmed it across the waves.

'I like the way she's changing,' said Robert. It was an understatement. He loved her new sexual adventurousness. He agreed to Paul's suggestion.

The idea had grown organically out of a theme that Paul had been working with for some time. There was an Englishwoman, Daisy, who lived in one of the cluster of cottages surrounding Paul's house on the harbour front in old Biarritz. She was the wife of Bertrand, a fisherman. Bertrand was also a hashish smuggler in a small way. Out at sea, beyond the prying eyes of the law he would take on board enough of the North African medicinal herb to keep his friends going.

It was a woman who ran the trade. She lived as a pirate outside the national waters of all countries. Several attempts had been made to catch her but she was as skilful a sailor as a smuggler and she eluded the Customs every time.

Bertrand went aboard once in a while to buy his hashish. She dealt opium and cocaine too but these didn't interest him. He heard stories of opium-induced dreams that went on for days and sex that broke all taboos.

Daisy would often come over to Paul's and they would smoke together from Paul's Moroccan hookah. Sometimes she would pose for him and they had been working on what was known as an oriental theme.

Daisy was the very essence of an English type of woman: all peaches and cream and pale brown hair. Her body was pear-shaped and petite. So far, she had not posed naked but with the arrival of Annette the scenes began to get more exotic.

Annette's knowledge of sexuality gave them ideas. Annette knew how men were turned on. She knew the species, man and boy. She knew the simple things that drove them wild and the way these fancies grew into obsessions as they became older. Men, she told them, do not let themselves be inhibited with a whore the way they do with women in front of whom they have to be fathers and suitors and sons.

She knew what turned women on too. She had lived in a stew of sex for most of her adolescence. She had a pale unhealthy pallor, as if her body, never seeing the light of day, was a china doll for the boys to play with in the darkened, over-furnished rooms of La Maison Rose. It gave her body a photographic value that Paul was quick to take advantage of before the fresh air and relaxation made her glow like an ordinary young woman.

She discovered a hidden talent for prop-making. They raided, wholesale, the ideas of the Orientalist painters of a generation before and pooled their collections of objects and fabrics from around the world. What they didn't have, Annette began to make and in her hands, ordinary fabric became mysterious curtains and exotic

132

sarongs. Scarves became turbans and veils. Feathers collected from the beach became fans. She made a fabulous snake from papier mâché and painted it and even changed the dustbin lid into a believable warrior's shield.

Michelle came by one morning and watched them setting up for a series Paul called 'The Odalisque'. The couch was draped with fabric and set by the window so that the light fell softly on it like the light of a dream. The snake was placed at the foot of the couch on the floor in the shadows. Daisy dressed herself as a harem guard and stood in the shadows at the back on a plinth, her figure veiled in mystery. Annette undressed and settled herself on the couch, fixing a velvet choker around her neck as she settled naked in the soft fabric.

Michelle sat spellbound and eventually plucked up courage to ask if she could join in but Paul insisted they ask Robert first.

And so it began in earnest. Michelle raided Aunt Violette's haberdashery shop for ribbons and braid and they spent a whole day together tying the beautiful strands to the body of one woman, then another, while Paul snapped away.

They chose dark ribbons for Annette, purple and black, saturnine colours to bring out her deathly pallor. They tied them to her wrists, to her ankles, to her hair. On the back of one leg she had a fine set of bruises left over from the roughness of the whorehouse. The purple and yellow injury was dressed up by the other women in a ribbon either side. They put an open yellow orchid in the cheeks of her arse and called it 'Aphrodite'.

Daisy they dressed in green ribbons like a hunter in the long grass. They found a knife and made a sheath that hung between her breasts.

Michelle they dressed in red and pink, with a turban around her head and a veil covering all of her face but her eyes. She wore red ribbons at her ankles and her wrists. She wore red lipstick on her lips and on her sex and did wonderful bendy dances, stretching now to the ground, now for the ceiling, leaping about with the freedom of it all and the drive of libido.

Paul encouraged them to do what they wanted to. His only input into the scenes at this point was to get the light how he wanted it, or to get them into the light that was available. He enjoyed the way the women took control of the ideas given the chance. The photographs took on an unusual, female interpretation of old ideas. Their burgeoning creativity stirred him. It was a kind of intellectual lust, he was so used to photographing women. Not that the naked flesh that filled his transformed studio day after day didn't have its effect in more physical ways but he was all too aware that these Three Fates were on loan to him. Daisy and Michelle were other men's women and Annette was too vulnerable to be seduced. He knew he wouldn't want to continue an affair with her and so he didn't start one. It cost him a lot of sexual frustration but he channelled all his energy into his work.

Daisy got it into her head that she wanted to be photographed naked, emerging from a net of freshly caught, silvery, flapping fish. The problem was getting the fish. Bertrand put his foot down. He wasn't going to have a catch wasted on a photograph. No. Definitely not.

Daisy took him home. The next day he not only brought the fish but was transformed by the women into Neptune. He refused to pose completely naked so Annette went and collected some fresh seaweed and he had it draped over his genitals and falling from his thighs. The studio smelled of the sea for days afterwards and Nefi, the cat, went into spasms of ecstasy. Annette scrubbed the place until it shone like a new pin.

Paul had an idea that Robert would be easier to get to pose naked so he searched his library for tales of famous kings of antiquity who were known for their luxurious tastes, and left the rest to Michelle. Robert was coy at first but the chance to show off the body that he had worked on for so long was eventually irresistible. The studio became a king's lair.

The women directed his poses, setting him here and there on cushions, on rugs. Gradually he became less self-conscious, more inclined to let his loincloth slip and reveal . . .

The photographs were phenomenal. Strange, almost breathing, erotic scenes covered the workbench in Paul's darkroom. They emerged mysteriously from the developing fluids in the small hours of the morning and the next day the women would look at them with him and start on new ideas.

Paul began to put something very small into each picture to indicate only to the most observant connoisseur that what they saw was an illusion. Shoes were his favourite. Poking out, barely visible from under a curtain in a perfectly re-created harem scene would be a modern shoe. Even the Three Fates didn't notice it until one night when Annette and Paul were on their own, poring over a new batch, she spotted it.

'Do you know,' she said, 'that there are drawings of shoes that they used to wear in the Middle Ages? They were like this.' And she proceeded to sit on the floor and draw a slipper. The toe was a long, erect phallus.

This began a whole new series of photographs of Annette drawing the things she had heard of during her days as a whore. Annette always naked, Annette surrounded by drawings of phalluses.

Paul's lens closed in on her face concentrating hard on her drawings that grew more beautiful as the days went by. His self-control was being stretched to the limit.

The days grew into weeks and the summer grew hotter. The studio seethed with heat and languor. The very walls seemed to sweat with sex. Paul padded around in bare feet, his beard growing for days before he had a shave. He wore a sleeveless vest and trousers that he rolled up when he went down to the sea and walked by the water when the day grew cool enough.

Annette made a huge fan and Robert would be employed as a slave to fan them. They were drifting into a demi-monde where nothing was quite what it seemed. Their sexual imaginations seemed inexhaustible.

One morning the Three Fates decided to dispense with props and form a naked ring on the floor, their bodies completely unadorned, their hands clasping each other's ankles. They stretched, their backs arched.

Paul was snapping busily, the fabric of his trousers stretched across his arse as he almost did the splits to get the shot. They heard a screech of brakes as a fast car pulled up outside. The door opened and a slender youth blew in. Daisy's lazy smile changed into a look of alarm. But Michelle and Annette, unaware of who the youth was, merely blinked.

Renée wore a yellow silk shirt and tie with plus-fours and silken brown stockings. On her feet were men's brogues. There was nothing to suggest she was anything other than a slender young man in a driving hat and goggles. Her yellow-green eyes surveyed the ring of naked women and travelled around the walls where Annette's drawings hung with their abundant interpretations of sex. The very air was heavy with erotic dreams.

There was mayhem. The Three Fates scattered, pulling on their clothes as Renée embarked on a spree of destruction. Paul's camera went flying and he caught it just in time to save it. But this infuriated Renée even more and she managed to tear two of Annette's drawings from the wall and rip down a flimsy curtain before Paul finally wrestled her to the ground.

She lay under him, her face close to his, a mask of anger, silent, hating, dangerous.

'It's not what you think,' he whispered. 'Calm yourself.' And he kissed her bloodless lips, kissed her temples, kissed the little red spots of anger on her pale cheeks. Tears began to form in her eyes.

'You bastard,' she said. 'You bastard.'

He kissed her again and felt her stiff, slender body begin to yield little by little. She kissed him back, her tears wet on his face.

The feeling of her body close to his made Paul into that strange male creature who is both putty in a woman's hands and master at the same time. Nothing would stop him from fucking her after all this time apart, even if she'd wanted to stop him, which she didn't.

He released her and pulled her shirt out of her trousers, pushing it over her nipples. Her breasts were a mere softness of the ribcage, hardly there at all. He adored them. He bit playfully at her nipples, licked them until they stood up.

But what he really wanted was in her trousers. Her belly was concave, her waistband loose on her. He undid her fly buttons and pulled her trousers and knickers down to her knees. There she was revealed. The uniqueness of her that was both awesomely beautiful and her ugly shame at the same time.

Paul pressed his lips to her enlarged clitoris and sucked.

Some hermaphrodites were born with huge penises; she ought to think herself lucky, the doctors had told her. But Renée knew she was anything but lucky. They told her a lot of women would be grateful never to have to menstruate. Renée didn't believe a word of it. She felt like a girl but her body stared back at her from the mirror, a mockery of those feelings. She just didn't know what she was. The real humiliation had been when her first lover, a boy of her own age, had been sick when she took off her knickers. He had left her naked, full of sex and ashamed, her overgrown clitoris sticking out of her pubic hair like some horrible half-grown thing.

It had been years before she allowed herself to be so vulnerable in the presence of another man.

Paul had adored her totally at first. He prized her uniqueness. He fed her a diet of undiluted love and she had blossomed with confidence. Her whole life had been affected. She realised her ambition to race cars and she became better and better at it. The speed satisfied her soul as nothing else.

And now? She had wanted him to be a slave to her all her life but he could never be that. She didn't understand his free-ranging soul. She grew jealous of his every move as their affair settled. He wasn't quite as enthralled as he had been at first. How could he hope to make her believe that he was hers alone when he spent his time with other, naked, normal women? She hated him now.

He dragged his tongue up her belly, to her breasts, to her mouth and manoeuvred his body to take her completely. She hit his big strong arms with her useless fists. She hated him. She wanted to hurt him.

Then he was inside her and she loved him again because he made her into a woman.

Her deformity crushed into the pit of his belly and gave her its gift of orgasm that left her almost unconscious underneath him.

Cheek to Cheek

With Renée back, the Three Fates laid low and Paul gradually brought her round to some kind of sanity. She had come home to train for the great August race held every year in the mountains in Spain. This was the first year she had been accepted, albeit in the guise of a man, for entry into the big-engine race. She would race against kings. She and her little team of two mechanics would take on the best in Europe. She knew she wouldn't win but she would compete. She made a fine sportsman and none of them even suspected that she was a woman.

The training kept her busy and Paul moved Annette out into one of the empty cottages without Renée even realising she'd been living there.

It was at this point that Michelle began to agitate for some more action to help Oruela. The hunt for the truth had been halted by the sudden, suspicious death of Dr Simenon.

The doctor's car had been found in a gully after mysteriously skidding off a mountain road in the middle of the night. There had been no obvious reason for the crash and it had scared Paul and Michelle. Their attempts to follow up Annette's lead on the coroner and the judge had been thwarted by closed doors and two of the mayor's henchmen had stopped Paul in the street one night as he was coming home from dinner at a friend's and warned him. It had seemed not only sensible, but a matter of life and death to lie low. Their wild burst of creativity had followed this warning and had restored them to life. But now it was time. It was no longer possible to put things off.

Through Bertrand's contacts they got letters smuggled in to Oruela, asking her to tell them everything she could think of that might involve the mayor. She had letters smuggled back to Paul by the same route but there was nothing she could think of to help him. Jean continued to refuse to answer Paul's calls.

Paul felt a sense of frustration that seemed to settle like a blanket of cloud over him. Even sex didn't lift it. He hated injustice and at the moment he wasn't sure which he hated most, the mayor's corrupted system or Jean's faint heart.

He was drinking a good deal of cognac, he realised, as if he was blaming himself. His common sense prevailed. He could do nothing. He made an effort not to drink so much and the discipline he imposed on himself gave him back his dignity.

One evening he came home from the market where he had bought some *saucisson* and Robert and Michelle were waiting for him. They sat on the wooden bench that stood outside his house under the low, shuttered window. He observed them for some few minutes before they saw him. They were talking close together, ignoring the world around them. The rythmic crash of the waves on the golden beach went unnoticed and unheard as they reached for the landscape of each other. They looked up, startled as two wild rabbits, when he said 'Hello.'

'We were waiting for you,' chirped Michelle. 'Robert's got an idea.' She looked at Robert with adoration as he spoke.

'There's a strongbox in Genevieve Bruyere's bedroom,' began Robert as Paul sat down on the warm bench next to them and put his shopping on the floor. 'She keeps her private papers in there. I've discovered how to open it without a key. I think you ought to come out to the house and have a look. There are a lot of official-looking documents in there. They don't make much sense to me but you'll be able to tell if they could give us a lead or something.'

Paul felt excited for the first time in days. 'When shall I come?' he asked.

'Tomorrow?' said Robert. 'She goes out driving a lot these days in the afternoons with that Alsatian policeman.' Robert scoffed. 'What a peasant that man is! I could throttle him with my bare hands. She can't even see that all he's after is her money. Still, what do I care?'

'You don't care at all,' crooned Michelle. 'Don't let him make you angry. You won't have to stay there very much longer. A job will come up, I'm sure.'

'Tomorrow's good for me,' said Paul. 'I don't have any plans. Right, now come and have some dinner with me, you two. I've just bought some of the most delicious *saucisson* in the whole of France.'

But Michelle and Robert made their excuses. Aunt Violette was cooking. Paul smiled to himself as they left and he opened his front door. Nefi appeared from nowhere and rubbed her lithe little body against his legs. He bent down and picked her up. He held her close to his chest with one hand and spoke to her in soft tones. 'Why do they make me feel so lonely, Nefi?' he asked her. 'Why am I so sad?' The cat purred loudly and pushed her head against his cheek as if to tell him that she loved him truly.

He ate a lonely dinner and gave Nefi Renée's share of the *saucisson* when she didn't put in an appearance. It was very late when she finally did show and she stormed out again when she discovered there was nothing to eat, announcing her intention to eat at her friend's café. Paul was asleep when she returned and got into bed. He had only the vaguest memory of her climbing in beside him when he awoke the following morning.

He left her in the dark, crumpled bed and closed the door quietly. Within the hour he was on the train for Bayonne.

The train clattered through the bright morning with its load of shoppers, business and tradespeople. Paul studied their faces. Which of them was really happy, he wondered? It was hard to tell. The mundane journey etched itself into their features. But what hidden depths of passion, of anything, were these façades concealing? The only two animated people on the train were a pair of matrons in the next bank of seats. They were different. They gossiped with relish, their lips glossy with glee, their eyes shining with salacious imaginings as they discussed people they were careful to identify only by initial. Paul wondered what the affairs they pored over were doing to their organs. Surely they were bursting with sex, he thought. They were such handsome, ripe women.

The train squealed to a halt at Bayonne and emptied itself with a gasp on to the platform. Robert was waiting beyond the smart ticket-office out in the sunshine. He leaned gracefully on the family Bentley with its top down. Robert wore a very handsome black chauffeur's uniform.

'You must be hot,' said Paul.

Robert made it clear that he was with an exasperated click of the tongue against the teeth. 'She won't have me drive this in anything else,' he said.

'How am I going to avoid being spotted?' asked Paul.

'It's all right,' said Robert, as he opened the back door and stood back for Paul to get in. 'She's gone out in the Citroën with the peasant again. They've gone in the other direction.'

Paul would rather have sat up front but there were no seats next to Robert's wheel. The leather of the passenger seats in the back was warm from the sun. Robert steered the car through the narrow streets and out of town towards the villa. The breeze refreshed Paul and modified the strength of the sun on his face. As they drew closer to the gates of the villa the trees were denser, overhanging the car, and then very suddenly the cool shade opened and the dazzle of the midday sun glinting off the lemon and white façade of the villa was too much for the eyes.

They drove slowly up the driveway and came to a halt outside the house.

'We had better not waste too much time,' said Robert. 'Her behaviour is unpredictable. I'll take you straight upstairs. But I'll put some coffee on for afterwards. Would you like some?'

Paul could have murdered a cup of coffee. He followed Robert up the surprisingly narrow stairway to the master bedroom. It surprised him. The room was sombre, not at all what he had imagined.

'She's going to decorate it she says,' said Robert. 'What she means is she's going to ask me to do it. She's a real skinflint sometimes.' He walked across the room to a wooden linen box by the window. He opened it and inside was a strongbox. He pulled it out and closing the linen box sat the metal one on top of it. Then he picked the lock with his butler's knife and said, 'There you are. I'll make that coffee.'

Paul made himself comfortable on the window seat. The pile of papers was mostly old financial documents, nothing that really leapt out as suspicious. But then he found Oruela's adoption certificate and along with it, her original birth certificate bearing the name of her mother. He had brought his Leica. He put the two papers on the window seat in the light and focused. He clicked the shutter at the same time as Robert burst into the room behind him shouting 'They're coming, look!'

Two figures were running hand in hand with gay abandon across the back lawn towards the house.

'Quite a girl, ain't she!' said Robert. 'Look at her. They're going to come straight up here, I bet you.'

Two minutes earlier and he could have escaped. 'Damn,' said Paul.

'We'll never get you out in time,' cried Robert. 'I know. Wait in here. Look.' He turned the key of Henri Bruyere's bathroom. 'She never uses it. I'll lock you in and take the key.'

So Paul sat on the edge of the bath and twiddled the strap of his Leica. He heard a lot of giggles, put the camera down and covered his ears. But nothing could block out the scream that a moment later, echoed round the whole house. He completely resisted the temptation to spy through the keyhole – for about thirty seconds.

Genevieve was pinned to the big wooden bedhead by Alix like a great drawing pin. His trousers were round his calves and his boots were still on. Both participants were wailing their way towards a very fast climax.

The temptation to take a photograph through the keyhole was overwhelming. Would it work? Paul uncovered his Leica and tried to focus. It might, he decided. He pressed the shutter button and it was all over.

In the peace Paul felt rather ashamed of himself. He straightened up and looked around. The bathroom smelt of disuse. A dried facecloth hung on the sink. The sun's rays fell in through the high window on to the edge of the bath. A blue chemist's bottle glowed on the side. Its label, half-turned, read '-blende'. In its neglect the once elegant bathroom had a touch of pathos about it that appealed to Paul's aesthetic sense.

He wound the film on under the muffling effect of his jacket and focused. The noise of the shutter seemed to echo round the bathroom like a thunderclap. He cursed under his breath and his heart raced as he bent down to the keyhole again. Alix and Genevieve were talking. Paul put his ear to the hole.

'Darling, this is more than just sex to me,' said Alix. 'It's on a higher, spiritual plane.'

'Oh, Alix,' she replied. 'We are as one!'

Paul breathed a sigh of relief. He amused himself for

a little while, taking photographs of the bathroom. Then he went back to the keyhole. Alix was smearing Genevieve's pussy with *confiture*. Oh dear, they would need the bathroom next.

He climbed into the bath and assessed his chances of getting out of the high window. They were not good. It would have to be a last resort. An hour ticked by very, very slowly. In the end he drifted into a kind of sleep, leaning on the side of the bath.

He was woken by the sound of another scream. This one curdled his blood. He was drawn to the keyhole again like a moth to a flame.

This time it was Alix screaming and Paul could see why. Still in his boots he was tied to the bed while Genevieve wielded a silver chain. It was a tiny instrument of torture, but torture it was. Alix's backside was red raw where she'd whipped him with it. The policeman begged for mercy but Genevieve's violet eyes had a fixed stare. She licked her lips and brought the chain down on to the pained flesh again.

Paul was really convinced he was about to witness a murder. The whole thing became clear to him. Genevieve had killed her unsuspecting husband in a bizarre sex game and blamed it on her daughter. But he was halfway out of the window, almost tearing his stomach on the catch, when he realised that the couple in the bedroom were laughing together. He eased himself back into the bath and went to the keyhole again. They were cuddled together on the bed, happy as lovebirds in a nest.

'Oh, Alix. I've never done anything like this before. All those wasted years. Oh, Alix, I feel alive,' breathed Genevieve. 'Let's do it again.'

'No, sweetest,' said Alix. 'Your lover needs some refreshment. Let's go downstairs and eat.'

Thank heaven, breathed Paul. It took another twenty minutes for Robert to unlock him.

* * *

Paul had heard of the English vice, naturally, among the girls at La Maison Rose. He'd heard of it in detail in fact. Especially tales of the rich Englishmen who came to Biarritz and paid handsomely for their humiliation. Some of the girls liked to do it, others didn't. But it didn't matter what they liked or what they didn't like. It had to be part of a whore's repertoire.

It had shocked him though, to see Madame Bruyere, naked, her pale wisp of straw at her sex, wielding the weapon. He'd never heard of a respectable bourgeois matron doing it. But then who ever heard what respectable bourgeois matrons got up to in their bedrooms? Paul steered clear of married women as lovers. He'd only slept with one and that was when he was an inexperienced boy. She had been a dark, Spanish temptress, a woman with a reputation, whose husband was a hotel-keeper with a heart condition. As a boy, Paul used to watch her doing the laundry of the small hotel in the open back-yard. He'd sat in the branches of a walnut tree watching her move as she carried the heavy baskets to and from the back of the building in the hot sun, her face glistening with perspiration, the sleeveless bodice of her dress revealing the dark hair under her arms, her heavy breasts moving in the thin material, all day. He would go home and dream of her at night.

The day she'd caught him watching her he'd almost died of embarrassment but he had not lost the stiffness in his pants! She made him help her like a little child but she knew he was ready to be a man and after days of their bodies brushing in the steamy laundry room she stopped him one afternoon, in his tracks, and suggested his shirt needed a wash. He peeled off his rough shirt and saw her eyes light up at the gorgeous boy's body underneath. He hadn't even started shaving but he was graceful and the promise of what he was to become was there in all its appeal.

She taught him, that day, how to please a woman. She felt it her duty, she told him, to let him know about a particular spot that needs to be loved if a woman is to

146

respond to a man. A whole treasure trove opened up to him before his very eyes.

She had a voluptuous body. Its curves, its softness, drowned him in the first delights of sex and once he'd started there was no stopping him. He couldn't get enough. Every minute of the day he was dying for love of her.

It was a rude awakening to find that she had another lover. It wasn't even her husband. It was a goatherd, a rough and ugly man that he'd always disliked. A man who got drunk whenever he came down with his goats from the beautiful Basque mountains and raised hell in the village where they lived.

One day he caught them together. His darling and this oaf in the same pile of laundry where she'd whispered sweet words to him only hours before. She was thoroughly enjoying herself. She liked it from behind with the goatherd. Paul crushed the little bouquet of wild flowers that he'd picked for her under his feet.

As he walked along the lane to the town of Bayonne, a man now, he remembered her and smiled.

The other thing he thought about was the name on the birth certificate that he had taken a photograph of. Euska Onaldi. Oruela's mother was the same woman Annette had talked of. She was here somewhere. What was she, some poor girl that had had her baby snatched?

It was pure instinct that drew him towards the graveyard. There was half an hour to wait before the train back to Biarritz. The town of Bayonne was busy with early evening shoppers. The churchyard was cool and quiet. The distinctive round, Basque gravestones of the older graves stood under the trees in the shade.

At the very edge of this community of the dead he saw a woman standing at a newer grave and before he admitted it rationally, he knew in his gut that he had found Euska Onaldi.

He kept back, leaning against a tall tree, peeping round it every so often to watch her. She seemed to be having

147

a conversation with the occupant of the grave. It crossed his mind that she might be mad by now. But madness didn't fit with the picture Annette had drawn of the beautiful woman who had visited La Maison Rose.

In due course she left the graveside and began walking towards where he hid. He sidled round the tree. She passed by, about two feet away, without noticing him. He could have touched her if he had just stretched out his hand. He wanted to.

She was dressed from head to toe in a pale shimmering grey. Even her face was obscured by a fine grey veil falling from a small soft hat on her head. He caught a glimpse of dark eyes under the veil. Her arms were bare and he surveyed them with a connoisseur's eye, judging her age more or less accurately. She walked with elegant sensuality and as she passed by he surveyed her fine, broad shoulders and long back with admiration.

As she reached the gate of the churchyard she turned and caught him. She held his gaze for a moment and then a sliver of amusement lit up her face before she turned again and was gone.

He started to follow her but as he reached the gate all he saw was her *derrière* disappearing into the back of a sleek black Hispano-Suiza. Her small, podgy chauffeur closed the door and walked round to the driver's door. Something about the man's movements told Paul he was homosexual. As the car pulled away Euska turned around and glanced at him through the window.

She was wondering what strange desires led the handsome young man to lean against trees in the churchyard and watch. He didn't look at all weird. In fact she had been rather flattered when she saw how fine-looking he was. It amused her to think that at over forty she could still attract those kind of glances. In younger days she might have got into her car and left the door open to see if he would climb in. But nowadays she wanted only one man.

148

With Henri dead she was free to join Ernesto in Rio. All she had to do was free Oruela. It was not an easy task but she was looking up old acquaintances one by one and calling in favours. Ernesto had insisted that his own chauffeur, Raoul, drive her down in his car to Biarritz on her dangerous mission. He would have come himself but he was too tied up with business in Paris.

Euska liked Raoul. He was a terrible queen. They talked girl talk and she told him where to find what he desired in the small private clubs of Biarritz.

The car sped along the road from Bayonne to Biarritz and her hotel on the Grande Plage. As she watched the people going about their business her thoughts turned again to the handsome young man in the graveyard. Perhaps he had wanted something else. The look from those gorgeous smoky green eyes stayed with her. Perhaps she would run into him again.

Paul arrived home to find Renée in a bad mood. She had returned the studio to its usual state. In other words, it was no longer a studio, it was a sitting-room. When she was in town she insisted. It was one of the things that irritated Paul and made him angry with himself. Why on earth did he put up with it? He poured himself a glass of country wine from the flagon he kept in the larder and while he was feeding Nefi he resolved to have it out with Renée.

She slung her magazine on the floor and glared at him as she walked into the studio.

'I want to talk to you, Renée . . .' he began.

'There's a letter from Paris,' she said. 'You've sold some pictures.'

'You opened my letter?' he said, taking it.

She merely reclined again, and lit a cigarette.

He looked at the letter. He had indeed sold some pictures. It was from a dealer that he'd sent the very first set of prints of 'The Odalisque'. The dealer had sent a money order for a sum that he could live on for at least three months! The joy of actually selling some work flooded through him.

'We're going to celebrate!' he said. 'Get your dancing shoes on, Renée.'

Even Renée was infected by his joyous mood and she smiled. She rose to go upstairs as he picked up the telephone and dialled Aunt Violette's.

As soon as he asked for Michelle, Renée jumped. She was on him, claws out, scratching at his face, tearing the phone away from him, screaming. He had to cut his call.

'You're supposed to be taking me out to celebrate! And you phone another woman! You bastard!' she screamed.

'Renée,' he said firmly. 'I'm not going to phone one woman, I'm going to phone three and a couple of men too. These are the people who made these photographs with me. Of course I'm going to invite them to celebrate with us.'

'No. No. No!' screamed Renée. 'I won't have it!'

Paul suddenly snapped. He'd had enough. Perhaps it was the image of Genevieve spanking Alix that did it. He'd certainly never done it before. He took her over his knee, reached for a slipper he saw poking out from under the couch and holding her firmly he gave her real solid spanking until she cried.

It didn't turn him on at all. It certainly quietened her though. He stopped and let her go. She stood up, a changed person.

'Go upstairs, wash your face, get dressed and be down here, ready to go out, with as many people as I choose to invite, in half an hour,' he said and she trotted off, meek as a kitten.

She re-appeared when he'd made his phone calls, in a beautiful black evening dress, her little velvet purse clasped demurely to her tummy.

As he dressed he thought about it. It was amusing to see Renée change like that. It was disturbing though. He was willing to try anything once but he wasn't the kind of man to get addicted to sexual violence. His whole being strained away from it. The women he enjoyed were beyond all that. He liked mature sex, real fucking. He liked his women naked. The thought of the trappings of sado-masochism just made him want to laugh. Poor Renée. When he was loving with her she just got in a bad mood. He understood why. The profound unhappiness that she carried around with her could, perhaps, only be relieved by violence. But it wasn't going to come from him.

He gave his hair a casual brush and walked downstairs without looking in the mirror. He wore his clothes like a second skin.

What a night they all had on the promise of money from the Paris dealer. They danced to the black American jazz band at the casino until dawn. They drank champagne and ate exquisite food. They toasted success and talked over new projects.

Annette looked stunning in her evening clothes and had a selection of beaux virtually kissing the ground she walked on. Michelle and Robert ogled the rich and famous and had the time of their lives. Renée behaved herself so well that Paul remembered the good times. He held her close as they danced and tasted the bittersweet love on her pale lips.

None of them noticed, among the comings and goings in the luxurious club, that Euska and Raoul sat in a darkened booth at the back. None of them saw her make enquiries of the waiter as to who they were, or saw her leave as the clock struck three.

They tumbled out of the club with the other bright young things as dawn was breaking and bundles of early morning newspapers were being delivered into shop doorways.

They were too tired and too happy to bother looking at the glaring headlines.

151

Put Your Foot Down, Baby
(and Turn My Wheels)

'CASPAR ALEXANDROVICH SHOT BY THE BOLSHEVIKS IN MOSCOW' glared the headline from the copy of the daily newspaper that came to the prison library. It was mighty strange for Oruela, having such an intimate connection with a man who was not only an international *cause célèbre* but most definitely dead. It brought her strange dreams and sleepless nights. The only way she could sleep was if she masturbated herself as thoughts of him skittered through her imagination.

During the day she was attracted to even the ugliest of the inmates who came into the library. She began to masturbate at night over them. In her dreams she would take all of them, two or more at a time. Desperate for the feeling of something inside, she stole a carrot from the kitchen and inserted it into her sex while she rubbed at her clitoris. She had the most violent orgasms.

She went to church and imagined everyone took off their clothes and bodies heaved in the pews.

Then one Sunday evening, when she was playing cards with Kim, Marthe came into the cell and, with a smug grin on her handsome face she said, 'I've discovered something.'

'Don't tell me,' said Kim, chucking a card into the

centre of the improvised table. 'You're going to get divorced and married again.'

'No,' said Marthe, still smugly smiling her smile.

'Come on then, Marthe,' said Oruela. 'Tell us.'

'Well,' said Marthe, 'I've found a way to spy on the men's shower.'

Kim and Oruela's four eyes lit up. 'How?' they chorused.

'Well,' said Marthe, 'you know that air vent next to the library building? You know how it has steam coming from it sometimes. Well, that's where the steam comes from. All we have to do is loosen the cover and crawl up the shaft.'

'You silly cow,' said Kim. 'We'll be cooked!'

'No, we won't. Most of the heat goes out of the window. It's only a trickle that comes out through the vent.'

'I wouldn't like to chance it,' said Kim.

'I already have,' said Marthe.

'You did?' they wondered.

'I did,' said Marthe. She wasn't just smug now, she was positively gloating. 'Boy, there are some honeys incarcerated in this place. Real peaches. There was this one with a body like a god. A real muscular type. You know what I mean? He strode in and took the jet right under my eyes . . .' She stopped.

'Go on!' cried the other two.

'No,' said Marthe. 'I'll spoil it for you. You'll have to come with me to experience it.'

And so they were hooked. The next day saw them up at the crack of dawn like model prisoners and out in the yard in dungarees. All three now had passes to walk freely within the inner compound. Oruela kept watch while the other two unhitched the grating. They crawled into the darkness one after the other and replaced it. Marthe led the way in the dark. They turned a bend and climbed up a metal ladder fixed to the wall. At the top it opened out and some light came from another grille. Below them was the empty men's shower room.

They didn't have long to wait. No sooner had they settled themselves to watch, their faces virtually pressed up against the grating, than an inmate walked in wearing only a towel around his waist. He was an Algerian, the same who worked in the church. He took off the towel, revealing his slender hips and his sleepy genitals. The three watching women sighed. He took a jet on the opposite side of the room so they could only really see the back of him. His arse was tight and paler than the rest of him. He turned on the water and it gushed over his body. Soon another inmate came in and another and another until the shower was filled with them. All shapes and sizes wandered sleepily to the jets and turned on the water. The water made their bodies shine. Rivulets of liquid covered their skin and ran through the hair on their chests down to their loins. Over their backs, it ran down arses of all kinds. It was noisy enough in the shower for the muffled groans of the three women to go unheard.

'Look at that,' whispered Marthe. 'That's him.'

'Christ,' groaned Kim.

Through the steam walked Marthe's honey. He really was something. His bulk was a delectable sight. His chest and shoulders were smooth and hairless with a slight film of steam glistening on his skin. His hair was long, to his shoulders, and beginning to curl damply. He stood right in front of them, a little below their grating and whipped off his towel. He was well endowed.

He turned on the stream as other men were leaving the room, and a look of pleasure spread across his face as he turned it upwards towards the jet and, unknowingly, towards the watching women.

'Oh yes,' groaned Kim. 'Oh baby, yes.'

Marthe signalled her to keep it down. With less men in the room Kim's groan was more audible. But the unsuspecting man below them carried on regardless. He turned under the spraying jet of water, round and back again and then he reached for the soap.

The foam slithered across his skin and dripped off him on to the floor. He soaped his hair and rinsed it. He soaped his underarms, his delicious chest, his belly and the water poured and poured. Then he soaped his cock. As he handled it it grew some.

Suddenly Kim went crazy. She began undoing her clothes.

'What are you doing?' hissed Marthe.

'I'm going in,' said Kim. And she began unhooking the grate. The man below them heard something. He left the washing of his cock and looked up. His face was a picture as out of the wall above his head came Kim, naked as the day she was born but all woman.

'Come here, big boy,' she said. 'I want you now.'

He didn't take any persuading. He didn't have a chance. She almost threw him against the wall. She climbed on to him without another word. He supported her arse as she fucked him under the streaming jet of water, their two bodies merging in the steam in one great, glorious celebration.

Oruela and Marthe nearly fell out of the hole in the wall with watching.

On and on it went, the two of them rutting like mad up against the tiled wall.

When at last it was over, Kim climbed off him and they stood for a moment smiling at each other. 'Help me back up,' she said, and he gave her a leg up. Oruela and Marthe pulled her in.

He hadn't expected to see the other two and he looked as if he couldn't believe his eyes. Oruela gave him a little wave and Marthe gave him the thumbs up. Then they refixed the grate. Kim pulled on her clothes and they crawled back down. Her skin was still steaming as she came out into the courtyard. They replaced the grating and walked back to the women's wing, Kim trailing wafts of steam like some glorious fiery demon.

As they waited for the guard to open the gate to let them in Marthe said, 'You bastard.' Kim merely smiled weakly back. After a minute she said, 'I'm sorry, Marthe. I just couldn't help it.'

Marthe grinned.

Paul had got permission to visit Oruela through sheer luck. Now the day had come he stood in front of the mirror worrying over whether his shirt was the right colour. Renée watched him from the bed. Her submissive mood had begun to crack over the past few days and they were becoming fractious with each other.

'What are you so fussy about?' she barked at him.

He knew damn well why he was so fussy this morning. It was the thought of seeing Oruela. If ever there had been any doubt it was gone now. He didn't answer Renée. He just looked over his shoulder. Her short brown hair was all tousled and she was reaching for a cigarette. She seemed so fragile; her ribs showed through her skin.

'Drive me out to St Trou,' he said.

'Is that an order?' she replied, her yellow eyes searching his.

'Yes.' he said, with all the command he could manage. Why not, he thought. The train journey would be deadly.

'OK,' she said, and she smiled.

While he was waiting for her to get ready he went into the darkroom and looked at the photographs he had tried to develop the night before. They were the ones on the film that he'd taken in Bruyere's bathroom. Every single one of them was fogged. He couldn't understand it.

He rummaged in a drawer and took out some photographs of a smiling family. His sister Marguerite lived nearby St Trou and he was going to deliver them to her.

'What do you think?' cried Renée, behind him. She stood in the open doorway of the darkroom in breeches of silky mustard, a soft jacket like a Battenberg cake and a vanilla shirt and tie. She clicked the heels of her tan suede brogues and saluted.

'We're visiting a prison, for Christ's sake!' he replied, ungallantly.

She looked at him questioningly.

He knew he wasn't playing the game correctly. He was thinking of other things. 'Get dressed more soberly,' he said. 'And bring me some coffee.'

'Get it yourself,' she said and flung off her jacket.

An hour later he stood waiting in the yard at the garage in the Avenue de la Marne while she went with the attendant to one of the small, green garages. The attendant drove the car out of its stable and handed Renée the keys. It was a Panhard-Lavassor, low and dark green with white-walled tyres. The spokes glinted in the sunshine.

'Jump in!' called Renée.

But Paul had seen something. The gleaming black Hispano-Suiza had just drawn up. Raoul jumped out and unscrewed the petrol cap.

Renée flung the keys into the front seat of the car and asked him if he was going to stand there all day.

'Look,' he said, nodding at the Hispano-Suiza.

'Beautiful,' she replied. 'It's the H6. Van Buren Body and four wheel brakes. It's got an $18\frac{1}{2}$-litre engine, you know. They weather the castings on those machine for two and a half years.'

'The chauffeur,' said Paul. 'It's the same car that was outside the graveyard in Bayonne.' But he was talking to the air. Renée had gravitated towards the Hispano-Suiza.

Paul watched Raoul's face soften as his gaze fluttered over Renée. He obviously took her to be a beautiful youth and Paul knew he'd been right about the chauffeur's sexual orientation.

He walked over to join them. Raoul gave Paul a queen bitch's dagger of a look and announced that he was late and had to go.

The road out of town twisted alongside the valley of the Nive. Beyond Bayonne the forest began, a green corridor winding into the foothills of the mountains. The new young leaves sparkled over their heads like stained glass. They turned off after about an hour, at Paul's request, and ordered coffee sitting outside a village bar.

Renée was fed up with listening to Paul's speculation about the chauffeur and Oruela and God knows what else. 'This is so pretty here,' she said, changing the subject. 'I feel I belong here in the Basque country. I'm not a native like you but I've adopted it.'

Paul shrugged. 'It's all very well romanticising it,' he said. 'It's beautiful and I'm glad this is where I came from, but I'd go mad in the country. It's nothing but sheep and gossip.'

'You're a fine one to talk,' she replied. 'All this snooping around and playing detective. You're like an old woman who twitches her curtains and gossips about what's going on next door.'

Paul slammed his cup down in his saucer. 'Are you serious?' he said. 'What do you mean? This is important. And while we're about it, let's have less of this old business. I'm only thirty-three. I know that's ancient to you at your tender young age of twenty-two but I'm not old. I only feel it with you sometimes because you're so bloody childish. And you're not the giddy young thing you pretend to be all the time. If you were more serious and stopped acting like a two-year-old . . .'

'I'm deadly serious,' she said. 'About my racing. But about you, well, I don't know. Why should I be? Where have you got these last ten years? What have you achieved?'

'I'm selling pictures, Renée, you can't bring that old knife out of its sheath,' he growled.

'Probably a one-off,' she said, nastily.

They sat in silence. He looked across at her. She was looking away. He hated her at that moment and at the same time, to his chagrin, he wanted her. Christ, this absurd game was getting to him.

They paid the bill and got back into the car in silence. The car began to climb towards St Trou. As they drove alongside the denser forest she sped up, skidding round the bends in the treacherous mountain road. The beeches flashed by, stretching away from the road like silvery columns in some fantastic outdoor cathedral.

Suddenly she drove towards the edge of the road and brought the car to a stop. The roof of leaves above their heads was made of green and gold. The sunlight barely penetrated the gloom. She was breathing quickly.

For a second or two he thought she was going to drive on but then she said, 'Come on, come on and get me.' And she cut the engine and was out of the car like a flash.

Paul sat watching her as she ran in and out of the silvery trunks like Pan. The keys were still in the ignition. He was tempted to move over into the driving seat and leave her. But he couldn't. His heart wouldn't let him. He leapt out of the car and went after her.

She was fast but he was faster. He caught her by the sleeve as she darted round a tree. She screamed and twisted her arms in his grip and escaped. It must have burned her arm. His hand stung. He watched her run deeper into the forest, deeper into her own fantasies.

He had a flash of inspiration. 'Forfeit the jacket!' he cried. 'I caught you!' His voice echoed throughout the forest.

She turned, hesitated and then took off her jacket and dropped it on the ground.

Paul took advantage of her pause and sprang after her again but she ran like the wind. Deeper and deeper into the forest they ran. He came to a small clearing and suddenly she was nowhere to be seen. His heart beat fast. He could see for miles in the solemn darkness around him but she had disappeared. He turned around and saw a flash of rust-coloured trousers behind a silver trunk. Then she ran off again.

He decided to change his tack. Let her run herself into the ground, he thought, and he sat down against a tree trunk and waited.

When she realised he wasn't chasing her any more she started coming back towards the clearing, tree by tree, until she was very close.

'Don't you want to play?' she called.

Paul pretended to pant heavily. 'Too much smoking,' he said.

She looked disappointed. 'Don't stop,' she wailed. 'I like it.'

He stayed where he was, silently, looking at her out of the corner of his eye. She came closer and closer until she was standing right next to him. He looked up at her slender legs. She crouched beside him.

'Gotcha!' he growled and he held her fast.

Her scream pierced the silent forest and echoed back at them. 'Oh, you tricked me!' she cried. 'That's not fair!'

'Take off your clothes,' he said. 'Now!'

Her eyelids drooped and she whispered, 'Yes. Oh yes.' Her fingers flew to her collar but he sprang at her like a tiger and wrenched her trousers down and pulled them off. He spread her legs. The leaves of the forest floor crackled under her.

'Raise your arms,' he told her.

As she dropped her arms back above her head on the leaves, a look of fear flickered in her eyes. He clasped her wrists in one broad hand and clung to them as he forced his cock into her warm and wet sex.

The feeling that he hated her guts was so strong in him that he said it. She squirmed under him as he fucked against her hard little knot of a clitoris, as the warmth of her cunt enclosed him and drenched his cock. He covered her breasts with his body and bit into her long, white neck, his teeth scraping up towards her ear. His tongue tasted the waxiness. He kissed her face but she turned it away from his lips.

Their rhythm began to slow. She lay under him like a dead thing, barely responding. He pulled away.

'Turn over,' he demanded.

She rolled over on to her belly and lay there, her arse moving from one side to the other. He slid his arm under her belly and lifted her up on to all fours. He parted the cheeks of her arse and for a moment he stroked her magnificent sex from her clitoris to her arsehole. His strokes grew rougher and she began to drip. Her glistening cunt swelled as he massaged it. And then he manoeuvred his cock into her and, driving it home he fucked her until she collapsed underneath him and he shot his load. He didn't give a shit whether she'd come or not and he rolled off her like a lout and lay spread-eagled on the forest floor.

He lay there until he felt her roll over on to his right hand and push herself into his hand. He cupped it and raised himself and slid one finger of his left hand into her arsehole the way he knew she liked it. She writhed like one of Daisy's fishes on the leafy carpet and then went stiff as a board for a moment. And then her release came in a great shudder. They lay for a while, the leaves rustling all around them and then Paul dressed himself, washed his hands in a mountain stream and walked back to the car to wait for her.

They arrived at the prison about half an hour later. They were a little crumpled and the guard on the gate eyed them suspiciously, refusing to let them drive through until he had telephoned the management. They stood outside while they waited like strangers, a little embarrassed, kicking their heels.

Eventually the man opened the small gate and beckoned Paul. 'Only you.' he said.

'Well,' said Renée. 'I don't suppose it would've mattered what I wore.'

But Paul didn't hear her. He had stepped over the threshold and was gone.

Inside, the grounds were dotted with the casualties

of life. Their subdued demeanour chilled Paul to the bone. In his mind he had a picture of a happy, laughing Oruela. But what would he find?

He was waiting in the dim, wood-pannelled reception when a black woman appeared from behind the stairs and meandered past him, looking him up and down. He thought he recognized her and wracked his brains. She smiled slyly at him as she passed him and went out into the courtyard.

He had no time to think about her further because Dr von Streibnitz came hopping down the stairs. He came towards Paul with one outstretched hand. The other fluttered in the air like a butterfly as he introduced himself. 'It is most unusual, Monsieur Phare to see – what is it you said you were? – a relative?'

Paul had to reply to the doctor's back as the man had started to lead the way back upstairs to his office. Paul tried to sound authoritative as he said, yes, he was her uncle.

The doctor grinned. 'I wish more people would take the trouble to visit these poor souls,' he said.

Paul entered the office and took the chair the doctor offered him.

'We shall effect a cure, you know. No need to worry about that,' said the doctor.

'Exactly what for?' asked Paul. 'What is your diagnosis?'

'Well,' said the doctor, 'I don't diagnose in the accepted sense of the word. Let's just say . . . well, a woman as promiscuous as your niece has been is probably capable of anything, even murder. Mind you, on the other hand, she's been a model patient since she's been here. No trouble at all. She's as chaste as a nun.'

Paul fought down a rising tide of disgust. 'Is she going to be charged with any crime?' he asked.

The doctor sniffed. 'I am not at liberty to discuss the legal procedure of this case,' he said. 'My job is to observe my patient. At present all I know is that

Mademoiselle Bruyere is here because her mother thought it the best thing for her. It is for the police to decide if and how they proceed further.'

Paul was beginning to find this tiresome. He was more than eager to see Oruela. He was almost on the edge of his seat.

'I say,' continued the doctor. 'Would you like to see my latest invention for curing the mind, Monsieur Phare? I'd appreciate the opportunity to show a man of culture. As I said before we don't get many visitors here, you know. People don't care –'

Paul broke in. 'I'd be pleased to,' he said. 'After I've seen Oruela.'

'Of course,' said the doctor. 'Excuse me just one moment.'

Alone in the doctor's book-lined office, Paul couldn't sit still. He went to the window. The row of cell windows in the next block squinted at him like caged eyes and a feeling of anguish grew in Paul's chest like a wave. He almost dreaded seeing her. What would this place have done to her?

When the call came for Oruela to come down she was still fiddling with her hair. She tugged at it with her brush in front of the old piece of tin that she used as a mirror. She was terrified of seeing Paul. She felt like an awkward teenager again. What would he make of her now? She'd been like this ever since the letter had arrived announcing his visit and Kim had been relentless in her teasing.

She had decided to wear her men's trousers. They were stitched back up at the crotch and they looked well on her but she hated them. She had pulled the belt so tight that it almost strangled her waist but at least she had a waist. Her shirt was freshly ironed but there was nothing she could do to make it more feminine. She was convinced she looked disgusting.

But there was no time to do anything more about it. She descended the iron stairs saying to herself that this

163   ·

was all stupid, that he probably didn't really fancy her at all. It was just some story Michelle had cooked up to make her feel better.

By the time she reached the gate it was the truth. And then, as she stepped out into the sunshine she suddenly thought of Caspar and the last time she'd seen him. She thought of the love they'd made and it gave her heart. It was as if his ghost was there, a friendly ghost, by her side, telling her that anything was possible.

The doctor greeted her at the doorway of the main building and she followed him up the stairs. She felt confident now. Whatever would be, would be.

The doctor opened the door of his office and there stood Paul, by the window. Her soul opened like a flower.

They stood looking at each other for a moment or two, unable to say anything and then the doctor discreetly disappeared and Paul smiled.

She sat down and he took a chair and sat opposite her at a short distance. The light was behind him. He seemed so fresh and clean and normal.

'How are you?' he asked. 'You look much better than anyone else in here.'

'Oh, thank you,' she said. 'It's nice to hear that. We haven't got any proper mirrors in here.'

She liked the way he sat at a distance. She would've died if he'd reached for her hand or shown any passion at that moment. Part of her wanted him to but she also wanted to study him a bit. She liked what she saw. There was a kind of dignity about him that was more appealing than anyone she'd ever met. She liked his clothes too, the way he sat easily on the chair. Her sex began to flutter in her knickers. She crossed one long leg over the other and swung it as she accepted the cigarette he offered her.

Paul watched her take a drag and blow the smoke slowly out. He studied every inch of her face and recognised beyond all shadow of a doubt that he was in love with this woman. His nervousness left him. She was easy to talk to. She thought clearly and she talked to his deeper self. He longed to touch her, to express his love physically but he could wait.

Eventually he told her that he thought he'd seen her real mother. She wanted to know every detail.

'Can I approach her for you?' he asked.

'Oh yes,' she said. 'Find out for me. My God, it would mean so much to me to know I had someone of my own.'

'You have me,' he said.

She smiled. She sat up straight, slowly easing back her fine shoulders. The curve of her breasts under the shirt swelled and he glanced quickly at them, appreciatively.

She caught the look and felt herself blushing like an idiot, but she knew in that instant that if she got free she would be his lover. The possibility of sex seemed to hang in the warm afternoon air between them.

They rose from their chairs, when the doctor returned, in unison and Oruela smiled again at Paul, through a sudden unstoppable film of tears. He took her hands in his and pressed them to his lips without another word.

When the door had closed behind her the doctor perked up. 'So, would you like to see my invention?'

'OK,' said Paul gruffly.

The grimness of the locked gates and the old buildings they passed through depressed Paul thoroughly and he marvelled privately at Oruela's strength.

'In here,' said von Streibnitz. He pulled a blind down over the barred window in the therapy room and unlocked a big cupboard with a key from the bunch that was always on a chain at his hip. With a great smile he wheeled out the hat.

'Here it is.' he said.

It reminded Paul of the iron mask in the Dumas novel and he fought down an impulse to laugh.

'It's a revolution and I tell you it works,' enthused von Streibnitz. 'It works on your little friend; she still comes here once a week, and she is most definitely changed by it. I question her and she gives me much better, more sane answers.

'Look, you see these little doors?' He opened and shut one or two compartments at different parts of the hat. 'The radium chloride goes in here.'

'Radium chloride?' asked Paul.

'Mmm. Isn't it exciting? The whole thing is made of aluminium. The metal acts as a filter. Some use of high doses of radium has caused burning, you see. I read all the papers written by the Institute in Paris, you know. They have been using it very successfully. It's capable of curing anything – papillomata, epithelial tumours, even syphilitic ulcers. Why shouldn't it cure the mind as well? Eh?' Von Streibnitz gurgled. 'It's going to be the answer to all of humanity's ills, you know. It comes from deep within the earth where the balance of things is as perfect as nature intended it. Now, these little chambers inside correspond with the parts of the brain that cause mental illness, this one is for murderous impulses, this is schizophrenia, you see it overlaps, and this one at the back is for overly developed sexual impulses, especially in women. It's a combination of sciences, a partnership, if you will, between phrenology and the Streibnitz method!'

The only thing that Paul could remember about radium was that it was astronomically expensive. He said so.

'Ah yes. It took a group of charitable American ladies a year to raise enough money to buy Madame Curie a gramme to work on. But I,' the doctor looked around as if checking that no one else was in the room, 'I have *a patron* and of course I use very very small doses, because the brain is very subtle. Then my private customers pay the proper price, so I'm able to give one or two patients here their treatment free. I believe in socialism, you see.'

166

Paul opened one of the compartments and closed it and wished he could get away. He was all churned up inside.

'Now don't go spreading the news about,' said the doctor. 'I don't want anyone picking up on my idea just yet. When my paper is written it will cause a revolution. I'm working on it now. Your friend is part of my research. You may depend on it that I am going to cure her and become famous for it.'

Take Me to the River

*L*ater that night Oruela, Kim and Marthe went on a raiding party to the kitchens. Their midnight feast was not solely food. Since the discovery of the shower room vent they had got more and more daring in their exploits. They could usually bribe one of the guards to let them out and almost every night they were out somewhere doing something they shouldn't.

The honey from the shower room had become a kind of pet. He couldn't believe his luck. By this time Marthe had had him too. Tonight it was Oruela's turn. They were going to raid the larder for the best food that the guards kept for themselves and he was going to meet them later.

But when it came to it she no longer wanted him. She gorged herself on a delicious breast of roast duck and told Marthe and Kim that she'd keep watch if they wanted him. They didn't have to be told twice.

Oruela sat against the bars of the gate, watching the night sky and dreaming gloriously romantic daydreams of Paul while her two friends had their fun with the hunk behind the warm ovens.

A few miles away Paul, Renée, Paul's sister Marguerita and her husband sat outside the restaurant in the village square. Paul's niece and nephew ran around on the cobblestones having an adventure. He watched them and remembered doing the same things with Marguerita.

His anguish was slowly dissipating under the canopy of the stars. The after-dinner cognac helped, and the warmth of being with his sister and talking about nothing and everything. He'd been in trouble when he left the prison. A feeling of sadness had hit him like a thunderbolt right in the solar plexus as he walked out of the gate and over to Renée's car.

Renée, surprisingly, was well-behaved. He was grateful. Eventually, Marguerita announced that the kids should be in bed.

'I'd like to sit a little while longer,' said Paul. 'You go back, Renée, if you like.' They were staying the night at the farmhouse.

'No,' said Renée. 'I'll stay.'

'I'll leave the back door on the latch,' said Michel, Marguerita's husband.

Renée and Paul watched them round up the kids in the pool of light in the square that gleamed from the porch of the hotel opposite. And then there was silence.

Renée looked at him. 'I know when I'm licked,' she said.

'What do you mean?' he asked.

'Just that I know you're in love with this girl Oruela and I have no hold on you any more.' Her voice broke as she spoke and tears glistened in her strange yellow eyes.

'Oh, Renée,' he said, reaching across the table for her hand.

'Don't,' she said softly. 'Don't pretend.'

'I won't,' he said. 'But – ' He was interrupted by the sound of a car. It was the Hispano-Suiza. It pulled into the pool of light and stopped.

'Oh, great!' said Renée as Paul's attention was lost.

'I promised Oruela I would speak to her,' said Paul.

Euska got out of the car on the hotel side and walked

up the steps of the entrance. Raoul got back into the car and the car started to pull away.

'I know!' said Renée. 'I'll talk to the chauffeur. That'll help you, won't it? I'll do something for you. Then you'll love me again, won't you?'

Before Paul could stop her she was up from the table in a flash and flying across the square. As the car sped up she ran nimbly alongside it and jumped on to the running board.

Paul was furious! He paid the bill and rushed out into the street.

Raoul noticed Renée as he looked into his mirror to turn into the hotel garage. Renée was glad he played it cool and didn't jump out shouting at her. All he did was stop in the yard and climb out to look at her.

She hadn't a clue what to say. So she smiled her most beguiling smile. He laughed. She jumped down from the running board standing tense, ready to fly.

'Don't run away,' said Raoul. 'Don't be scared. What a funny little thing you are. Get in the car, come on. I have to drive it in there. We can talk.'

Renée felt terror in every pore of her skin. But he sounded nice. She opened the passenger door at the front and climbed in. The car smelled of leather and polish.

'You take good care of the car,' said Renée. 'I would too, it's beautiful.'

'Well, I like cars. I take care of my boss's car in Brazil.' He drove it smoothly into the garage and switched off the engine. 'I mean that's what I do, take care of cars,' he said and turned to look at her.

'You're from Brazil?' she asked.

'What do you care where I'm from or where I'm going? The moment is now,' he said, turning off the lights.

'Come for a walk with me,' she said, in the darkness, before he made his move. 'By the river, I love the wetness down there, the smell of it.'

Raoul started fumbling around under the dash. 'Wait in the yard,' he said.

He wasn't long. He came waddling out and took her by the hand. 'Can I have a little kiss?' he said and put his lips to hers.

She kissed him lightly and looked into his face. He was really very nice-looking, kind. 'Do you have a dark side?' she asked.

He laughed. 'I've got whatever side you want,' he said softly.

Wait till you find out what I've got, thought Renée. They reached the gate that led down to the riverside. The sound of the water rushing over the precipice was too loud for them to talk. Renée took him by the hand and led him along the path past it. But he pulled her back at the noisiest point and began to kiss her.

It really was lovely with the water roaring beside them but she manoeuvred him away. She had to talk, to tell him what to expect if he touched her sex, which he would. She stopped him and pulled him on, along the path.

Meanwhile Paul was having kittens. By the time he got to the garage it was all dark. He called softly but there was no answer. He walked back to the hotel. There were a few people in the bar, all local men. He recognised one he had known years ago and dropped into a surreal conversation. The man was really pleased to see him, but Paul said he was looking for his friend and left.

'City dweller,' said the men in the bar, to each other, sagely.

He went back to the garage. Nothing. Surely Renée wouldn't have gone somewhere with the man if she had sensed danger, would she? He walked up the main street, eyes peeled, looking into the dark shadows and crevices. He turned and came back down the other side. She could, of course, be back at the restaurant by now and not know where he was. She'd go to Marguerita's probably. There was only one more street in the town. He walked up it and down again. He went back to the restaurant. She wasn't there and they were closing. No. They hadn't seen her. He went round the square once more. Surely she wouldn't have allowed herself to be taken down any of the lanes.

And then he stopped in his tracks. He was doing it again, wasn't he! The pull of her particular madness had sucked him in. Damn her! He hurried back to the hotel and asked for Euska Onaldi at the desk. The clerk phoned up to her room; who wanted her? Paul told the clerk his name and received permission to go up . . .

'Oh, it's wild! Oh, you wonderful little freak! Oh my God, you've got both. OH MY GOD!' squealed Raoul.

Things had progressed.

Renée was so relieved he wasn't angry that she almost cried. They were leaning in the crevice of a rock.

'So what are you? I mean you, really, in here?' He pointed to his heart.

'I'm a woman,' she said. 'I think.'

'Oh, and you can be, can't you. Oh, you lucky devil,' he said.

But he had lost his erection. Renée began to cry.

'Oh, love. Oh, sweet thing. Don't take any notice. I like men. That's all. Don't be . . . Oh, I'm sorry.' He put his chubby arms around her. 'Come here.'

'I've only ever met one man who isn't revolted by me and I've grown to hate him,' said Renée. 'The affair's worn out. He kind of ignores my difference. He worshipped it at first but now it's . . . oh, I don't know. He's not, well, ideal.'

'Well, no one's ideal, darling,' said Raoul. 'I mean all that love and marriage. How many happy couples can you count on one hand?'

'I wish you could have made love to me,' she blubbered.

'Oh dear, you're hurting, aren't you?' said Raoul. 'You're lovable. Someone will love you.'

He was certain he could introduce her to some people in Paris who would really appreciate her and he had heard of a Greek island (the name escaped him) where hermaphrodites were worshipped as the ultimate human being.

'Well,' said Renée, 'worship would be nice!'

Paul knocked on the door of the room on the second floor. He heard her footsteps on the tiled floor.

Euska opened the door and smiled warmly. 'Come in,' she said. She was dressed in a long orange gown. The colour against her skin and her dark lustrous hair gave the impression of southern fire. Around her neck was a heavy, gold necklace with a topaz at her breast. 'I'm going to order something to drink, would you like to join me?'

He said he would and he wandered out on to the balcony as she telephoned room service. Below, in the square, the brightly coloured umbrellas of the restaurant swayed a little in a breeze. The trees rustled and the gas lamps sprinkled their light on the cobblestones.

'Would you like to sit out here?' she asked. 'It's lovely, isn't it?'

'Wherever you please,' he replied.

'I'm sure you'd like to smoke,' she said. 'I'll just get my wrap.'

He did indeed want to smoke. He took an American cigarette out of his packet and tapped the end on the railing of the balcony before he lit it.

She reappeared, wearing a black shawl and sat in one of the cane chairs. 'Well,' she said.

'You're Oruela's mother?' he asked, still standing.

'I am,' she replied, with a slight frown. 'And what are you to her?'

'I don't know yet,' he replied. 'I only have hopes.'

A big smile lit up her face. 'A suitor?'

'We're talking as if she were in the next room,' said Paul.

They were interrupted by the waiter at this point and

they waited until a bottle of cognac had been set down and two drinks poured.

Paul watched her as she picked up her glass. The resemblance to Oruela was most definitely there, and if Oruela aged like this then he knew he would never tire of her. Metaphors of ripe fruit came to his mind but they were inadequate. There was something strong, an excellence about this woman, that was most desirable.

'I saw her today,' he said.

'What is she like?' asked Euska.

'She's strong and beautiful,' said Paul. 'She's magnificent, considering what she's been through.' He paused. 'What exactly has she been through? Do you know any more than I do?'

Euska was obviously delighted to hear him praise Oruela. Her face shone. 'My guess is that Jacques Derive has colluded with Genevieve Bruyere to have her incarcerated.'

'That's self-evident,' said Paul. 'But why? And more to the point how do we bring them to justice and get her out?'

'The answer to the second part of your question is easier to say than the first part. I know why, but . . . well, let's say I'd rather tell the story to Oruela herself first. That's why I'm here. I am going to the prison tomorrow to see her and introduce myself.'

'I've told her that I think you are here,' said Paul.

'Yes, good. I was worried about that. I didn't want to give her too much of a shock, – ' said Euska. She seemed nervous.

Paul warmed to her. 'You said the second part . . .?'

'Yes. It's simple. Jacques Derive thinks I'm dead. I am going to give him a shock. I'm going to simply go to his office and tell him that if he doesn't release Oruela I am going to spread my story all over France. That's why Oruela has to know first, in case he calls my bluff. I don't think he will though. I've been to see some of the other people involved and at least one of them is on my side and will corroborate my story.'

'He's a dangerous man,' said Paul. 'I think he's killed one man already and I was warned off in a pretty ugly fashion.'

'I know. I know. I won't say I'm not nervous. But if he did harm me in any way he'd be dead.'

'Would you like me to come with you?' said Paul. 'It'll be too late for us all if you're dead.'

'You would come?' asked Euska, smiling. 'It could put you in danger, too!'

'I don't do things by halves,' said Paul.

Renée was awake, sitting up in the big old iron bed when Paul finally arrived home, quite drunk and very happy. She was in a strange, skittish mood. Neither of them could sleep although they hardly spoke. And then, in the darkness, she wriggled her arse into his groin and enclosed his prick. He immediately became rock hard.

She manoeuvred him inside her from behind and settled on to him. He closed his eyes and thought of Oruela as Renée's warm sex enclosed him. He reached around her smooth skin for her strange and wonderful malformation and cupped it in his hand. He took some of the juices that flooded from her and lubricated it. It hardened and Paul held it tighter.

Suddenly she said: 'This is goodbye, Paul.' She said it to the darkness, into the pillows. He couldn't hear her.

He stopped fucking her. 'What did you say?'

'I said this is goodbye.'

Paul felt his freedom being born in his gut. It hurt him and excited him at the same time. He pushed her down into the bed so that she lay underneath him and he rose on top of her like a Titan, the strength of him bearing down on her now, fucking her one last time, thighs on thighs, belly on her buttocks, madly. He hated her because she couldn't live up to him and he loved her because she was weak.

Unforgettable

Oruela began to cry before she reached the end of the document that Euska had left her. Von Streibnitz had allowed only a brief visit.

'Try to forgive me,' her mother had said as they parted. Her very own mother! This is what Euska had written:

'I grew up on the Calecon estate near Navarre. My father managed the estate for Anton Calecon and I spent my girlhood as free as a bird among the vines and the animals.

'When I was fourteen my father died and Anton made a promise to him to look after me. Anton loved me in a fatherly way. Women did not attract him. His taste for boys was his weakness. He used to travel to certain private clubs in Biarritz to indulge his tastes.

'When I was sixteen I fell in love with a boy from Navarre and one evening we were caught making love in the barn.

'Soon after that Anton and Madame Jaretière, the housekeeper, concocted a plan to show me another side of life. Anton needed a camouflage to indulge his developing tastes. It wasn't exciting enough for him to go always to the private clubs; he liked to court danger in society. He dreamed of a real man who would see him by chance across a crowded room and fall in love. A man with whom he would have the courage to declare his love to the world.

'He never found it, poor Anton, but it was a romantic dream that he had and the mere chance that it could be realised excited him.

'He bought me gowns and jewellery and we went to the casino, to the opera, to the races. It certainly did show me what the world had to offer but I loved my Navarre boy. I continued to see him and eventually I became pregnant.

'While it was still unnoticeable I decided not to tell anyone. I continued going out with Anton and he treated me well.

'Then one night, Anton thought he had found his man. This man was part of a gambling party that had continued long after the casino had closed, upstairs in one of the suites. The party included Jacques Derive, Rosa – his mistress at the time – Norbert Bruyere, Armand Pierreplat the judge and Everard, who is now the coroner. They were all young hell-raisers in those days and when they gambled they were completely outrageous.

'I never knew who Anton's man was but I remember his face. He was an ordinary-looking man but he had lovely eyes. I found out later by chance that he was a Greek and that he went mad and died in the arms of a Hungarian countess after an overdose of opium. I have no reason to suspect that he knew what havoc he caused that night.

'Anton was taken by a total madness. He gambled everything, just to impress his Greek god. But when the last chips were down and the fate of the whole of the Calecon estate was laid on the turn of a card, his man merely yawned and left.

'The cards were turned. Anton had lost. He was out of the game and it dawned on me that all my dear friends on the estate were going to be homeless. Then

Jacques Derive and Norbert Bruyere whispered to each other.

'"Anton," said Norbert, "you have one more chance."

'Anton looked up. He was coming back to his senses and realising what he had done. He was as white as a sheet.

'"The girl," said Norbert, looking at me.

'I urged Anton to agree to it, on the condition that the old servants on the estate would be looked after for the rest of their lives if we lost. Anton put this to the other men and they agreed.

'When Anton lost again I was sad but not desolate. I thought I would be taken somewhere and I would escape and be with Lauren, my lover . . .

'But that was not what these men had in mind. Henri was drunk. He staggered up to me and shoved me against the wall. He tore my clothes and they all laughed. All except Anton who tried to help me. But it was no use. They beat him up and called him names and threw him out.

'Norbert dragged me into the bedroom next door and, thinking my life was at stake, I allowed him to have me.

'He left me crying on the bed. Then in came Derive, then Pierreplat. By the time Everard was shoved into the room by the others, all laughing and jeering, I was in such a state that he took pity on me. He didn't touch me. He tucked me up in the bed and called Rosa.

'She came in and sat down and that's when we heard the shot. I didn't know Anton had a gun and I wish he'd had the sense to threaten those bastards with it. The police came and I don't know how the affair was kept quiet.

'I spent the next few days with Rosa at the apartment Derive kept for her. We didn't see any of them. They didn't come near us. Rosa was kind, but the future looked bleak. I couldn't think of facing Lauren. I felt as if I'd betrayed him. I never saw him again, ever. I heard he was killed in the war but for me he was dead long before that.

'Henri eventually paid us a call. He was a strange mixture of remorse and threat. When he saw my bruises I thought he was going to cry and he begged my forgiveness. But then he said that if I ever opened my mouth about what had happened I would die. With some prompting from Rosa, he agreed to rent me an apartment. It was the only way for me to stay off the streets at the time.

'So I became his mistress. It was the only way to survive. And I wasn't his mistress in the usual sense. I never made love to him again. He taught me that there are some men in the world who take their pleasure from pain. I gave him plenty of what he wanted and I later made my fortune practising the English vice. I only had a small number of clients but they paid me well.

'This was a long time after I had given you away, Oruela. You were born in Paris. Hearing I was pregnant Derive put pressure on Henri to get me out of Biarritz. I was lonely and frightened in Paris. There was only the visit from Henri every fortnight and his demands. You were young and you would sleep through it in the small bedroom. But I feared for you. I didn't want you to grow up in that tawdry life.

'Henri's marriage to Genevieve had been barren and he thought he could place the blame on her now. He was sure you were his child. Some fantasy led him to believe that I was a virgin before he raped me. I didn't disabuse him of the idea. I couldn't. I feared being put out on the street.

'When he first suggested he take you and adopt you and bring you up as his own, I resisted the idea with all my heart. But gradually he persuaded me with the practicalities of it. You would have a stable, normal upbringing, he said, with the best education that money could buy and all the things a young girl could want.

'The reality was different but I thought I was doing the best thing. I never stopped loving you and I was Henri's friend until the day he died because I could never break the link with you. If anything happens to

179

me I urge you to contact Ernesto Medejar, at Villa Carioca, Rio de Janerio. He is my dearest friend and will vouch for the truth of my words.

'During this past year, Henri's health has been failing and he has paid a king's ransom to some bogus doctor to cure him. I believe he had nothing left. I suspect he was trying to blackmail Jacques Derive with the events of long ago and I suspect he was killed because of these blackmail attempts. I cannot prove this but I am going to try the same thing, with a different motive. Should I die in the attempt, a copy of this document will be in safe hands and someone will contact you.'

By the time Oruela read this, of course, she also knew that Paul was involved and that Euska felt safer. Nevertheless the ruthless mayor was dangerous and the tension gripped her like a torturer's rack. Her body felt like ice.

Kim advised her to come on their nightly adventure as usual, especially as tonight the honey was bringing a friend and it was definitely Oruela's turn. The thought of anyone other than Paul still revolted Oruela but she knew she needed distraction.

The five of them met in von Streibnitz's well-upholstered office in the main building. Getting in here past the guards was the latest dare they'd set themselves. It went off without a hitch. The two men were waiting for them. They had already undressed down to their shorts.

The second man was another strong-looking beauty. He looked a bit nervous though, as if he wasn't sure what was expected of him.

Marthe locked the door behind them.

'Our friend is tense,' said Kim. 'She needs relaxing.'

The honey looked at Oruela with obvious lust. He was longing to get his hands on her.

'No, really!' said Oruela. 'I, er . . .'

'We'll give you a massage if you're tense, won't we, Alphonse?'

His mate looked Oruela up and down. 'Sure,' he said.

Oruela had a delicious feeling deep in her womb. She knew if they massaged her she'd want more, but she didn't want to know for certain that it would happen. 'Well,' she said. 'Just a massage then.'

'On the couch then, young lady,' said the honey. 'I'll need your clothes off if I am to make a thorough examination.'

A shiver went down Oruela's spine. She began unbuttoning her shirt.

'Here,' said Alphonse. 'Let me help you.'

She sat on the psychiatrist's couch and allowed him to undo her buttons all the way down. Kim and Marthe were busy picking the lock of the booze cupboard.

He pulled her shirt out of her pants and slid it off her shoulders. She was naked underneath and both men, she could tell, liked the look of her breasts.

She undid her belt and slid her trousers down and off. Then she lay on her belly and closed her eyes.

Someone's hands, big strong hands, massaged her back, at the shoulders first, then down her spine vertebra by vertebra until he reached the elastic at the top of her knickers. Then his hands made a great sweeping motion over both her hips and up and held her waist gently before smoothing up her ribcage, just brushing the curve of her breasts as they went. Down her spine again went his palms and up the same way, again and again and again.

The other man began on her legs. He had some kind of oil on his hands that made them soft and he massaged her feet with it, lifting each leg up and bending her knee so that he could get a good rub going on first one calf, then the other, first one shin, then the other. Then he bent her toes about and massaged around and in between each one.

It was heaven. They were so good at it that there was no threat in it. She began to relax and really give herself over into their hands.

Each time the hands on her back touched the elastic

181

of her knicker waistband she felt more and more that she wanted him, the next time, to touch her arse.

The second pair of hands let her lower legs down gently on to the soft leather couch and then started on her thighs. Up and down he massaged, both thighs at the same time and with each stroke upwards she felt as if her thighs were parting little by little, and her sex was opening. And then, instead of rubbing down her thighs, his fingers travelled up a little bit higher on to the cheeks of her arse. Now, each time, they went higher, massaging her glutes and her knickers were pushed up so that the fabric was tight against her sex and each time he squeezed her arse her clitoris got a tug.

The other man – she looked up and saw it was the honey – started on her arms. He massaged her shoulders in their sockets and then stretched her arms out in front of her, rubbing them, loosening them. She felt as if she was flying, her torso was stretched, her breasts cupped in the soft leather.

'Turn over,' said Alphonse, at her heels. She eased herself over and he pulled down her drawers in one decisive act.

She lay before them totally naked. Honey began to massage her torso, avoiding her breasts at first, like a professional. But Alphonse was more daring. He slid his hands right up her legs, touched her triangle of hair and, bringing his hands to rest on her belly, he bent his head down and kissed her right on her clitoris. It was a light kiss, testing the water. Her eyes were full of the beauty of his shoulders, his arms, big and strong.

He parted her thighs and slowly massaged them with both hands, up and down like before. Honey's hands circled her breasts once and then stopped, caressed her ribs and then went back to her breasts, massaging them firmly. It felt so good, so very very good.

She wanted sex. She wanted Alphonse. There was something about the slight perfume of his skin that she liked. She liked his hungry mouth too and the curiosity

182

of his blue eyes. And then he moved his body closer to her and she felt the hardness of his sex through his shorts. It pushed at her thigh. He couldn't help it. He was so turned on by her and what could she do, now, if he decided to fuck her? Nothing. Her sex was wide open.

She saw him issue a silent command to the other man to get lost – just with his eyes. Then there were just the two of them. He climbed on to the couch and held her.

The weight of his body was energising after all this time without a man. He buried his face in her shoulder and struggled with his shorts. She felt his cock spring out and it was so warm and friendly and he was so dying for her. She let her legs fall right apart, and he entered her with a 'Mmmm' and kissed her. No sooner was he inside her than she felt herself on the brink of coming. She was so excited to be in the hands of a complete stranger. And in his hands she was, so completely. His belly was hard like a board. She wrapped her legs round his waist. Her arse pressed into the soft leather.

'I love you,' he said.

She heard him and knew he had to say it. Her lips were close to his ear and she licked it.

'I love you. I love you,' he repeated and she felt him coming and let herself go . . .

They lay together in bliss afterwards.

'Thank you, little girl, you're a peach,' he said. Then he kissed her nose.

There was, thankfully, no sign of the others. Oruela and Alphonse got dressed and he kissed her again and again, little pecks in between each piece of clothing that he put on.

He was acting as if he expected that this would happen again. But Oruela didn't want him for a regular lover. The anonymity of it had turned her on. He seemed sweet but she didn't want him any more. She thought she had better tell him.

'This was a one-off,' she said.

He looked at her suspiciously.

'It was unique. It can never be repeated, it was so fantastic,' she said diplomatically.

'We'll see about that, little lady,' he said.

'We'd better find the others,' said Oruela.

They looked for them in the adjoining office. There they were, drunk as skunks, arguing politics in loud whispers.

'Don't look at me!' said Kim. 'He started it.'

The man they called honey was looking decidedly gloomy. He glowered at Oruela.

'We'd better get out of here,' said Oruela.

They tiptoed to the door and along the hallway to the stairs where they split up. Alphonse gave Oruela's arse a healthy slap as they parted, which for some reason shocked her much more than the sex . . .

Euska and Paul ascended the steps of the town hall just as the great clock struck twelve. The door at the top opened and Jean and his father Etienne stepped out into the sunlight. Etienne was more handsome than his son. The hard edges of youth had disappeared from him but he had the same irresistable air. He was solid, a rock of a man. He spotted Euska instantly.

'Hello, Paul. Haven't seen you lately,' said Etienne. He was looking at Euska.

'Let me introduce you to Euska Onaldi. Euska, this is Etienne and Jean Raffoler.'

'My pleasure,' said Etienne.

'Father, I'm going to be late,' said Jean and he ran away.

Etienne passed the time of day and then followed his son.

'Who were they?' asked Euska.

'Jean might have been your son-in-law,' said Paul.

'Better tell me later,' said Euska.

They had reached the door and Jacques Derive was in the ornate entrance hall, talking to some other politicians. Paul opened the door for her and she sashayed into the dim interior. The look on Jacques Derive's face was a framable picture.

Euska went straight up to Derive and stood inches away from him, not making a sound. The look on the mayor's face showed that he recognised his nemesis in the form of this beautiful woman he had thought long dead. The whites of his eyes flashed.

Paul watched from a discreet distance as planned, but Euska's voice was loud enough for him to hear.

'We have a long delayed appointment,' she said to the stricken mayor.

He nodded, fixing a smile on his face and excusing himself from the rest of the politicians, most of whom were busy looking Euska up and down. But then Paul saw the mayor's eyes flicker a signal across the room. Paul followed the direction of it and saw a flashily dressed man move quickly across the floor towards Euska's back.

Euska seemed to sense danger. She turned and saw the gangster. 'Why not hear what I have to say?' she said to Derive. 'Better you, than the whole of France.'

The gangster hovered as Derive said something to Euska that Paul couldn't hear. Immediately she beckoned him and Paul steeled himself to walk over to the group. The look that Derive gave him was venomous.

'You had better come up to my office,' said the mayor.

As they ascended the great ornate staircase, Paul suddenly saw their strange party as some absurd ceremonial procession. He looked across at the gangster. The man's eyes were blank and deadly.

Once in the office, Derive sat down behind the huge leather-topped desk and lit a cigar. He didn't offer Euska a seat but she took one, calmly. 'I will get straight to the point,' she said. 'Either you release Oruela or I will send the full story of what happened to me at your hands to the newspapers.'

Derive leaned back in the mayoral chair. 'I don't think anyone would be even slightly interested in a story that old, much less believe it. We were all just youngsters at

185

the time, having fun the way youngsters do. I've held office in this town now for a long time. People won't believe their mayor was ever a criminal, if that's what you are trying to say.'

'Interesting,' said Euska. 'I haven't told you yet how I would describe you. But criminal will do. And you are obviously out of touch. Do you surround yourself with sycophants, or has no one told you how unpopular some of your policies are? This new road, for example. Everyone knows you've given the contract to your friends. It's a perfect time for the newspapers to run something from your past. It will put the last nail in your coffin.'

'That's outrageous!' said Derive. 'The newspapers in this town would never stoop . . .'

'Oh I wouldn't bother with the small papers, she interrupted. I assume you've either got them in your pocket or under your thumb. But the national papers, now they would. . .'

'You'd have difficulty finding anyone to corroborate your story. The big papers wouldn't dare to run such a story unless you could back it up. I don't think they'll readily take the word of a –'

Euska cut in. 'I have witnesses,' she said. 'I've spent the last few days talking to them. Everard was never happy about it, you know that. Even Pierreplat has been nervous since you killed Norbert and locked my daughter away in a prison for life. Anyone would be revolted by what you have done except you. *You are despicable!*'

Derive pulled one cauliflower ear and his eyes narrowed, as if the two were connected by some mechanism. 'I didn't kill Bruyere. Your daughter did. Her blood is bad. St Trou is the only place for her!'

'It's not her blood that is bad,' shouted Euska. 'It's yours. She has none of you in her. Her father was a boy from Navarre. I was pregnant when you all raped me!' she spat.

Paul felt anger and pity in his breast as he listened to

her words. He had guessed it was something like this although she still hadn't told him. But to hear it spoken was a shock.

'You filthy bitch,' said Derive. 'You filthy, lying bitch.'

'That's enough' barked Paul as he stepped forward.

The gangster moved forward at the same time, ready to fight. Paul glared at him.

Derive ignored them both. 'You made poor Bruyere believe that she was his child. I knew all along she wasn't. She has the mark of the devil on her.'

'He believed what his guilty conscience wanted to believe,' said Euska. 'And you are forgetting something. I was an unwilling participant that night. It was you. You Bruyere and Pierreplat that were the devils. Don't you dare twist it around. You are the filth! *J'accuse!*'

Paul could see her hands shaking in her lap and he knew that it cost her all her strength to face the man who had stolen her life. But she had won. Derive was squirming.

'Give the order for her release, now,' said Euska. 'Give it because you know that what you did was wrong.'

Derive sneered.

'Failing that,' she continued, 'give it because the whole story is in document form and is held by my lawyer, and if I don't telegraph him tonight telling him I am safe and all is well, he will contact a certain national paper whose editor is my friend . . .'

Derive was silent for what seemed like an age. Then he picked up the telephone. 'Von Streibnitz,' he said into the receiver, 'I want you to release the Bruyere girl. Yes that's right. New evidence has come to light. New evidence. Release her. Don't question my judgement, man. As mayor, I am also chief of police. Release her. Very well then. Tomorrow morning.' Derive replaced the receiver.

Once they were outside in the hallway, Euska and Paul walked quickly towards the top of the stairs. Only as they descended into the ordinary day to day bustle of the foyer did they turn to each other and smile.

The next morning Marthe came to say goodbye. She was dressed in her own clothes. She looked lovely in the red dress. She seemed happy. When she'd gone Oruela and Kim went along to the shower together.

'You know, I don't even know what she did,' said Oruela.

'She shot a man, killed him,' replied Kim.

'*Crime Passionnel*?' asked Oruela.

'I doubt it,' said Kim. 'She'll probably be executed.'

'What? She's not going free?' cried Oruela.

'No. She's going for trial.'

'Oh God!' cried Oruela and she ran back to the end of the landing. She was in time to see Marthe being taken out through the gates. She called her name. Marthe kept on walking.

Oruela went back into her cell and sat dazed. Kim came back from her shower and stuck her head in. 'Why didn't you tell me?' said Oruela.

'It wasn't my business to tell you,' said Kim, simply. There were tiny droplets of water on her shoulders still.

'It's going to be boring round here without you two,' said Kim.

'We don't know that I'm going yet,' said Oruela.

'It's only a matter of time.'

'I'll come and see you,' said Oruela.

'Don't,' said Kim. 'It'll drive me mad.'

'Write to me then. I'll write back,' said Oruela.

'Give me an address then,' said Kim. Oruela wrote down the address where she sent letters for Paul. It was his home he told her, but she'd never seen it. She longed to.

Oruela knew something was going on when she wasn't called for work, but she didn't dare hope that this was really it. She went and had her shower. More of her hair snaked down the plughole. It really was getting alarmingly thin in places. What if she was going bald with the worry? She had heard of such things. It made her feel sick.

It wasn't until the middle of the morning that the news came. She was going home, they said. She didn't contradict them, but in her heart she knew she wasn't going home to the house where she had grown up, ever. She was starting a new life.

She had no clothes! Her only personal clothing was the nightdress they'd brought her into the prison in. And then her cell door opened and a guard threw in a package.

'Your people sent this,' he said.

Oruela opened the brown wrapping paper. It was a dress. It was green silk. She pressed it to her cheek. It was so long since she'd felt the touch of silk. As she dropped it over her head and the fabric settled next to her skin she felt good.

The guards came for her and led her downstairs. She stopped by the serving hatch where Kim was bringing warm plates on to the counter.

'I'm going,' she said.

Kim put the plates down and came round to hug her. 'Nice,' she said. 'Nice dress.'

'Look me up when you get out,' said Oruela.

Kim nodded.

They hadn't allowed Euska's car to drive into the prison that day. Raoul sat in the front seat while Paul paced up and down by the gate and Euska sat on a shooting stick under a tree. The flies buzzed around. Paul felt he wouldn't believe it until they had her in the car and they were driving back to Biarritz.

On the other side of the gates Oruela fought down the impulse to run and walked slowly and calmly across the courtyard. Von Streibnitz shook her hand in a fatherly fashion and told her to be a good girl. She didn't reply.

She kept on walking and didn't look back. She held

the thought of Kim tight in her heart as she went up to the guard at the gate and showed him her pass. He opened the door for her and she stepped out into the lane.

Let's Face the Music – and Dance

*E*rnesto was at the Miramar when they arrived.
  'Better late than never,' said Euska and she gave him a kiss.

It gave Oruela pleasure to see the woman who was her mother reach up to her lover and kiss him.

They all ate a delicious lunch in the luxurious suite, overlooking the sea. The sounds of holiday-makers drifted up from the beach and the promenade on the hot and heavy late August air.

'I'd like to give you a party,' said Ernesto. 'But I expect you'll want to wait a while.'

'I'll be fine soon,' said Oruela and her gaze strayed to Paul. It would be their party. He knew it too. His eyes said so. They would dance and afterwards . . .

'Where would you like it to be?'

'At the casino,' replied Oruela.

The way Paul grinned was boyish and she loved it. He was delighted that she'd chosen the place where they had first set eyes on each other, she knew. This time they would do it right. He sought to cover his delight by talking to Euska. He obviously didn't want to let her know it all, not right away. She admired that. It was exciting to be almost certain, but not quite.

'Ernesto, I want to do some shopping. Come with me,' said Euska, rising from the table.

'I ought to come too,' said Oruela. 'I must get some clothes.'

Euska frowned at her. 'Don't you think you should rest?' she said. 'I'm sure Paul will stay with you if you don't want to be alone.' And she looked at Paul with wide, innocent eyes as if the thought of leaving them alone together had just occurred to her.

Not for the first time Paul found himself on the point of sexual arousal at the thoughts that were going through his mind. Ernesto had gone to the bathroom and there he was, alone with the two most delightful women he knew, and they were mother and daughter. Two dark-haired, dark-eyed playful beauties. He was aware of every movement they made: the way Euska picked grapes from the fruit bowl, not using the pearl-handled shears, the way Oruela's eyes seemed rimmed with red as if the world outside prison was too bright . . . These details he watched and because he had knowledge of them that the women hadn't themselves he knew he had power.

And yet he was rendered totally powerless by them, helpless and awash in his desire, his soul bumping against the hard fact that he daren't express his thoughts and his hardening sex pressing against the buttons of his underwear.

'Well, I'll get ready,' said Euska, seeing that Oruela was not going to stay behind.

When they were alone Oruela went out on to the balcony and looked down at the people below. Paul joined her.

'She's angling to leave us alone.' said Oruela.

'I'm glad I have your mother's approval,' replied Paul, leaning with his back on the railing.

He looked good enough to get close to but Oruela held back. 'Strange to think I have a mother after all this time,' she said.

'How do you feel about that?' asked Paul.

She could have melted. She could have touched him just then. Green eyes, square jaw, blond hair and a brain too. How did she feel? She felt like taking his hand and putting it to her breast. She felt like nuzzling in his neck, opening the buttons of his shirt and seeing, feeling his stomach. She felt like undoing the leather belt and feeling the warmth inside his trousers. It was so strong, her attraction, it was hard not to act upon in some accidental way. Her gaze dropped involuntarily to his shirt collar. She loved the way it was loose at his neck.

'I have mixed feelings,' she said. 'I don't quite know what to think.'

'I'm sure it will come right,' he said. 'Just give it time.' He turned around and looked out to sea. 'Your mother is a great woman.'

Oruela felt a sudden quick flame of indignation. Something about the way he said it. Did he think of Euska as a lover? But the indignation turned to amusement just as quick as it raised its head. Doubtless her own sexual adventures had done her good. So what? She liked a man with broad-ranging tastes. Just so long as he didn't act on them.

'When can I next see you?' he asked, cutting into her thoughts.

'Tomorrow?' she suggested.

'Dinner?' he replied. 'Just us two?'

'*Pourquois pas?*' she said, shrugging her shoulders as if she didn't care.

The afternoon was spent in the *haute couture* houses of Biarritz. Big fans in the ceiling turned lazily, merely stirring the air as the bony mannequins paraded before them in the latest designs. Euska ordered Oruela more than a dozen outfits. But when Ernesto got bored and went off to have a beer Oruela confessed that she needed something ready-to-wear in the meantime and something special for the following evening with Paul.

They went to Oruela's favourite little shop where she

bought a deep blue cocktail dress off the peg and some linen trousers.

'Trousers!' wailed Euska.

Oruela jumped on her firmly. Euska wouldn't dare comment again.

'I know,' said Euska, as they came out of the shop. 'Let's go to the Turkish baths.'

The sight of her mother's body unwrapping itself was extraordinary. Deep feelings stirred in Oruela that confused her. Euska's breasts were the fuller. They rested heavily on her ribs. Her posture was good and so she looked well for her age. Oruela peeped at her furtively. She looked at her dark and lustrous triangle and the thought that she came out of there sent shivers into the very fibre of her being.

In the steam room she lay on one of the benches, higher than Euska, still drawn to watch her mother's body as she talked of how Oruela could live in her apartment in Paris if she wanted. She found it difficult to answer her. She wanted to say that she didn't know what she would do. It depended on Paul but she felt too vulnerable to pour out her heart.

In the pool afterwards they swam and Euska complimented her on her body. They swam lazily. Oruela floated on her back, letting the water wash over her. There was a great glass roof to the indoor pool. The sun baked their skin and made the water warm.

Euska's body cut through the water, droplets glistening on her fine brown skin as she paused and trod the water. Suddenly she called 'Race you!' and they swam fast and strong up and down the pool. The exercise cleared Oruela's mind and she felt better. They dived and played like a couple of dolphins.

Paul came for her the next evening and drove her along the coast in Renée's open-topped Panhard-Lavassor all the way down south to St Jean de Luz where they chose a small fish restaurant overlooking the sea. The sounds of the plates clattering in the kitchen mingled with the talk of the other diners. They ordered champagne cocktails to start with and the bubbly went straight to Oruela's head.

'How's it going with Euska?' he asked, as they sat down to their crabs' claws.

'It's difficult to talk about what I really want to talk about with her,' said Oruela. 'Have you read her story?'

'No,' said Paul. 'I think you're supposed to give it to me.'

'She was a whore,' said Oruela. It was difficult to say it out loud. She felt like she'd dropped a bomb into the middle of paradise.

Paul merely smiled. 'Does it make you feel uncomfortable being the daughter of a whore?' he asked her.

'Well, it's not every day you discover that your mother was a dominatrix!' she replied.

'A dominatrix? Was she Norbert Bruyere's mistress by any chance?' he asked.

'Yes,' said Oruela. She felt on edge, as if everything she said was a matter of life and death. But he was smiling again.

'That's irony for you,' he said.

'Why?'

'I got the impression that Genevieve and Norbert Bruyere never had any kind of sex.'

'They didn't,' said Oruela. 'How did you know that?'

Paul told her about being locked in the bathroom and the policeman being whipped raw with his own whistle-chain.

'It makes you wonder though,' said Oruela when they finally stopped laughing, 'how those two lived together for all those years and never discovered each other. I wouldn't live like that for all the security in the world. I would want to explore love with the man I . . .' She trailed off and attacked her last claw.

'Do you imagine yourself wanting to tie a man up and whip him?' asked Paul. He was pulling the flesh out of a claw with a tiny silver fork.

'No,' said Oruela, sucking on the meat. 'I've seen

enough punishment to last me a lifetime. I hate the thought of narrowing everything down to such a trickle. In prison, the whores used to talk about how certain men wanted a procedure to be followed and never diverted from. Only this way would they get their pleasure every time. I hate the idea! It's like the only path to the child within, to the human being who is free and sensual and alive, is down a tiny crack in the rock underneath which they're buried. There are footholds that have to be followed: pain, fear, belittling – horrible.

'Myself I want mature sensations. I want to feel all the different colours, sounds of love. I want breadth and depth, the smells and tastes that are waiting, unknown, to be discovered.'

Paul was looking at her, she realised, the way a man looks when he is utterly smitten.

After dinner they walked along the seashore for about half a mile under the craggy rocks, the darkness enveloping their bodies, the sound of the sea on the shore a lilting music behind their conversation. They talked about everything under the crescent moon. He told her about the photographs he'd sold and she listened with excitement as he described their content. But there was no hurry. She felt as if all she had to do was wait. And she must wait. He must come to her. He would come, she knew, eventually.

They climbed down on to the dark beach and walked barefoot for quite a way before he asked if she was tired. She was, but she wanted the night to last for ever.

As they turned she found him watching her again, looking into her face and this time she gazed back, lazily, at his lips.

They were soft and full as they met hers. He held her tight in his arms, her breasts pressed against his chest. Her hands felt his back, under his thin shirt. It felt good, well-formed.

They kissed for a long time, tasting each other's skin, caressing each other's hair, lightly touching each other's body with their hands. They were absurdly proper. He didn't touch her breast, she didn't grab his arse. It felt right like that. She had never felt so purely romantic before.

Eventually they drew apart and they walked back along the beach without saying very much. They held hands.

Then he said. 'I have nothing very much to offer you, Oruela, in the way of material things.'

She held her breath. It sounded like he was leading up to something else. It was too soon. She almost said 'Don't!' But luckily she didn't. He wasn't that simple. He continued: 'But I might have more of a chance to make money in Paris. I should have gone there a long time ago but I got stuck like the needle of a record. If you were there . . .' He paused.

'Oh, it would be wonderful!' cried Oruela, forgetting herself.

'It would,' he said, grinning.

The next day Michelle came to visit. Oruela noticed a change in her friend. She was more self-assured. She carried herself better, her posture, usually a little hunched, had improved and she walked tall, carrying her high breasts with a sexual confidence.

She was never going back into service. Robert had been offered a job in a garage and they were going to get married. It was everything she wanted. Their sex life was fantastic and she thanked Oruela for setting her free with the letter.

'I've discovered that when I reach a climax if I let myself pee at the same time, the strength of my orgasm is intensified. If I just let myself empty completely my body feels wholly alive. I like to be on top of Robert and do it all over his belly. He really loves it, although the first time it happened we were in bed and we had to sleep on the floor. Now we do it in the open air wherever we can find a secluded place. I was always frightened that I would do it before but now I'm no longer frightened and I know he wants me to, every-

197

thing is better. Everything. A trust has grown through that simple thing.'

Oruela listened closely, her own sense of excitement rising. The room was shady and cool. The electric fan droned on. She told Michelle about Caspar, about the anonymous sex with the woman at the hen night, about Alphonse.

Michelle told Oruela about when they had posed for Paul's photographs, about the freedom she had begun to feel.

'That's what it's all about,' said Oruela. 'That's what life is. It's stepping out and doing what you want to do. It's seeking experience for its own sake. I wish you were coming to Paris. Paul might come to Paris as well.'

'I'd bet my life on it,' said Michelle, smiling. 'He's besotted. You're lucky. He's a lovely man.'

'Did you ever . . .?' Oruela stopped.

'Did I ever what? Have sex with him? No I didn't, none of us did. He never made a move. It was all art to him. I used to wonder sometimes what it would be like.' Michelle stole a glance at Oruela's face. 'You don't mind me saying that, do you?'

'No. I don't think so,' said Oruela. 'I expect I'll have to get used to the fact that he makes his living that way.'

'Renée didn't like it,' said Michelle, and she told her about the day the photographs stopped.

Oruela fought with her feelings. 'How much of a hold do you think Renée still has on him?' she asked.

'None. Annette told me they have broken up for good,' said Michelle.

But even as they spoke, Renée was sitting in the big, old armchair by the open shutters in Paul's studio telling him what had happened.

She had run into Raoul again at the garage on the Avenue de la Marne and invited him to the track. He was thrilled to go. He was fascinated by the atmosphere and the paraphernalia of the big teams. They had their own caravans for the mechanics and prepared food on the spot. 'It's like the circus!' whispered Raoul gleefully.

It was nice to have someone around who paid attention to everything she did with a kind of awe.

'Oh, well I never, there's someone I know,' said Raoul, waving over the fence. 'It's Victoire! I must go and say hello. Excuse me, darling.'

Renée watched him. He met a tawny-haired young man at the fence and waved to her to come over. She left the mechanic to his job.

'Here, this is Renée, my special friend. Renée, this is Victoire, the little devil. He's playing the gigolo to the rich woman.'

Renée gulped.

'Oh, look, isn't she sweet, she's shocked,' said Victoire. 'Don't be, love. It's a living. Do you know the countess, dear?'

'No, but I've met her driver and of course I've seen the team at races,' said Renée.

'Oh, you *must* come and meet her, she's such a sweet,' said Victoire, giggling. 'She's such a naughty sweetie.'

'Renée's embarrassment was growing. It wasn't the done thing to climb the fence and introduce yourself. She had her dignity as a fellow team leader to consider.

But the countess herself saved the day. Seeing her boy chattering away, something drove her over. Renée wondered if it was jealousy. The countess was a thin but handsome woman of about forty-five. She was dressed for the terrain in flat shoes and a green dress that reached her calves.

Introductions were made and the countess enquired how the two boys knew each other. Victoire said they'd been at school together. The countess smiled sweetly at Renée. Renée, of course, was dressed in her boy's clothing and the countess obviously thought she was of that sex. She complimented her on her driving.

'Do come and have champagne with us,' she drawled.

As they walked across the grass Raoul whispered that he wasn't schoolfriends at all with Victoire, that Victoire was an *habitué* of the Biarritz night clubs and quite a brilliant dancer, and he'd only met him last week.

Renée's sense of dread was heightened by this remark. 'How long has he been her gigolo?' she asked.

'Oh, ages,' said Raoul. 'At least a month.'

Under a candy-striped awning a flock of young men and women, fashionably dressed, not a sign of grease on any of them, laughed too loudly and sized up the newcomers in a flicker of drawn steel. This was the party crowd, explained Victoire. They all lived off the countess one way or another. Judging by the attention Renée herself was receiving, she guessed that most of the men were homosexual. How on earth did they please the countess?

'But *you'll* be a star when she finds out what you've got, dearie,' said Victoire.

Renée felt like she'd been struck a blow in the face. 'Raoul told you?'

'Don't be shy, darling. We're all a little freaky, you know.' Victoire smiled kindly at her.

'Well, *don't* tell anyone else. Just *don't*. My career will be ruined if you do, understand?'

'Oh dear. I think it's too late.'

At a distance, Raoul was in conference with the countess.

Renée took her courage in her hands and marched over. 'Forgive me, Countess, but I hope Raoul isn't boring you with silly stories.'

'My lips are sealed, my dear,' the countess crooned. 'He thinks you're wonderful, you know.'

'Please don't tell anyone else these lies, Raoul,' said Renée. 'My career is at stake.'

Raoul looked embarrassed.

'Run along and leave me alone with Renée,' said the countess. 'Come and sit in the shade, my dear. We'll leave this crowd of ghouls and talk.'

What choice had she, now her secret was out? She

followed the countess to a little table parked by the side of the caravan. They sat down and a servant brought them cakes and more champagne.

'Would you drive for me?' said the countess.

'I prefer to be independent,' said Renée.

'I understand that, but do you have the money to keep going?'

'I . . . I have enough,' said Renée.

'Couldn't you do with more?' said the countess, a smile playing on her bright lips.

'Undoubtedly.'

'Well, I could give it to you.'

Renée's heart was pounding. 'In return for what?' she asked.

'Your affection.'

'Really?' said Renée sarcastically.

The countess's eyes travelled over Renée's face, her tiny breasts and her legs. It gave Renée the feeling she was standing in the line of a falling tree.

'I have the heart of a woman, madame,' said Renée, deliberately using a lesser title.

The countess winced. Renée felt a little sorry. She hadn't meant to be unkind.

'You have everything I want,' said the countess simply.

In truth Renée was sorely tempted, not by the woman, but by the chance to drive with money behind her. But the thought of becoming one of the crowd of dependants didn't appeal either. She would rather walk off now into poverty and obscurity.

But she sat still. 'I'd be happy to be your friend, Countess.'

The countess seemed amused. 'How näive you are and how very, very charming.'

Renée rose to leave.

The countess stood up and looked her in the eye. 'Why not leave it to chance? Race my best driver. Cars of your choice. If you win I will back you for three years. That will be enough to get you famous and have car manufacturers falling over themselves to back you. You'll be independent and probably very wealthy. If you lose, you'll drive for me for the same length of time. There, how can you refuse, you're a sportswoman?'

Renée stared at the gleaming cars in the paddock. Pierre Suliman, the countess's driver, was there, working and as greasy as the rest. A man who loved racing, passionately. A man respected worldwide.

'I might agree,' she said slowly. 'On one condition.'

'Oh?'

'That if I lose you treat me with respect, you don't consign me to that crowd . . .' She nodded to the candy-striped tent.

'Oh, don't be silly. I don't know who half of them are, they change every race. They amuse me, so I pay their bills. My drivers are a completely different thing.'

'How do those people amuse you?' asked Renée. Her voice came out a little wobbly.

'I'll tell you if you agree to my wager.'

'I agree,' said Renée.

'That's the spirit!'

As they walked back towards the candy stripes, the countess said, 'They do whatever I ask, you know, anything for a crust of bread, poor loves. The naked wrestling can be rather fun. If you lose I'll give them to you as a consolation prize! Oh, look at you, your eyes are as wide as saucers!' the countess cackled.

Renée's knees were a bit weak as she walked back to her own car with Raoul. They got into the Panhard-Lavassor and she drove out of the compound.

'Well! I'm absolutely dying to know!' said Raoul.

She told him. 'But don't tell anyone else!' she said.

'Look,' yelped Raoul. 'My lips are like a buttoned fly!'

'She doesn't care about your friend, you know,' said Renée, thinking it only fair to tell him.

'Of course she doesn't. God, you have led a sheltered life, haven't you. He doesn't care about her either.'

Renée put her foot right down on the gas and Raoul screamed with delight.

She told the story in a diluted form. Paul was disturbed. He wasn't angry. In his love for Oruela he felt he had left Renée far behind. But he worried about her now, like a father.

'When is this race to be? Don't you have enough to worry about with the big-engine race only two weeks away?' he asked.

'Oh, I knew you'd disapprove,' she said. 'I don't know why I bother telling you things.'

'I'm not disapproving, I'm just worried,' he retorted.

'You're a liar!' she said, raising her voice. 'You just don't want me to get on in my career. You're jealous.'

'That's absurd,' he said, and he threw the coffee spoon in the sink. It clattered on the crockery that had sat there all day and Nefi turned and looked sleepily from the pool of sunshine that she was basking in on the kitchen windowsill.

Renée picked up her coffee from the counter and sipped it. She looked up at Paul. Her yellowish eyes gleamed. She had him and she knew it. It was the only way she knew anything about him now, when he showed signs of disturbance. She craved his violence and she would make him violent even though she hated him and didn't want him at all. She had meant it when she bowed out in favour of Oruela but now she wanted to sleep with him again. She missed him.

'That's right,' she said. 'Call me absurd, insult me. It stimulates you to do that, doesn't it? Go on! Admit it!'

Should he, he wondered. There was a part of him that responded. Even now, as he looked at her angry little face, the temptation to reach out and soothe her, to pin down her wild ego, was tempting. He was even beginning to get hard.

But then she said, 'You only care about yourself, you do.'

He knew she was wrong. 'I've cared too much about

203

you,' he said. 'Far too much. You wear your difference like an open wound. You use it as an excuse to abuse those who love you.' His tone was deadly. Renée began to cry.

He ignored her. He went and opened the front door and sat on a cane chair outside. The afternoon was waking up again after siesta. A woman he knew nodded to him as she passed by with her shopping bag. It was all pleasantly normal. But as he raised his coffee to his lips he heard Renée's crying get louder and louder. He'd never heard her cry like that before. It sounded as if her heart was breaking. He went back into the house and shut the door. He went to her and put his arms around her.

Her closeness suffocated his reason. She clung to him moaning his name over and over again. He stroked her hair, he held her as he had held her a hundred times before. He tried to soothe her, to make her whole. Her fingers searched his clothes and reached between his legs and before he knew it they were naked on the couch in the dark cool of the studio and he wanted to fuck her.

He took her hands in his grip and held them fast. She pushed on to him with such strength that the struggle took over. It was all he could do to hold her. It excited him so much. She moved on top of him like a woman possessed, her deformity sliding into his belly. He watched as it worked its magic and its spell drew him in. He was hers once more, she was whole. But he was empty.

The following morning Paul's telephone rang. Renée had just left, threatening to come back later, after training. He picked up the phone and heard Oruela saying: 'We've arranged the party for Saturday evening, just a few of us. I would like to ask your friends, Annette and the people that helped us get the letters through. I was thinking of taking a walk. I thought I might drop by and see you . . .'

But he knew he couldn't face it. He made an excuse and put the phone down, after promising to ask their friends himself and saying yes, he would love to come, he looked forward to it.

Saturday was two days away; by then surely he could free himself of Renée for good.

Oruela felt as if he'd slapped her face. She instinctively knew it was an excuse. With her feathers ruffled she sat pondering. Had she fooled herself over this man? The clerk at the reception desk told her someone wanted to speak to her. She waited a moment while the phone was transferred. It was Jean! He'd heard she was out, he said. Would she like to come over to his house for a swim?

And so, on the rebound, she said yes.

He was waiting for her in the lobby, looking gorgeous in linen trousers, a pale cream silk shirt, a straw boater. His eyes fluttered over her body as she walked towards him.

It was strange, walking with him through the busy streets. He acted with exaggerated politeness; every time the holiday-makers barred their way he led her, considerately, through. The crowd thinned as they walked up the slight incline that led to his villa.

'I owe you an apology,' he said, when they were alone in the street.

What she thought was, you bet your life you do. What she said was, 'What happened?'

'I don't really know,' he said. 'I got sucked in by the stories I was told about you.'

Oruela looked sidelong at him and saw a cloud of shame in his eyes.

When they reached the villa, a servant showed her where to change. It dawned on her as the woman opened the little cabin door by the pool that she didn't have a swimming costume.

The exit from the house to the pool was hung with pale cream muslin curtains that shimmered in the breeze. Over the top of the wooden door of the cabin she saw Jean's form as if through a mist. The curtains parted for him as he stepped out into the sun. He wore a striped bathing suit with thin straps that followed the contours of his muscles. The bulge at his crotch was well-defined by the jersey fabric.

Oruela slipped on the wrap that hung on a hook and stepped out. The blue and white tiles under her feet were cool.

'You're not swimming?' he asked.

'Not yet,' she said.

He pulled a chair out from under one of the tables for her and they sat down and ordered drinks from the waiting servant. 'Bucks fizz,' he said.

'Why did you ask me over here today?' she asked, as the servant walked away.

'Well,' he said, 'the pool is new, I thought you'd like it. I have all my friends over.'

'Are we to be friends then?' she asked. 'After what has happened?'

'Oruela,' he said. He looked sincere. 'I can't ask you to forgive me, because I'm not sure I wouldn't do the same thing again. Perhaps we can't be friends but I wanted you to enjoy this.' He swept his hand over the luxurious pool. 'I know what a terrible time you've had and I just wanted to share it with you.'

Oruela felt her toes itching with anger. He sounded so calm, sitting on his wealth like a fat chicken on an egg. The servant brought the drinks with fresh flowers in the glasses and then left them. The pool was still, like glass. She sipped her drink. 'Are we alone in the house?'

'Yes.' he said. 'Hélène's in Cap Ferrat and my parents have taken a trip to America.' He looked at her.

She stood up, let the robe slip off her shoulders and dived into the pool. Her naked body shot through the water, white and slender.

Jean practically fell over himself in the rush to join her and they swam leisurely. Eventually she rolled over on to her back and floated, her breasts bobbing in the sun-sprinkled water, the dark hair between her legs floating like a drowning animal.

It was too much for him. He swam over to her and held her around the waist. She kept her eyes closed. He felt like a stranger as he pulled her close to him in the warm water. She felt the hardness between his legs and pressing at her buttocks as he pulled her to the side. They reached the steps and emerged from the water, glistening. He held her and kissed her breasts. He picked her up and carried her through the curtains into the conservatory. He laid her down on the couch and stood up to peel off his soaking wet costume. Still she kept her eyes closed. She heard the flutter of the breeze outside and felt his wet body close over her own, felt his kisses on her damp skin. Her hands felt his dripping hair, and slid down the well-remembered back to the protuberance of his fine buttocks. In her chest, something opened, a door into her soul. There was nothingness inside. Nothing at all. His head disappeared from her grip and he kissed her white belly. Further down went his face into her wet pubic hair, seeking her clitoris and finding it. His tongue circled it, sucked it. Familiarity seeped in through the door that had opened. She took his head in her hands and moved herself against it, her sex open, her thighs stretched apart. She pushed and pushed. He sounded like a pig at the trough, greedy for her, greedy as hell. He took the whole of her sex into his mouth and gobbled at her. She felt the swell of her climax approaching and pushed down on to his tongue as she had pushed down on to the anonymous female head in the hashish-thick room that night, and a great wave of laughter welled up inside her. He was nothing more than a tongue. Nothing. Nothing. She felt him move his body as if to come up and get ready to slide into her but she held him there, made him suck her until she came in a great physical relief that bolted through her and relaxed her.

Realising she'd come he looked at her and smiled.

'There hasn't been anyone else, has there?' he said. His voice had a note of triumph in it.

She smiled at him lazily and he raised his head to kiss her. 'Oruela, I knew you'd still be mine,' he said as he came close to try and kiss her.

She averted her head, swung one leg over his body and stood up. She said nothing as she glanced over her shoulder and then she walked out through the wafting curtains, her legs feeling a little shaky underneath her.

He was still kneeling at the couch, kneeling at nothing. 'Don't leave me like this! Look at me!' he called. He was holding his penis in his hand. It was stiff and red.

Oruela walked away.

He came to the cabin door, slobbering something about how he understood and he knew she'd make it up to him next time.

She dressed herself and came out. He was still naked, his cock had gone down a bit but it perked up as soon as he saw her.

'Darling,' he said.

She went to him and gave him a little peck on the cheek. 'Oh, touch me,' he moaned, 'touch me.'

'Just stand there,' she whispered. 'Let your arms drop to your sides. Just stand.'

He did as he was told. It was shady on this side of the pool. His upturned face was dark and at the point of no return. She held his cock, massaged it. She could feel him responding. She held his cock, pushed it. She put her other hand on his chest and pushed him hard. He fell backwards into the water. She got a good look at his amazed face as he fell, still loaded. The surface of the water broke on his back.

He phoned her solidly for two days after that. He sent flowers, he made a nuisance of himself in reception but she felt things were resolved enough for her and she ignored him.

By Saturday though, Paul still hadn't been in touch

and she was beginning to feel that perhaps she would be going to Paris the following week without hope of seeing him again.

Euska told her not to worry about it. She had heard about Renée through Raoul and she told Oruela everything she knew. Oruela felt as if she now shared the knife-edge that Paul was on. She had to wait for him to jump her way towards a new life, and if he didn't then she had to believe he wasn't worth it.

She spent the afternoon writing her agonised thoughts to Kim and regretting she'd let Jean anywhere near her body. When it came to the evening Ernesto poured her a stiff drink.

She had come to like Ernesto more and more. It was impossible not to appreciate his mature sexuality. It was in his every movement, in his eyes. He appreciated her too. When she came out of her room in the evening gown he complimented her with just the right amount of enthusiasm.

She did look marvellous. Her black dress was floor length, very simple. It followed the contours of her figure without being too tight; a slight train that fell from her thighs at the back in folds gave the suggestion of an exotic creature just come from the sea to live on land. The dress stopped at her breasts in a classic neckline. Her broad milky shoulders were displayed to perfection and her hair, which had stopped thinning, shone glossily.

Euska came out of the bedroom. She was also in black. Her dress was clasped on one shoulder with a huge, single diamond and it fell in folds, the shape of a finely wrought J, down and across her full breasts. It clung to her waist and slithered over her belly down to the floor.

'I'm the luckiest man in the world!' exclaimed Ernesto, picking up his dinner jacket.

Euska was staring hard at her daughter's bare neck. She went back into the bedroom and came out again with a diamond-drop necklace. 'I want you to have this,' she said, fixing the clasp round Oruela's neck.

'Thank you,' said Oruela. But in truth she felt uncomfortable. It was such a personal present. It was as if Euska had hung herself round her neck. But when Oruela looked into the mirror over the fireplace, she saw how nice it looked: how simple and fabulously expensive and she decided she rather liked it.

'It was the first piece of jewellery I bought when I had enough money of my own,' said Euska.

Oruela went to her mother and kissed her on the cheek. Euska held her fondly for the merest moment but it was too long for Oruela. The moment was supposed to be beautiful but it didn't feel it. Having a new mother was all very complicated.

'Let's go then,' said Oruela.

'But where's Paul?' whispered Ernesto to Euska as Oruela went to the door.

She told him to ssshh and followed her daughter.

Heads turned as they stepped out of the elevator into the palm-lined foyer. As they crossed it the revolving doors spun and in whirled Paul, in a heated state, his tie askew.

Oruela certainly admired her mother's presence of mind. Euska immediately took his arm and told him he was her date, leaving Ernesto and Oruela to follow. Paul looked over his shoulder not once but twice on the short walk through the balmy streets to the casino but Oruela kept firmly to her conversation with Ernesto.

Annette had brought a date and so they sat boy, girl, boy, girl once the introductions were over, around the best table the casino had to offer. There was great excitement because the show was from America. A new show, on a try-out before Paris – *La Revue Negre* with Josephine Baker.

Oruela took to both Diane and Annette immediately, especially Annette, whose delicate beauty was blooming again. The seating prevented her from talking to Paul but as the meal was eaten and the wine drunk their infrequent eye contact grew more. As soon as they finished the show began.

First came the chorus girls, their long legs flashing in the dance, their barely covered breasts swaying under feathers and beads. The men too, with their superb physiques. The music was like nothing anyone had heard before, with drumbeats that stole into the heart and opened it. A table of elderly diners got up and walked out. Michelle, who had moved next to Oruela, kept exclaiming, 'Look at that!' Oruela felt warmer and warmer as the dancers whirled now far, now close to their table on the edge of the dance floor.

Then on came the star. She had the longest legs anyone had ever seen and her bottom was high. Her breasts were bare and high too. She leapt into the centre of the stage and began her incredibly elastic dance, her legs bending in impossible ways, her arms floating freely. She wore high-heeled white shoes with thick anklets, thick bracelets at her wrists and ropes of white beads that flew and bounced off her breasts as she bent and flung her extraordinary body around. All the time she smiled, her broad white-toothed smile that flashed in the glinting stage lights. Her dark-rimmed eyes smiled too and the kiss curl in the middle of her forehead gleamed black and damp on her coffee-coloured skin. She placed her hands crosswise on her knees and pulled them back and forth. It was the most riveting display of dance that had ever pounded the boards of the casino floor and she looked as if she enjoyed every moment of it. She stomped around, wiggling her tail-feathers, lifting her legs and shaking her barely covered sex. This was a different sensuality. This was life and joy and raw passion.

It roared through Oruela's veins, through every cell in her body. It made her want to dance too. She joined in with a passion as the audience thundered its approval and the delightful dancer bowed gracefully to her admirers.

The white band and singer that came on afterwards

felt a bit like an anticlimax but as soon as the first note sounded and the singer began to croon her song, Paul was on his feet asking Oruela to dance.

Not yet crowded, there was room on the dance floor for them to move and he surprised her. He was a graceful dancer, leading her expertly.

'Wasn't she wonderful?' he said.

Oruela replied, 'Yes.'

'Oruela,' he said. 'I haven't been to see you because I've had some unfinished business to take care of.'

'Me too,' she said, looking over his shoulder.

They stopped speaking, with words at least, and let their bodies speak, let their bodies sing to the music. They moved easily together. Oruela felt at peace with him. There was no need to talk. She felt the movement of his shoulder beneath his jacket and it spoke of his body. She became acutely aware of his hand that held hers as they danced and gradually the dance floor became more crowded and they closed the gap between their bodies.

She lost track of the number of dances they'd danced. She lost track of everything except the music and the feel of him. He had her hand close to his breast now. Her cheek brushed his chin, his lips close to her ear and, lower, her belly close to his. Closer still as they moved to the delicious tune, she felt the curve of his hip touch her lower down, her thighs on his. They moved together in perfect harmony, each movement of his sparking off a tenderness of her flesh under her clothes.

His lips brushed her neck and he held her closer. Her sex rested on his thigh now; it came alive as she swayed her body close to his, now touching, now not, tantalising her, building a cocoon of love around her that made her invisible to the other dancers. She closed her eyes and floated in it, feeling his sex at her own hip, not hard but swelling. The rhythm of the dance took her on to it and then away. The rhythm had first his sex then hers, brushing against a hip bone. She felt sex in her

212

fingertips, in the cleft between her shoulder blades, in her buttocks.

'Let's go upstairs,' he said as the music sped up and became a rag. So they went up to the gambling lounge and he put money on the number she chose and won. Then they left the table and went out on to the balcony. Biarritz was below them, twinkling in the indigo night.

'Do you think they'll miss us?' he asked.

'I don't mind even if they do,' she said. 'I like your friends.'

'I wish I could take them all to Paris with me,' he said.

Her heart leapt. 'So you're definitely coming?'

'Oh yes,' he said and he took her hand and led her into the shadows where they couldn't be seen from the room. He drew her to him. His lips were close to hers. 'I want to be where you are,' he said simply.

The relief was overwhelming. She raised her lips to his and they were met with a kiss that touched her everywhere she could feel.

Anything Goes

*T*hree days later she boarded the train for Paris with Euska, leaving Ernesto and Paul on the platform. It was torture to tear herself away from him. With every moment of waiting for him the desire grew more intense. She seemed to exist in the same cocoon of love that he had woven round her on the dance floor, immune to everything. The bother of packing, of leaving, of arrangements, existed outside. She was immune to everything except his next touch. As the train pulled out she sank into the cloth seat feeling the wrench deep inside.

The train was a fast one but every turn of the iron wheels seemed like an hour further away from him. Finally Euska brought up the subject, and Oruela poured out her heart.

'A man like that is always worth waiting for,' said Euska. 'Ernesto didn't touch me for three months. I thought I'd go mad! But he wanted to be sure we could be friends. Now he's my greatest friend in the world and the sex is still wonderful.'

'What if it's not that? What if he's just not much interested in sex? Michelle said he didn't make a pass at any of the models when they were working on those pictures.'

Euska was too busy laughing to hear most of that. 'You must be joking. If I'm any judge of men, that one is as sensual a man as you could hope to find. He's serious though.'

And with that Oruela had to be satisfied. A few hours later the train pulled into the station in Paris and the great city consumed her thoughts.

They stepped down into the crowds as the steam hissed from the tired locomotive. Porters dodged this way and that through the crowds. Their baggage was coming in the car with Ernesto who had to make a stop in La Rochelle on business. So they had the luxury of walking out into the wide boulevard free of concerns.

Euska was tired so they took a taxi and Oruela rode with her gaze glued beyond the windows, watching the hustle and bustle of the streets. The number of beautiful women made her feel a little insecure. They all seemed so certain of where they were going. Her lack of sophistication overwhelmed her and she became gloomy.

Euska's apartment building was swish from the outside and no disappointment inside either. The peaceful modern vestibule was manned by a young handsome attendant who had difficulty taking his eyes off Oruela's legs and backside as she walked in. She felt him looking and it cheered her. If he was sufficiently impressed when there were fashion-plates wandering up and down on the street outside his window every day then things weren't as bad as they seemed.

Euska took her out to dinner to La Coupole in Montparnasse and they talked about the people they saw. She learned from her mother's knowledge of Parisian life.

The next morning she lost no time. After breakfast she looked at the street map and excitement filled her to overflowing as she realised that they were living on the very edge of everything she wanted to see and do. She dressed in her trousers and a silk vest and flew out of the apartment building: the nice young porter stared after her in wonder.

Instead of taking the Boulevard St Germain, with its fashionable shops, she walked south along the pretty Rue Mabillon and at St Sulpice she turned towards the Place de L'Odeon and her Mecca. Almost every street name she saw brought some historical fact to her mind. The sad death of the English poet Oscar Wilde, Beach's bookshop 'Shakespeare & Company' on Rue de L'Odeon where James Joyce's *Ulysses* had been launched upon an unsuspecting world. Then suddenly she was on Boulevard St Michel, the Boule Miche as it was known to the students who flocked around the Sorbonne.

The cafés were only just waking up. Sleepy waiters in long aprons brushed soapy water in the morning sunshine. And then along the street came a man dressed in purple and yellow, sporting a lustrous moustache and a lobster on a leash. Oruela's mouth dropped open and then she closed it quickly and tried to be sophisticated. After all, this was Paris.

She crossed the road and walked into the Place Sorbonne almost on tiptoe. Students, up early, hurried along the streets towards the great building and she followed their direction. It led her into the foyer of the university which was crowded with people all talking and shouting. On the walls great boards announced the subject and place of the morning lectures. She crept to the wall, keeping out of the way of the jostling crowd, aware of their bodies. One or two young men smiled at her and she smiled shyly back. She looked up at the boards towering above her head.

L'historie de la revolution. Socialisme et change en Europe. La nouvelle francaise 1812–1889. La nouvelle anglaise. Les philosophies anciennes. La philosophie–Henri Bergson. If her mind had had a sex of its own it would have been creaming her eyes.

Suddenly a sharp bell rang once and galvanised the crowds. Within a minute she was alone in the echoing hall. She felt silly. How would she ever become part of this great institution? There didn't seem to be anywhere to go to ask about enrolment. She stood there, against the wall, staring blankly at her stupid little shoulder bag that swung against her legs.

'Are you lost?' said a voice.

She looked up. An old man stood there. He was dressed in a black suit, a cravat at his throat. He carried a couple of books and a sheaf of notes.

'What lecture are you due in? Perhaps I can show you the way,' he said, kindly.

'No. Thank you,' said Oruela, excusing herself. She headed for the glass doors.

'Wait,' he said. And he took her gently by the arm. 'Don't run away. You shouldn't be frightened, you know. This is a friendly place. Are you a student?'

'No,' she said, eaten up with shame.

'But you would like to be, is that it?'

She managed a smile. 'Yes, but . . .'

'Knowledge is here for the taking, my dear. Come. What subject interests you?' he said.

'Philosophy,' she said.

'Which particular philosophy?' he asked. 'We have a variety. It's like a shop, look.' He gestured with a broad sweep of the hand to the lectures on the board.

'I would really like to hear Henri Bergson,' she said, still shy. 'I used to dream of it when I was in pris–' she stopped, horrified.

'Were you going to say prison?'

'Look,' said Oruela, 'I really don't think . . .'

'On the contrary,' said the man, 'I expect you have thought a lot. Come. I will get you into the lecture. And we will talk more, afterwards, about your dreams, *n'est-ce pas*?'

He hurried up the stairs and she followed him, like a virgin walking to a strange crowded bedroom where all her half-formed desires would blossom.

Other students turned to look at them as he settled her in a seat at the back of the stepped auditorium and made her promise that she would not run away afterwards.

Then he trotted down the steps to the applause of the room and took up his position at the lectern.

Oruela spent the next hour listening to the great man in a kind of trance that lived each word he spoke as he spoke it. Bergson was the great irrationalist. In his vision, the great force of life struggled to break a way through inert matter and the universe was a clash between these two vital forces. Life organised itself according to need, unknowing beforehand but driven by want and satisfied only by action. Life, for Bergson, was creative, like the work of an artist.

Yes, yes, yes! cried Oruela's soul and that wasn't all. She fidgeted in her seat, feeling hot between her legs, as if God himself had taken her by the hand and led her into his den . . .

The signs were not lost on a young male student sitting in the next row. His eyes travelled over her body and her hair. He scribbled on a piece of paper. When the lecture was over he thrust it in her hand and rushed off into the crowd. She opened it. It said 'Venus lives!' It would have been rather amusing but for the fact that he waited for her at the bottom of the stairs and clung to her like a leech. She stamped solidly on his foot and went off in search of Monsieur Bergson.

The old gentleman wanted to hear her story and listened attentively. He decided there and then that she should be enrolled at the university. He cut a swathe through the tedious bureaucracy and got her a date to sit the entrance exam. Then he took her to a café and introduced her to some young gentlemen who were his best students, and left.

The café was in the heart of the Latin Quarter and was crowded with students eating their lunch. Her companions were rather morose but she took it that they were thinking great thoughts. The women seemed sexless. They wore shapeless clothes that hid their bodies completely and thick stockings even though it was still hot outside in the September streets.

On another table was a much more colourful group of people, Americans. They spoke in a slow lazy drawl and although Oruela's English was not that good she picked up a few words here and there. They were talking about sex.

They seemed to radiate sex. The women's eyes were hidden mysteriously in the shadows that fell from the cloche hats pulled low down on their foreheads; the men, hatless, made big gestures. Other people joined the group, a black couple, an oriental man in dark glasses, a dissolute and hungry-looking man in a faded, crumpled suit. They changed their language to French. A woman with bare arms and a deep, sensual voice complained about a famous painter who was taking advantage of the women that flocked around him. He made them race, naked, across the floor of his studio and the first one to grasp a thorny rose that he dangled in front of them won him. Then he drew her with distended misshapen muscles, with her sex where her eyes should be, grotesque forms that jolted the mind.

The others derided her, even the other women. Sex, the subconscious, the passions and the gross realities were the stuff of art, they said.

The conversation was hypnotic, it drew Oruela in. She wanted to be turned inside out. Her excited mind longed for the complementary stab of sex, with all its physical and emotional openings.

Her studious companions left to return to their lectures and she sat alone, self-consciously, listening to the gossip and ideas of the artists at the next table. Then she left and wandered the streets, hoping to be picked up.

In the days that followed she seemed to split into two people. On the one hand she was Oruela with her new friend and mother. They went to Maxims for cocktails and saw *tout Paris*. She met politicians, sportsmen, film stars and talked small talk. Underneath this Oruela was another, powerful creature who roamed the streets on her own. The animal that passed by the apache bars and longed to go in, who walked quickly along the low-life streets absorbing the forbidden atmosphere but too timid to step over the line into this *demi-monde*.

Then she failed the entrance exam to the Sorbonne. The test was cloaked in the tricks of academia and she had answered the questions too simply. She didn't find this out till much later. She thought she had done well and so the letter was a shock. That day, out on the streets, she stepped into the half-light.

The man who showed her the way was a young apache. His face was etched with the violence of his life. He approached her on the street from behind and spoke crudely, in a low voice, of what he would like to do to her. She knew, from the moment he approached her, that she wanted him, but she played a game with him. It was as if she were enacting a grotesque carica-ture of the broader give and take of sexual dynamics. She made a half-hearted attempt to walk on but he was relentless. They were passing a bar and he invited her in.

It was dark and almost deserted inside. One or two other Arabs were drinking at the tables and a woman wearing too much make-up sat at the bar, her skirt was split at the thigh and her blouse was stretched over big breasts. No one stirred when they entered. The barman served them drinks. The liquor was strong and slightly sweet. Her apache grinned at her as he led her to a dark corner.

His clothes were tight on his body and as they drank more of the liquor she became absorbed by the way his torso moved, by his smooth brown hand that clasped hers across the table. Everything was drowned but his touch. She remembered dancing with Paul at the casino; the drink gave her the illusion that she was experiencing something similar.

Eventually he led her out of the bar, along the street

and up some iron stairs at the side of a bakery to a grimy room without much light. The windows were open and the sound of a family arguing in one of the rooms off the courtyard at the back accompanied his love-making. He kissed her violently. His body was taut as if tensed for flight. As he broke off his kiss and fondled her breasts she saw, over his shoulder, a murky fish tank with big, black fish slumbering in the water. She thought of Paul as the apache undressed her and she closed her eyes and tried to pretend . . .

The physical sensations overtook the fantasy. He threw off his clothes and pulled her to the small cot that was his bed. The sheets smelled evil. There were no preliminaries. He stabbed her sex with his cock, leaving her to warm to him as he moved inside her. Her heart and soul never opened to him but her sex did. The delicious knowledge that this was a stranger, that this was the one and only time, gave her feelings an impetus. She opened her legs wider and wider, stretching her thighs. Then he pushed her knees up to her shoulders, so that her knees were forced into his shoulders and her sex protruded between her thighs. He fucked her hard. She felt him deep inside her, so deep there were stirrings of pain. It frightened her and she tried to move her legs but he held her fast. Her fear made her aware of where she was and made her stronger. She got her way. Her legs were wide again, she could push her clitoris towards him. But he had no idea of what she needed. He was bent solely on his own climax and she realised that she was not going to have an orgasm, that she didn't even want one with him. She gave up trying and lay there soft and pliant as a pillow.

The experience cured her. She almost thanked him. He said he had to be somewhere afterwards and left her alone in the room, telling her to slam the door as she left. She doubted that the room was even his own. She dressed and listened to the sounds in the courtyard at the back of the building. Just as she was about to turn from the window she saw a man sitting on the fire-escape across the way, on a floor higher. He was staring straight down at her. He was sketching and she realised with horror that he could see right into the room.

She left the room and ran down the fire-escape quickly and out, between the buildings into the street, turning to look over her shoulder once only before escaping.

That evening, to cheer her up, Euska suggested they go to the opening of a new show by some fashionable artists. Euska and Ernesto were always receiving invitations but they rarely went. Ernesto got bored too easily.

Euska was aware that Oruela was disappointed about the entrance exam and pining for Paul who had not written or telephoned at all in two weeks. She knew nothing of the afternoon's adventures in the seedy room.

Oruela spotted him as soon as they walked into the gallery. He was studying one of the paintings. Her heart jumped. It was the man she'd seen sketching on the fire-escape earlier. Every instinct told her to avoid him and she excused herself, deserting Euska, and went to the back of the gallery and tried to look at the work. But the place was too small, the drink was flowing and everyone talked to everyone else. She found herself in a group that included him. He gave no sign of recognition until chance stood them next to each other.

'My guess is that you have afternoons free,' he said. 'Would you consider sitting for me?'

So she began a stint as an artist's model. It was one of the happiest times of her life. It brought her back from the edge of disillusionment like a lifeboat brings back a survivor from a wreck. He brought her back. He was the opposite to what she expected of an artist. He was calm, quite rational, he had a quick intelligence that stimulated her and she trusted him. Once more she had found someone who would help her grow.

He didn't seem to want sex with her. He painted her

naked but he tasted her body only with his eyes. He touched her only with his brush. He had a wife in the country who adored him and he went home to their houseboat at weekends. He was only in Paris temporarily. His name was Albert.

They became good friends and in the evenings they went out to the cafés and bars. Oruela began to meet other interesting people. Everyone she met was talking about sex or doing it with whoever they chose or were addicted to. She heard stories and wondered. But her own sex drive had retreated into the safety of merely being looked at and appreciated.

One man she met was a brilliant linguist and academic. He lived with his mother who cooked for him and kept him comfortable. He was unable to make love to a woman and he couldn't with boys. He had an ingrown testicle that was such an embarrassment to him that it had twisted him. He was like a spider. He wove webs with words. He distorted stories that people confided in him until they became sordid and cheap. No one trusted him and it had made him bitter. He sat in his room translating scientific papers into all the known languages of the world but he couldn't speak the language of love. Oruela felt enormous pity for him.

There was another man who had a young wife who constantly slept with other men. He was desperate. People laughed at him and told him he should slap her. But he was kind and gentle. He'd been duped into keeping her but he held up his part of the bargain until it got too much and he took to drinking, and when he drank he cried bitterly. Oruela comforted him too.

These men were on the edge of a brilliant group of people, writers, artists and academics. Everybody told Oruela she should take the entrance exam again if she really wanted to but she wasn't sure now. Other artists asked her to pose and she became something of a favourite with them. Then a young, experimental filmmaker asked her to be in a film.

She was instantly addicted to it. It was such fun.

There was an energy about the people who made films that was unlike anything else. In one she appeared in a cage, wearing a mask, with only flowers to clothe her. In another she was a hat stand that came alive.

Albert complained that she was no longer around to model for him and that she was not using her fine mind but she ignored him and drifted away from him. He was soon to leave Paris and return to his houseboat. But what he was saying was true. She was drifting, but she was not free. Paul had been silent for weeks and she was learning that she didn't have to be locked up to be in a kind of prison. Her new acquaintances provided her with a daily carnival of colour, excitement, stimulation that lasted briefly. Once again she felt drawn to have some deeper experience. She found herself thinking about the apache.

This time she slept with a writer who had a domineering wife. He and Oruela escaped together one afternoon to a cheap hotel and locked the door against the world. He was very gentle, almost passive. He seemed overwhelmed that, as he said, such a beautiful woman would want to make love to him. He had a deformity of the spine which made him self-conscious and he was ugly. But as he warmed to her he was a good lover. He spent an age at her breasts, sucking, crooning. He touched every part of her body with light fingertips, he made the fine hair on her arms stand on end because he made love to her arms as much as her breasts. He touched her body for so long that when he eventually got to her sex, she was streaming with anticipation. He fucked her for an hour, never coming himself, but giving her orgasm after orgasm until the shocks were deep inside her, momentous shiftings like the movements of continents, that merely tremor on the surface.

They took a break and he ran out to the shops to buy wine with her money. When he came back they drank the dark red liquid together and she begged to be allowed to make him come in whatever way he wanted.

'Do you mean that?' he asked.

'Of course,; she replied. She was so full of sex, so dreamy that she meant it.

'Get dressed then,' he said. 'We're going out in public.'

He told her to leave off her underwear and she stuffed it into the paper bag that had held the wine. They walked out into the street and took a tram to the *Exposition*. Tourists still flocked to the pavilions where the decorative arts of twenty-one countries were on display. The crowds were ordinary people, families, soldiers on leave, a few businessmen.

They went into the Bon Marché pavilion and spent a while moving though the crowds, looking at the sumptuous and imaginative Art Deco displays of furniture, clothes and interiors and touching each other surreptitiously.

One display was of an executive suite from America. The huge black wooden desk stood on chrome-plated semi-circles. The lamp was made of aluminium. Oruela found out this detail because they went up close to the display and hovered until there was no one looking. Then quickly he pulled her behind the scarlet curtains that formed the backdrop to the display. They were in a small space next to the wall, so small that one step backwards and their bodies would be visible to the world under a skin of scarlet.

'Here,' he said. 'Lift up your dress.'

She lifted up her dress as she was asked and he unbuttoned his trousers. The sounds of the tourists outside their curtained world continued as he took her against the wall. His climax came quickly, almost as soon as he penetrated her and moved in the swollen walls of her sex. She felt like a vessel but she was happy to be one this time. He had satisfied her so well already.

They saw each other every day for a week. They ran over Paris. He had a whole list of places that appealed to him. They were always just out of the public gaze. There was always the chance of getting caught. There

225

was a nook behind the museum at the Palais de Lux-embourg, a shrubbery within sight of the Arc de Triomphe, an alleyway just off the Quais. They spent hours and hours together touching, stroking, cajoling each other's bodies into heightened life and then they rushed out and fucked like dogs in the street.

Their adventures were stopped by his wife who discovered them at the hotel. He apologised fifty times as she led him away and Oruela waved goodbye. She had grown philosophical. It didn't matter. She could find another lover.

But there had been no word from Paul for weeks and as she sat up in bed in the cheap hotel she had the uncomfortable realisation that she could no longer fool herself. She got dressed quickly and sat by the window facing on to the street, watching the writer and his wife arguing as they walked down the street. At least they had each other. There was no getting away from it; Paul had deserted her. She hated him at that moment. She hated him for being such a coward as to leave her without telling her. He might have written even if it was only to say that he had changed his mind. In the moment of hating him she also knew that this was a point of no return. Her heart was closing to him and with it, all her other feelings. It was a dreadful release. It made her cry. Everything was one big mess.

Life Could Be a Dream

*J*acques Derive jumped up from the mayoral seat in the council chamber and fled out of the door. The members of the roads committee looked at each other in perplexity and debated what to do in his sudden absence.

Meanwhile, in his office, Derive was pouring himself a stiff drink. He grasped the glass with a shaking hand and slung the liquid down his throat in one go. It made no difference. The fiend was still there, hovering in the shadows, he knew it.

Ever since that hell's bitch, Euska Onaldi, had risen from the dead and come to see him, he had been seeing things. He saw them out of the corner of his eye, creatures like little black cats underfoot. It kept happening and the delirium tremors were getting worse. He had begun to see things everywhere. Before tonight's meeting he had seen what looked like a bat hanging from the highest bookshelf in his office. They regularly sat under his chair, whispering and tugging at his socks. But this evening was the first time they had followed him into the council chamber.

He knew she'd cursed him. She was a devil in woman's form. He'd been loath to tell anyone, but now they were coming out in public he knew he must. She had cast her spell on him. She had forced him into a moment of doubt that he, Jacques Derive, had been in the wrong, and once that spell had entered his soul he was doomed unless he could get help. He remembered how the jewel around her hag's neck had flashed in his eyes that afternoon, blinding him to the truth. That was when she must have bewitched him.

He made his excuses to the deputy mayor and left the building. He climbed into the back of his limousine and instructed the driver to take him to a church in one of the poorer neighbourhoods behind the railway station. The priest at St Jude's was well known for being a successful exorcist.

But as the car rolled down the street, Derive suddenly realised a devil had smuggled itself into the upholstery. It was sitting in the corner grinning and ready to leap at him.

He shouted at the driver to stop. 'I'll walk,' he said. 'Take the car home and disinfect it immediately.'

The chauffeur scowled and drove off. Derive pressed on towards St Jude's. The clock above the railway station struck two into the still, hot night as he passed by. At the back of the station he needed to relieve himself and he squeezed in between a bush and a wall and unbuttoned his fly. There was one in his trousers! It flapped its wings and flew at his throat. He screamed and grappled with it until he flung it off and dashed it to the ground.

Gasping, he continued his journey. He turned up the long dark narrow street that led to St Jude's. In the distance the solitary spire of the big church rose into the inky sky. The area was more than just poor. It was Biarritz's most dubious quarter. Its population was mostly transient. This was where unlucky gamblers holed up, waiting for their luck to change. The only natives of the place were the commonest of streetwalkers who plied their trade in the shadows.

A blousy redhead stepped towards him but, seeing who he was, stepped back and snarled. Once he had passed she gave a low whistle. Derive was well known. More than once, during an election campaign, he had made the lives of the women who depended on the street trade a misery, locking them up and having them beaten just so he could gain the votes of the respectable hypocrites in Biarritz society.

In response to the whistle, eyes peered at him with hatred. Women, usually inviting, seethed with anger. As he passed, the local people came out of their doorways and watched. They sensed something was wrong; that he was weak. They laughed at him. One or two began to follow his stumbling tracks up the street.

He could hear them, their soft devil footfalls. He knew it was the devils following. They were almost silent, but he could just hear them. He knew he daren't look back lest they turn him to salt, but it was hard not to. They had him in their power. He willed himself to concentrate on the dark shape of the church in front of him but the power of the devils was too strong. They forced him to look back. They forced him. He turned.

He was so surprised when he saw the grinning women behind him that he tripped. He fell backwards and there was one almighty crack as his skull hit a sharp stone protruding from the kerb.

One of the two women took her chance and reached inside Derive's thin, linen jacket, even as he lay dying, to rob him of his wallet.

'How much is in it?' asked her friend.

'Only ten francs.'

'Pig,' she said, and gave him a kick in the ribs.

The pair disappeared into the shadows and the street was once again quiet and still as Derive's life blood seeped slowly into the gutter.

His death dominated the news for several days. Murder was suspected and almost every resident of the St Jude's district was questioned. No one came forward. No one was caught.

Alix Peine was not directly involved with the murder

investigation team but he had his own ideas and tried to tell his superiors that they were on the wrong track. No one wanted to listen to him. He would prove them wrong. Alix had had feelers out for a long time. He was always on the look-out for anything that might serve to give his career a boost. He knew that Oruela had been freed through the machinations of a mysterious woman. A few notes in an hotel clerk's hand and he knew who the woman was. It was as plain as the buttons on his uniform to Alix that, not content with being free, Oruela, and probably her mother too, had murdered the poor mayor.

On the strength of this, he immediately moved into Genevieve's house to protect her. They decided on separate rooms, for the sake of the servants, but their evenings were spent in the twin pursuits of detective work and debauchery. Genevieve had invented a new game that he loved. Just thinking about it now, as he sat by the window in the station house, looking out onto the street, made his cock grow stiff.

He left the office early and rushed to Bayonne with anticipation in his heart and his loins. Genevieve was waiting for him, as she had been for the past three evenings, with a bottle of cognac on a silver tray on the coffee table, ready to pour him a drink after work. He didn't immediately go and see her, however. He passed by the door of the salon without so much as an acknowledgement. He went straight up to his room and changed into something more comfortable. While he was changing he thought about her. She was always more appreciative of him when he kept her waiting. She was so pliable in that state. He enjoyed being the master of the house when she was like that. As the evening wore on, though, the balance would change subtly. She would become mistress and he would be putty in her hands.

Eventually he came down that evening in his smoking jacket and his patent leather slippers and sat down next to her on the couch. Even before he had sipped the drink that she handed him lovingly, he was elaborating on his plan for tricking Oruela, once they found her, into confessing to the mayor's murder.

Genevieve held up her hand. 'Be quiet,' she said. 'Stop. There is something you have to know, my dear Alix, before you proceed with this plan. Oruela didn't murder her father. She wouldn't hurt a fly. I found that lizard on the seat of her car and I lied about finding it next to Norbert's bed because I wanted the little brat off my hands.'

Alix was struck dumb by this. The words wouldn't come out. What was there to say? What he did know though, was that his cock was stiffening even as he sat there gaping at her. She had such a marvellous neck. Her head, as she spoke, was held high. She had such a firm chin. He was truly at her mercy now. He wanted to bury his face in that neck. He reached for her. 'You're so vicious. I love you madly,' he said as he brushed her skin with his lips. 'Tell me. Did you kill him?'

'Oh good God, no,' said Genevieve. 'He died of his own accord, I suspect. He was always being ill and vomiting. I used to hear him. It was absolutely disgusting.'

Alix drew back. The thought of Norbert Bruyere vomiting had destroyed the mood somewhat. He took a sip of his drink.

'Do you want to play doggy now?' she said, suddenly. She held her head high again. Her lips were a little pursed.

'Oh yes,' he groaned. It was his favourite game. They played it only when she allowed it.

'Go upstairs then,' she said, 'and get prepared. I will join you.'

Alix ran up the stairs two by two and threw off all his clothes. He rummaged in her wardrobe and found the mink that he was to wear to be her dog. The feel of it was heaven to him. The lining was cool on his skin. He slipped it on and crouched down on all fours waiting for her.

'Fetch your leash,' she told him, when she entered the room.

He crawled off into the wardrobe and expertly fished out the leash with his teeth.

She put it round his neck and led him around the room threatening him with the direst punishments if he was a bad dog. The things she would do were too tantalising to resist, so he bit her leg and she immmediately put her threats into action. She beat him severely with the leash until he cried for her to stop.

'Undress too!' he pleaded.

Eventually she gave in and undressed and pretended to be a doggy too. He liked to sniff her and she did the same to him until they were both so excited he mounted her, just like a dog and took her. She howled fit to bring the house down.

After dinner in the dining room, when the servants had withdrawn, he reached for her hand, and said, 'We have to get married soon. The waiting is driving me to distraction. When will it be the proper time?'

Genevieve smiled at him. 'It happens that I am going to see my lawyer tomorrow. The final accounts are ready. This time tomorrow I will know exactly how I stand. Once I have control of Norbert's money, then, my darling, of course I will marry you and make a politician out of you.'

Alix was overcome with emotion. 'With Derive dead, there is bound to be room for new blood in the town hall. We will go far together, my dearest one.'

'Yes, my sweet,' she said and she took a morsel of pudding between her two fingers and popped it in his mouth.

The next day at the office Alix told the sergeant to make his own damn coffee. The sergeant replied that he would be out of a job if he didn't do what he was told and Alix laughed at him. The police station was just over the road from the lawyer's office and he saw

Genevieve going in just minutes after the coffee incident. She looked delightful. She wore her floatiest of floaty black dresses. Just thinking about what that respectable looking woman got up to under her big iron bed at home gave Alix a stiff cock in his trousers.

Inside the lawyer's office, though, things were grim. He came straight to the point. He told Genevieve that Norbert's accounts were in such a bad state once they were finally unravelled, that everything would have to be sold to pay off his creditors. There was nothing left. Not a sou.

'What about the house?' asked Genevieve. Her voice was little more than a frightened whisper.

'It must be sold,' said the lawyer. 'I suggest that as a matter of urgency, you get in touch with your family. I will hold off the sale of the house for as long as possible but I'm afraid eventually the creditors will have to be paid.'

Genevieve composed herself before she left. She crossed the street and made straight for Alix's office. The sergeant was rude and nearly made her burst out crying but she kept hold of herself as she sat on the wooden bench and waited. Eventually, Alix came out and led her into an office that looked out on the street. It was one he shared with another man, he told her, the other man was out at lunch.

Genevieve plucked up her courage and told him what had just happened. He was very sympathetic. He was marvellous, in fact. He took her in his arms while she had her little weep and told her everything would be all right.

Then he made sure she was comfortable in the car and told her to rest during the afternoon and not to worry.

'I'll have your cognac waiting for you at – ' she began.

'Oh, don't go to the trouble, my dear,' he said. 'I have an engagement this evening. I won't be back until late.'

Genevieve went home and spent some time going through her jewellery box. There were a couple of expensive pieces and she must be sure they didn't fall into the hands of creditors. That done she tried to fill in the hours until he came home, but it was hard. There was so little to do. Then it got dark, the clocked ticked on and he still didn't come. Eventually she went to bed and fell into a restless sleep.

Alix, meanwhile, was at La Maison Rose with the sergeant who he had offered to treat him to the services of a whore for being so bad tempered earlier that day. The sergeant had accepted his apology and they were having a great time. But even as he had his hand up the skirt of a pretty little whore, Alix was pondering his next move. He'd spent the earlier part of the evening with the widow Derive. She was so charmed that a young man like him should take the trouble to visit an old woman like herself that she gave him plenty to drink and listened as he told her the story of his life. She dimpled when he chided her for saying she was old. Why, fifty wasn't old, not for a woman as handsome as the widow Derive . . .

All in the Game

*A*nnette had been very busy. She was training to be a croupier at the casino. Her plan was to travel once she was good at it, to work the transatlantic liners. She had been so busy that she hadn't seen much of Paul at all, apart from saying hello in the afternoons as she rushed off to work. Nevertheless she had noticed how sad he looked and she had made an effort to invite him over to eat. As soon as he arrived, while she was still preparing the meal, he spilled out his heart. Annette listened and then she rounded on him.

'You're a fool,' she said. 'I can't believe you can be such a fool!'

'Hold on,' he said, a little peeved. 'Just hold on. I'm not really such a fool. She's gone off to Paris to have the time of her life. If she wanted to include me she would have written. She would have told me about all the exciting things she's been doing! I think it's pretty damn obvious by now that she's just too busy to think of us down here, of me. I can understand it. This place holds terrible memories for her. She's probably put it all behind her.'

'Rubbish,' said Annette. 'You'll get nowhere sitting on your fine *derrière* understanding, my friend. I think that twisted little fiend has eaten away at your brains.

Hasn't it occurred to you that Oruela will be expecting to hear from you?'

Paul drained his wine glass and grinned a rueful grin. There was an element of truth in Annette's prognosis that Renée could twist his mind. He didn't like the idea but it could be true. She had pressured him not to go to Paris until the outcome of the race with the countess's driver was known. 'Renée needs me,' he said. 'She's in above her head.'

'I'd watch her drown and say good riddance,' said Annette. She detested Renée.

'She hasn't changed my mind. I still love Oruela,' said Paul.

'Well, for goodness' sake tell her then. Write to her and explain your duty or whatever you call it. Otherwise you'll lose her. I warn you.'

And with that they closed the subject and ate dinner. That night Paul went home and wrote. He wrote eight pages. He explained exactly what was happening, the whole of it. All he left out was that Renée was still sleeping in his bed. But it was there, between the lines for anyone with insight to guess at. He knew Oruela had that insight. But he was making his own gamble – with his hopes and dreams, his love as the stake. He rose early the following morning and posted it in the box at the end of the road.

At first, when Renée had asked Paul to stay, she was telling the truth that she was in over her head. At first she needed an escort to be seen with. The countess kept her promise. She showed Renée, and Paul, what her entourage did for their keep. When they arrived at the first 'party' in her luxurious, specially furnished hotel suite, the young men and women whom Renée had first seen at the racetrack were already semi-naked.

The theme was 'Rome'. Paul and Renée were unaware of this when they were asked and there were other guests in ordinary evening dress. It was only the countess's employees who were in Roman attire, showing off their fine limbs, a breast here, a flash of hip there.

There was a meal for twenty or so people, the ones dressed in their own clothes. A whole pig was carved in the room and served by the young slaves. There was an abundance of wine, of fruit served Roman style. It all quite appealed to Paul's sense of theatre.

But there was an undercurrent of abuse. The way the countess ordered the slaves about, the way, as the guests got more and more drunk, they too ordered the slaves to do certain things . . . It was getting out of hand. Paul wanted to leave.

But Renée insisted they stay. After the dinner was over the slaves had mostly been undressed. Some still wore a belt or a sash or anklets. The guests had taken to pulling them by these pieces of bodily decoration. One middle-aged man was being given fellatio under the tablecloth.

The countess clapped her hands and the slaves rearranged the furniture so that the guests could sit on chairs around the perimeter of the room and the centre was a mass of cushions. The gorgeous young people arranged themselves on the cushions and the orgy began in earnest. The carpet became a mass of naked bodies, clawing and sucking, rising and falling with sex and sweat. The other guests were invited to join in if they wished. The young slaves came and encouraged them to do so. They draped themselves over portly middle-aged men and women. Two young men stripped a perfumed matron of her evening clothes, her corsets, and plunged into her rolls of flesh with glee.

The countess merely watched. So did Renée and Paul. And the countess watched them.

Later, when they got home, Renée and Paul had savage sex. Her pale skin glistened in the moonlight that filtered through the unshuttered window and her taut little body writhed under him with an urgency that was irresistible. She called him a hypocrite the next day when he said he didn't want to go to any more of the parties.

'You were just as turned on as anyone,' she sneered.

'Of course I was,' he said. 'How could anyone not be? But I didn't like the abuse of power.'

'You're stupid,' she said. 'It isn't an abuse. It's their job. It's what she pays them for. If it wasn't for her, those talentless fools wouldn't have enough money to eat. She told me, she finds them virtually in the gutter.'

'Exactly,' said Paul. 'And that's where you'll end up if you get more involved with this absurd set of people.'

'They're not a "set" as you call them. They are nothing. It's the countess that creates it all, pays for it all. She's just amusing herself. She could walk away from them at the drop of a hat. She told me so herself. You're just jealous.'

That little discussion ended predictably, with Renée slamming out of the house. She told the countess about it and the countess agreed, to a point. She didn't think Paul was jealous, just full of bourgeois inhibitions.

Renée knew she wanted more. She felt sultry all the time she was with the countess, knowing she could have anything she wanted because the countess had the money and the set-up to order anything. The countess encouraged Renée to try out being a master. She presented her with a couple of young boys one day and told her they were hers. Renée ordered them to wrestle and she and the countess watched as their firm naked bodies gripped and pulled and mauled at each other. Renée liked being a master; it was the other side of the coin from being spanked and it was just as captivating.

The countess had a special thing she liked. She called it a private ceremony, but she had about five or six of the young slaves with her when she did it. She wanted Renée to join in. Renée dithered a bit and tantalised her by not agreeing immediately. Renée was well aware that much of her power over the countess was dependent on her not giving away too much too soon.

'I might agree,' she told her, 'if it doesn't involve me undressing. I'm very shy of anyone seeing my body.'

'No,' said the countess. 'It's only me that undresses, me and the slaves. All I would ask you to do is touch me when I shout for it, with this.' And she unwrapped the silk scarf from around her neck. 'Please, Renée, say you'll do it. I must do it. Even if you don't want to. I must. It's a compulsion. It's time.'

Renée couldn't resist finding out what it was and so she agreed. The slaves entered the room and undressed the countess down to her garters and stockings, which they left on her. She had a fine body for a woman in her forties, if a little too skinny in places. The slaves helped her arrange herself on the couch where she proceeded to masturbate. The slaves stared at her intently, as, presumably, instructed before.

'I like to be watched,' said the countess. 'When I tell you, you must tickle my skin with the scarf here,' and she raised her legs and touched her squashed buttocks.

She closed her eyes and rubbed herself harder and harder. Suddenly she shouted 'Now!' and Renée draped the scarf lightly at the place where she had been asked to. The countess's body convulsed. Tears streamed from her eyes as she orgasmed.

Every night at first Renée went home to Paul and cuddled up to him in bed and he put his arm around her and held her. Almost every night she whispered long into the darkness, 'Don't leave me. Don't leave me. You keep me sane. Your body is the world I must keep touching. Your hands are the ties that keep me here. I would be lost. I would be lost without you . . .'

After a while she no longer whispered these things. She merely clung to him. And then after another little while, she stopped coming home every night. The race was drawing near, she told Paul, and she trained every day and camped out by the track in a tent the countess had provided for her. She came back sometimes and she cuddled up to him silently. They no longer argued at all.

It was the day of the race that Paul posted his letter to Oruela. Renée had asked him to be there for the start at eleven.

Renée woke early and tried to shake off the grogginess of the champagne of the night before. She had escaped making love with the countess by a whisper. In the fireglow the air had been heavy with desire. The countess had dismissed her retinue and they were left alone. Renée felt the power she had and revelled in it. She knew she must win today to avoid losing that power. She was nervous.

She ate breakfast and went across to the car. The mechanic was under the bonnet.

'Everything all right?' she asked. She suddenly had a sense of how mad this was, how unequal. The countess and her circus were all out, milling around Pierre's car. Here was she, just herself and her mechanic. Where was Paul? It was 10.45 and he had promised to be here. She felt so terribly alone.

But there he was, walking across the field. He seemed so ordinary to her. He was an embarrassment. Why hadn't he brought any of his friends with him to give her moral support?

'Jump in,' said the mechanic.

Her nerves were so taut she sprang into the car like a cat. Paul stood next to the car.

'Gas,' called the mechanic.

She put her foot down. The engine roared.

'Right,' said the mechanic. 'She's as good as she can be,' and he lowered the bonnet, twisting the silver catch shut and giving it a little pat.

Renée slipped on her hat and goggles and adjusted them. She glanced over towards the countess. Paul wished her luck. The mechanic ran with the car out of the paddock and on to the track.

She took the car round once, coasting, listening to the engine, feeling it, becoming part of it. One twitch of her toe and this magnificent machine would respond as if it

240

was an extension of herself. She coasted to the start grid and did some regular breathing.

He was coasting now, too, the countess's driver. She didn't think of him as a person, although she knew damn well who he was. She thought of him as a mythical beast, half-man, half-car, her sexual opposite . . . This was going to be fun. A surge of excitement went through her. The flags were waving. He drew alongside. The leader car came on the track. They would follow it round once and then the race would begin. There were twelve laps.

It began and the leader car slowly picked up speed. They were half way round, coming up to the start line.

Her foot went down hard as the leader disappeared. Hard but smooth so that the engine appreciated it. She knew how to control this car. She knew what it liked. She took the lead and a glow of satisfaction descended on her. It shouldn't be too hard to hold on to a lead for twelve laps; all she had to do was prevent him from overtaking. She had the prime position and she knew it. She set the pace lower than full speed.

He made his first attempt to take her on a bend. She felt him coming up on her flank, but she had the reserve power to pull away and block his chances. He went down in her estimation. Fancy trying it on a bend!

They settled like a needle on a record player, into a groove, for the next four laps. Then he tried again, this time on a straight. He pulled alongside her, glanced at her and grinned. She ignored him and pulled ahead, but this time, instead of hanging back, he was right on her tail, forcing her to go faster than she wanted to. Her adrenalin pumped. It was impossible! He couldn't do it! It was a bluff. She steeled her nerves and raised her gas toe very very slightly.

He hadn't expected it, obviously, because she felt the terrifying brush of rubber on her tail. The steering wheel wobbled. She held on tight but did not increase her speed forcing him to drop back before the bend.

Now they had a race! She was prepared for anything!

On the sixth he tried the same trick again but she was prepared for him this time and she fought him off with panache. Ha! Let him sweat! She took the seventh and eighth with nerves of steel. Then, on the ninth, he came right up close again, right on her tail, bumper to bumper. She felt a moment of disbelief. Surely he wouldn't continue. She had to go flat out this time. He seemed determined to force her off the road! They raced the tenth at full speed.

On the eleventh lap, on the straight, he pulled alongside her. She put the throttle down full but the bend was too near! She had to slow or die. He took her, the bastard!

She caught up with him again on the penultimate straight. But the next bend was now in sight. A moment of doubt seized her. She couldn't do it! She didn't have the skill to take him on the bend so she sat on his tail as they hurtled round it, reserving all her energy for the final straight.

As they hammered into it she pulled out and floored the throttle. She got alongside, inching forward, inching. The finish line was in sight. She willed the car to go faster. She pushed and pushed, concentrating with all her resources.

The car responded. She was even surprised herself when she crossed the finish line just feet in front of him. The two cars coasted off the track and came to a halt. Pierre Suliman jumped out of his car and came over to congratulate her. The countess was there too. Renée stripped off her goggles and her hat and climbed out of the car.

'Congratulations,' said the countess.

Renée went to her and hugged her. She felt the woman's body thrill at her touch. Renée gave her a long, outrageous kiss on the lips and then they walked, arms around each other, to the big tent where champagne corks were already popping.

Paul stood at the trackside. It surprised him that she didn't even give him a backwards glance. He considered going into the tent, just to say goodbye, but then he thought better of it. He left her car where it was and thumbed a lift back to Biarritz.

Back in Paris Paul's letter sat in the Onaldi pigeonhole along with the rest of the mail. Euska and Oruela had gone to the country. They had taken a small cottage near Albert's houseboat and were enjoying the ease and beauty of the clear autumn days. The river slunk like a gleaming snake through the plain, reflecting the sun. Small patches of orange and gold appeared daily on the trees, heralding winter. Morning mists rose from the land and hovered, fruits began to drop.

When they had been there for a couple of days Euska announced that she was planning to sail to Rio with Ernesto. He wanted to get married at sea.

A deep indefinable anger took hold of Oruela. She became irritated with every little thing. They bitched about household tasks, about what to do for the day. Eventually Euska asked her to come out with what was really bothering her.

'I feel deserted,' said Oruela. 'I feel deserted by everyone. First Paul, now you. What am I going to do with my life?'

One of the crowd in Paris had suggested she have analysis, that she go to Vienna. She didn't want to. She had always imagined Vienna to be a cold, soulless place. But she didn't know what to do. Paris was not turning out as she had hoped.

'Come to Rio,' said Euska. 'At least for the winter. You can decide what you want to do after that.'

'I don't think I want to,' said Oruela. 'I want my own life.'

'Why don't you write to Paul?' said Euska one afternoon as they were walking along the river towards the houseboat. 'Why don't you ask him what is going on? My instincts tell me there's a reason for all this. I suspect he's trapped in something that his honour won't let him desert.'

243

So Oruela tried to write, but each time she wrote a few sentences she ended up in tears. It was pathetic. Her pride wouldn't let her ask the kind of questions she wanted to ask, not of Paul, not even of Euska. Why have you deserted me? Why? The wound inflicted by Euska was an old, old one. She dreamed of a misshapen child sucking at the breasts of a wolf. The wolf changed into a man, the man was Norbert Bruyere. She woke up covered in sweat.

The local men watched her as she walked the countryside, like cows watch, turning from their business to stare impassively and chew. They had time on their hands. The harvest work was over. In the village bar they played chess and a young man offered to teach her.

He was very young, too young to leave home and go to Paris. He was a farmer's son but he was a poet, he told her. He wrote in cramped handwriting. He had pale skin with a fine down on his chin and around his eyes was the palest mauve. He was slender and fit and his movements were graceful, a touch feminine.

He explained the pieces to her in human terms. The king, he said, was stolid. Seemingly powerful, he was in reality very vulnerable whereas the queen was emancipated and bold. She had licence to roam wherever she wanted to. The power was largely hers. He reserved his pity for the pawns, the mass of humanity allowed to advance only to get them playing the game and then restricted. The bishop, tricky like any cleric, attacked from an angle and the knight, the impetuous gallant, could jump to the lady's rescue. The rook he described last; the rook he said was decisive, an officer in the royal guard, making his decisions and going straight to the heart of the matter.

As he finished explaining he looked straight at Oruela, took her hand and made her move a pawn.

Oruela played her first game intently, unaware of his quick little *double entendres* except on the periphery of her consciousness. He didn't let her win. He showed her her mistakes and advised her to learn by them.

She was amazed at his wisdom. For such a young man, a boy really, his intellect was so acute. She played on regardless, thinking of him as sexless, his beauty yet unripe. He was precocious, nothing more. But every day spent in the misty autumnal countryside took her more and more into a dreamlike state, a sultry, full mood. As they played in the evening in the quiet café getting used to each other, she began to notice him and wonder if he had ever tasted the rich fruits of a woman's body. She began to respond to his little jokes, to his cleverness, less as a mere companion, more as an older woman.

One evening it grew cold and the proprietor of the café lit a fire. It roared in the grate and was too hot. Oruela took off her jacket and as she turned back to the table she caught him looking at her bare arms. She felt protective towards him, naturally, because she was older. That evening he told her about his frustration living under his parents' wing, of his dreams. She began to muse on the fantasy of taking him under her wing, taking him to Paris. He would, she thought, become a real friend to her. He would be so grateful to her he would never leave her side. She didn't examine her fantasies. They gave her pleasure.

He walked her home each night if Euska wasn't in the café, back to the cottage where a light would be burning in the darkness. They would draw closer and see that Euska was reading. Oruela opened up to him on these walks, told him about the unusual relationship with her mother, the frustrations that she still felt. Her admissions made her feel that they had common ground, that they were equal in a way more profound than mere years. Their friendship stepped outside the boundaries of the evening's games. He defied his father and took time off from the autumn work of the farm to walk with her. He taught her to perfect her techniques in horse-riding. They galloped through the lanes and across the fields. One day they went deep into the woods. The horses' hooves thundered through the sweet-smelling forest as they raced along the track. There was tension in her knees and thighs as she stood in the stirrups; the body of the mare she rode was warm with exertion underneath her. She was hot herself.

Lauren beat her, as usual. She chided him as they led the sweating horses to drink at the river.

'You should let me win something!' she said, laughing. 'You're better at everything than I am!'

He told her off. 'Women need to strive to be better than men. If they are going to have real power in the modern world they need to be pushed to the limit by men like myself who believe in their power.'

As he spoke she knew that there was one area of human experience that she knew much more of than he, one thing that she could teach. Something he needed.

She walked away from him, back in among the trees where no eyes could see them. She walked slowly. He caught up with her. When she came to a glade she stopped and lifted her face to the misty sun above. He stood in front of her, looking at her. 'You're so beautiful,' he said. She looked into his eyes. He came close and touched her face with his fingertips. Their lips were close. She waited. His kiss was long and wet and explorative. His tongue searched for hers.

His fine brown hair at his neck was soft and young, his shoulders and back were firm and slender. She slid her hands into the warmth between his jacket and shirt and held him lightly. She was excited by his inexperienced desperation. When he kissed her neck, pausing on her Adam's apple, tickling it, she bent back her head and exulted in her maturity and power. His hands unbuttoned her waistcoat and her blouse with terrible urgency and he fed at her breasts like a baby.

His hands were less certain as they touched her hips' roundness. They fluttered down to her thighs and she imagined he had never touched a woman there before.

246

But he raised the hem of her soft woollen skirt forcefully and grasped her soft thighs in between her garters and her knickers strongly, pushing his still clothed hips into her sex.

'Let's see what you're made of, little boy,' she said, unbuttoning the rough woollen cloth at his fly.

He glowered at her and looked down to see his own stiff sex emerge from its shelter. 'What do you think? Will it satisfy you?'

It was huge! She was secretly amazed at the size of it. Her whole body was amazed; alarm bells, tiny ones, rang in her mind, in her womb.

'Suck it,' he commanded, pushing her shoulders down.

'No,' she said. 'I want it here,' and she held it and pushed her own sex towards it. In truth she thought it would choke her if she took it into her mouth.

They searched for a soft, leafy spot under the trees and lay down. He pulled off his trousers and kneeled between her legs. He spread the rosy folds of her sex with a strange precision that echoed in his young face as the twisting of his cherry-red lips. His lashes shadowed the pale mauve of his eyes. He opened her sex so wide she felt the cool air chill the inner folds. She felt tight at the same time, she anticipated pain.

Then he was in, a little at first, pushing against the resistance of her panicking vaginal walls. And then the soft walls relaxed, opened and she took him all. The surprise of finding that her sex could stretch to give him a home was delightful. He moved with a frantic passion, undiluted passion. She held his downy young arse in her hands and marvelled at the firmness of it, the way the muscles moved. She opened, curled her legs over his calves, stretched her body to push her clitoris against the board that was his belly.

She had expected him to come quickly but he seemed to be in no hurry so she relaxed, she opened yet more, felt him deep inside her, pushed against him and had her orgasm as he had only just begun to emit the sounds of endings. With his final thrust he tore into her, like someone leaping over a cliff. Then he was quiet and he quickly rolled off her.

She lay alone, looking up at the sky between the leaves for a moment or two, then she felt his hand on her arm, stroking it like a little puppy wanting attention. She looked at him, his eyelashes sweeping his pale skin. She reached for him and took him in her arms.

They rode back slowly. He chattered nervously about all kinds of things. She wanted to ask was that his first time but he chattered and chattered.

The next time they played chess he was more damning in his criticism. He was sarcastic and hurt her feelings. She told him and he apologised. She felt as if he were acting like a woman who has lost her mystery to a seducer. It didn't endear him to her, it irritated her. She made an excuse for the following evening and went out to dinner in a nearby town with Euska. They went to a small theatre and laughed at the farce that was playing.

The next time she saw him she told him about the farce and he laughed at her for going to see something so unfashionable. She was really a bourgeois at heart, he said. She was happy with the mediocre.

Oruela felt hurt but she was still insecure. The failure that she felt she'd made of Paris so far had left her unsure. She imagined her clever little chess player was right. Her tastes were perhaps, dubious, unrefined as yet. Her doubts made her want his instruction and her body remembered his, how easily she had reached a climax with him. They stole into a barn on the way home and he took her in the hay.

Euska began to talk about going to Paris. Ernesto would be there soon. She had a lot to organise. They would be flying to London first. The liner they had chosen sailed from Southampton. Everything would be a rush.

Oruela thought there was something else that Euska

wasn't saying. Her little chess player had taught her to watch every move the other player made very carefully.

'I might stay here a while,' said Oruela casually.

'No!' said Euska, betraying herself.

'I'm going out for a walk,' said Oruela haughtily.

Euska rose to her feet. 'Oruela, please stay. We need to talk to each other. I thought that being here in the country we would be thrown together and we would have to. I have spoken to Albert about this. He agrees with me. It's no use – '

'What do you mean speaking to my friend about me?' shouted Oruela.

'Why shouldn't I?' said Euska, calmly. 'We both care about you.'

'I resent it,' said Oruela.

'I think Albert resents the fact that you've hardly seen him at all since we've been here.'

Oruela walked out of the cottage and Euska kicked herself for not keeping to the point. Her motherhood was lying heavily on her shoulders. It wasn't easy picking up the threads. The threads that had been broken so many years before. She didn't for one minute disapprove of Oruela's sexual experimentation but she observed that whatever was going on, of which she knew very little, was not making her daughter happy. She cursed Paul Phare, she cursed her own naïvety in thinking that Oruela, free of the Bruyeres and of the disastrous consequences of her own fateful decision, would find the path to a sense of herself an easy one.

Oruela walked to the village and found her little chess player in the café. He drank more these days, she noticed. He used not to drink during the day. When he saw her a slow smile spread across his face. He was playing a game with one of the old men and he went back to it.

Sitting, watching them and thinking, Oruela knew she didn't want this life at all, out here in the country. When the game finished she asked him to come to a

249

corner and talk. As he stood up from the table he was swaying.

She told him quietly that she was leaving, that their affair was over.

'No it's not,' he said, grabbing her arm roughly. 'No it's not. Not while I have life in my body.'

His words, the way his slow stare rested on her, chilled her to the bone. 'I'm sorry,' she said. She got up and walked out.

'No you don't!' he shouted.

Heads turned. He ran up the street after her, shouting, 'I love you. I love you. Don't leave me.'

She walked quickly and broke into a run but he was faster than her and fleet of foot. He caught up easily and held her arm again, tightly. He spoke loudly. A woman cleaning her doorstep stopped and stared at them.

Conscious of the attention they were drawing Oruela told him to keep his voice down.

'I won't!' he cried. 'I want the whole world to hear how much I love you!' His grip on her arm was hurting her. She pulled away but he held her tight. 'It's not over,' he said. 'Understand? It's not over.'

She struggled with him and eventually broke free. She walked quickly back towards the cottage. He kept up with her. 'You can't just use me and then go back to your comfortable life in Paris. You can't.' Over and over he said the same thing until she began to cry, even as she hurried along. His voice felt like torture. She ran into the cottage only to find it deserted. He followed her in and kept on talking. She became afraid he would force himself on her but he didn't, he just kept talking in that same voice, accusing her. Then he left, slamming the door after him.

The tears that flowed from her came from a deep well of sadness. She cried and she cried and she cried. Euska came back and found her still weeping.

The following morning dawned bright and they packed quickly and took a taxi to the station. Oruela looked over her shoulder frequently to see if he was following them, but the train drew in and they got on without bother.

Only when it was drawing out did she see him running alongside it swiftly, running, running, just running. She knew it was a threat, a gesture, no more, just to torment her.

That same evening the slop cart went as usual to the prison in St Trou. The driver parked the funny little three-wheeler under the kitchen chute and called at the kitchen door. The chef opened it and let him in.

The darkness of the compound was broken only by the single lamp burning at the porchway of the reception. The rooftops stood black against the deep night sky.

Kim caught her breath and waited behind a big chimney-stack until she heard the gate below locking up again. Then she ran at a crouch to the edge of the roof of the cell-block and looked down. The kitchen roof was a drop of about ten feet. She sprang into the air.

The roof hit her feet and she went into a roll, coming to a stop at the edge. She crawled along to the drain-pipe. Testing it first and finding it firm she swung her leg down on to the brick and carefully began to climb down. She dropped the last couple of feet into the slop car and flattened herself on the floor. She waited.

The sound of the mechanism of the chute door opening at the other end broke the quiet. She heard the men's voices as they lifted the bin. She heard the slop sliding down and the next moment she was buried under a huge mound of stinking pigswill.

The cart drove out of the gate and down the small country road towards the farm. As it reached a bend a figure leapt out of the back and stood gulping the air for a second or two. She stumbled into the wooded bank and dropped down into the river.

* * *

Paul had been to an old friend's house for a wonderful dinner. He was saying farewell to people he knew. His letter hadn't been answered but he had decided he was going to Paris anyway. A collector had bought more of his photographs, so he had plenty to live on and he had been reading about the new films that were being made in Paris. The dealer said he would introduce him to some people. Paul was unhappy that he hadn't heard from Oruela but he thought that perhaps if he was there and they should happen to run into each other he could at least explain and renew their friendship. He had new strength, new purpose. Whatever the future held, it was his and he could only try . . .

He was too drunk to find his key easily and he fumbled around on the doorstep looking for it. When he did locate it he muttered to it because it wouldn't go in the lock. Finally it went in and he turned it. He was about to step into the hallway when he felt a pair of hands on his back and he was pushed roughly inside.

In the darkness he fell against the wall and swore. He could hear her breathing hard. 'Damn it, Renée!' he cried.

'Please don't be frightened,' said an unfamiliar voice in the darkness. 'I didn't mean to hurt you.'

Paul sobered up immediately and punched the light switch. Kim stood there, filthy and blinking in the electric light. He looked her up and down and was not impressed. 'Who are you?' What do you want?' he demanded.

'I'm Oruela's friend. She gave me your address and I thought I might be able to trust you. I've escaped.'

The sense that this girl's whole life depended on his next words touched Paul's compassion. 'It's OK,' he said.

'I'm sorry I pushed you. I didn't want to have this conversation on the road,' she said.

Paul had a flash of recognition. 'Are you the dancer?' he asked.

'Yes,' she replied.

'Well,' he said. 'You'd better have a hot bath!'

She staggered, the relief and tiredness hitting her all at once. He took her arm and showed her upstairs. The water was not very hot but it was warm and when he had found her something to put on he tottered downstairs and brewed some coffee. He took it, on a tray, to the armchair by the window, closed the shutters and fell asleep.

Kim got half a tubful out of the geyser and washed the accumulated grime of the forest from her body. Her skin was scratched and torn in places and discoloured with bruises. She applied some of the witch hazel she found in the bathroom cabinet and wrapped herself in Paul's second-best dressing-gown. She padded down the stairs to find him still asleep.

She decided to drink the coffee without waking him up. It was delightful but it made her realise how hungry she was. She looked about in the kitchen for something to eat. There was bread but not much. She hesitated.

'Eat it!' said Paul behind her, yawning.

She turned to him with a grateful smile and he realised with a start that, without the dirt, she was gorgeous. He suddenly got very nervous and fled up to bed.

Kim's night's sleep was so sweet and so comfortable that it was really late when she got up. Something wonderful was cooking downstairs. She wrapped his dressing-gown round her and followed her nose. Paul had made fresh brioche. They ate it with butter and *confiture* and drank coffee. Kim filled in the details of her escape.

'How on earth could you hold your breath for so long?' he asked.

'I used to do it as a kid,' she said. 'In Martinique. We used to dive for coins and jewels that fell from the rich people's boats. We became a legend. The children that do it now are famous in America and tourists come especially to see them and throw them coins for luck.'

She had stolen a bicycle and rode all the way. She

planned to escape France, she told him, exactly the way she had entered it, by stowing away at La Rochelle on a ship. It would be easy enough if she could find one with a Caribbean crew who would help her. The hard part would be getting to La Rochelle.

'I'm too visible to travel in the open, even if I had the money to do it.' She paused and looked him straight in the eye. 'I don't plan to inconvenience you more than necessary. I shall be gone tonight. I just needed a rest.'

'Oh, don't go!' said Paul. 'I mean not before you want to. I'll be going in a week or so but you can stay here.'

'Thank you, I'd like to stay a little while,' she said 'But they may come looking for me.'

'I doubt if they'll come here,' he said. 'And I think I know a hiding place in an emergency.'

He led her upstairs to the darkroom. 'Under here,' he said and he removed a board from the underside of the developing tank. The space was small but she was slender enough. 'Try it,' he said.

He held the board while she wrapped herself around the U-bend like a handsome snake. His eyes lit up at the sight of her lithe legs. He repositioned the hardboard and pushed it back in place. But it wouldn't quite go.

'Wait,' she muffled from behind the board.

He stepped back as she rolled out from among the cobwebs lightly and stripped herself of the robe. She was entirely naked underneath and unselfconscious.

His gaze struck her like a wave strikes a beach. She tried not to think about it as she wrapped herself around the pipe again. This time the board fitted back nicely. She could be safely hidden.

Paul repeated that it was very unlikely they would come. In fact he repeated everything he'd already said twice more and went on about all kinds of rubbish, physically maintaining as much distance from her as the small darkroom would allow. He stood holding the board like an advertisement for a department store and

ooked stolidly at her feet. They were long and flat, the
skin irresistibly paler on their underside.

She pulled on the robe and belted it and stood looking
around her as he replaced the board.

'Alternatively,' he said, once she was dressed and
they were back down in the studio. 'You could come to
Paris. It would be easy enough to disappear in a large
city. I'm sure Oruela would love to see you, if she's still
there.'

'How is she?' asked Kim. 'I haven't heard from her in
a while, a long while, in fact. I'm not very good at letter-
writing I'm afraid. I suppose she got fed up of writing
and not getting a reply.'

Paul was stroking Nefi, who had come to see what
was going on. 'I don't know how she is. I haven't heard
anything at all.'

'Since when?' asked Kim.

'Since she went to Paris. Oh, I know I should have
written to her earlier, but I wrote a fortnight ago and
she hasn't replied,' he said sadly.

'It doesn't make any sense,' said Kim, almost to
herself.

Just then there was a knock at the door and Kim flew
upstairs to her hiding-place. It was Daisy and Annette
with some fish for Nefi and a little something for the
human spirit. Paul made an excuse and left them in the
studio while he went to tell Kim it was all right to come
downstairs if she wanted to. 'They're safe,' he said, 'but
I haven't said you're here.'

Kim decided there was no harm in it, if they could be
trusted. There might be advantage in knowing a few
more people, in case she decided to stick with her
original plan and not go to Paris.

Daisy took to Kim immediately. Her forthright way
of approaching things was easy to like. And Annette
remembered her dancing.

'Still no word?' said Annette.

Paul shook his head.

'There's a telephone here, isn't there?' asked Kim.

Paul nodded.

'It's a relatively new invention, Paul,' said Daisy, 'but you pick it up like this, see and you dial the number . . .'

'Look,' said Paul, 'I want Oruela to make her own decision, can you understand that? Anyway, I need some air. I'm going for a walk. Come on, Nefi.' Nefi trotted like an obedient dog out of the front door with him.

The three women exchanged looks as he left, expressing varying degrees of impatience. Men!

'In a way I can understand it,' said Daisy. 'She does have to make her own decision now. He's written to her.'

'Trust an Englishwoman to say that,' said Annette. 'Fair play and cricket, what? I wonder how you lot across the water ever get together.'

'What do you think I'm doing here?' said Daisy with a dirty grin.

'A man who lets you make your own decisions and isn't trying to mould you all the time is a rare thing,' said Kim. 'Worth having I reckon.'

'True,' said the other two sagely.

All I Want

Oruela arrived back in Paris feeling beaten and exhausted. She trudged up the stairs leaving Euska to collect the post, and opened the door of the apartment. As she walked into her mother's living-room it suddenly dawned on her how much she hated this place. It represented a life she had missed, one that could never be replaced. She made a decision. She would move out. She would find work. Anything to shrug off the awful sense of loss she felt in these rooms.

'There's a letter for you,' said Euska, as she came in. 'From Biarritz.'

Oruela went to her own room and opened the envelope. She curled herself up in the chair by the window to read it. It stirred mixed feelings within her. When she saw his name on the last page, which naturally she looked at first, her heart leapt and she willed it to be good news. But as she read, she grew angry and upset. If her own charms, if the love that she'd thought they had, weren't enough to pull him away from his sense of responsibility to a dead love affair, what was she supposed to do? What use was there in waiting? Only a nice girl would wait and she didn't feel nice. She felt betrayed.

She tossed the letter on the coffee table and left it

there. Over dinner that night she told Euska that she was going to find her own apartment and go back to modelling to pay the rent.

Euska agreed it was a good idea. 'But you don't have to get a job,' she said. 'I can give you an allowance. Let me, it will give you time to make a decision about what you really want to do.'

It wasn't easy to resist. Why work when you can be kept? Oruela rose early the next morning to go apartment-hunting.

The nice young porter stopped her on the way out. There was another letter. When she saw Paul's writing on the envelope she felt happier. It was a good sign. She put it in the deep pocket of her coat.

She called at a place that was advertised in the newspaper and didn't like it. She read the letter over coffee at her favourite café.

He told her about the result of the race, about Kim, and said he was arriving in Paris on a date about a week away. He hoped, he said, that he could visit her.

A smug little smile crossed over Oruela's face as she replaced the letter in the envelope and drank the remainder of her coffee. Yes, she thought. You can visit. But you are going to have to work very hard if you want anything more.

When she got back to the apartment she took out the first letter again and read it with new eyes. She could hear his voice as she read the words, see his face. It was all genuine, she could see that now, as her anger was softened by her growing sense of power. He really had stuck it out with Renée until the bitter end, until he could walk away honourably. A man like that, one who would always be there, standing in the shadows while his woman made her own mistakes, although hopefully not too many, a man who would let you live your own life . . . could be marriageable.

She emerged from a pleasant little daydream about ten minutes later and clapped her hands on her head. She knew she was hooked. Steady on, she told herself.

You'd better not let yourself be reeled in without a good struggle.

The afternoon post brought yet another letter, this time from Kim, who was worried in case Oruela had left Paris and wouldn't be there when they arrived. She felt bad about asking, she said, but she was hoping to stay with Oruela. She needed somewhere where she could lay low for a while. She had given up the idea of sailing back to the Caribbean straight away because the next boat with a Caribbean crew was not due to leave for another six weeks. With Paul coming to Paris she felt her chances were better if she accepted his offer of a lift.

Oruela put it to Euska who was more than happy to give Kim shelter. She also suggested that she invite Paul until he could find somewhere to rent. Oruela didn't think it was a good idea.

'How am I going to appear distant if he's staying here?' she asked her mother with exasperation.

'There'll be too many people around for you to be alone,' she said with a smile. 'And just think what it will do to him to be in such close proximity and unable to touch. You can't give him a completely cold shoulder now, can you? It's ideal really, for your purposes.'

So later that afternoon Oruela picked up the telephone and dialled Paul's number.

'Hello,' he grunted.

'It's Oruela,' she said.

'Oruela,' he cried, his voice leaping to life. 'Oh, thank God. I was beginning to think you had left Paris.'

'Well,' she said, wickedly, 'Euska's asked me to go to Rio with them.'

'And what have you decided?' he asked.

'Well, there are things to consider . . .' she said, trying desperately not to lie outright.

'I'm sure you'll come to the right decision,' he said.

God, he was a cool customer, she was thinking. But he was saying something else. 'When is she going? When do you have to decide by?'

'She's going in two weeks,' said Oruela.

'We'll be there before that,' he said. 'We'll be there next week . . .'

There was a brief silence between them. She wanted to hear him beg her to stay but even as she wanted it she knew a man like him would never do that.

'Euska's invited you both to stay here,' she said.

'Oh, that's really nice of her. Thank her from me,' he said.

There was another momentary silence.

'Well,' he said. 'See you next week then.'

'Yes,' she said.

'Kim wants to speak to you,' he said. 'I'll say goodbye.'

Kim came on the line and asked her to tell Euska she would be grateful for ever. She dropped her voice.

'And I want to hear what you've been up to. In detail,' she said. 'If there are any broken-hearted men in your wake tell them I'll soothe them . . .'

Oruela put the phone down and sat staring blankly into space. Euska came back into the room a moment later with a pile of clothes to go to charity.

'What's the matter?' she said, putting the bundle on a chair.

'I feel bad,' said Oruela. 'I told him you'd asked me to go to Rio and let him think I hadn't made a decision about it. I virtually lied to him. I don't want to start out by lying to him.'

Euska dropped the bundle on a chair and sat down next to Oruela on the couch. 'If it makes you feel any better,' she said, 'I don't think what you did was really wrong. I suppose it puts us in a bit of an odd situation because we'll all have to play along with it, but it's just a little mistake. Ernesto doesn't know. It's only you and I and I'll play along.'

'I thought I was so clever,' said Oruela. 'But I was stupid.'

'No, you weren't. You had your first taste of power and you made a very small mistake.'

'I don't feel comfortable with power,' said Oruela. 'I'm no good at it.'

'What's the alternative?' said Euska. 'You left it in his hands when we came here and it didn't work because he didn't write to you until it was almost too late. Do you want to live like that?'

'No. But I want a marraige that isn't about power,' said Oruela.

'*Ma chérie*,' said Euska, 'if it's a marriage you want then you had better keep the power in your own hands. Only a woman who has it knows how delightful it is to relinquish it in the right place at the right time. Women who let men have control are fools. Men don't know their ABC when it comes to love.'

'But how can you respect a man that you have such power over?' said Oruela.

'You already love him, don't you. You already respect and admire him? You won't lose that unless you lose respect for yourself. Besides I don't expect he'll be easy to rule. You won't tire of him quickly.'

Oruela felt thoroughly confused. She picked up her apartment-hunting without enthusiasm. But it was when she saw the third place, early in the evening, that the confusion cleared. It was lovely. It really was. It had a glass roof at the back. It was a storey higher than the other buildings around it and so it looked down on the world. The glass roof sloped to the floor and had a little door in it that led out on to a flat balcony. It was just perfect.

But she kept looking at it through Paul's eyes. How he would love the light. How he could change that room into a darkroom. How that would be their bedroom and she would have her desk in the corner there . . .

She wanted him. She wanted to live with him and wake up in the morning in his arms. She wanted to make love to him under the stars as they shone through the roof.

'I'll take it,' she said to the landlady.

'Good,' said the woman. 'I think you will be happy here.'

Euska approved of her decisiveness and they formed a plan. Oruela wouldn't move in. She would stay until Euska had gone and then would move in with Paul. She would pretend to have just found it. If he didn't want to live with her and make love to her under the stars then she would move in and find somebody else who would. Oruela had made up her mind. She knew what she wanted.

Ernesto came home the following morning and caught her humming the wedding tune.

'Is there news I should know?' he asked.

'No,' she said, giving him a hug.

'All will be revealed,' said Euska, taking her turn.

'I'm going out to buy a dress,' said Oruela. 'Back for lunch.' And she closed the door behind her.

When Euska and Ernesto were alone he asked, 'What kind of dress? Is there a second wedding in the offing?'

'You'll know what happens when the times comes,' she said.

'Hmmmm,' he said. He came close to her and held her hands. He edged them round the back of her body and held them there. 'You know what is going to happen to you right now, don't you?'

She smiled. 'Show me,' she said.

And he edged her backwards into their bedroom and closed the door behind him.

Oruela spent her allowance for the week on a beautiful cashmere dress that felt like a dream and clung to her shoulders and breasts like a second skin. It fell straight to her hips and the skirt was cut on the bias so that it drifted round her thighs and swayed when she walked.

She bought some new lingerie, some silk and lace camisoles and soft, handmade knickers with delicate little ribbons. She bought beautiful lace garters and fine silk stockings. She even bought chocolates, dark, bitter-sweet little nuggets of pure heaven.

That night she went out with her friends from the café to the Bal Negre and watched the African men dance with the society girls around the floor, gradually loosening them up. The men gave everything to the dance, to the women, while their white men sat and talked with each other at the tables, seemingly and perhaps genuinely unperturbed. Why should they be? They owned the goods. There were a few African women too, not as many as men but to Oruela's eyes they seemed to be setting the pace. The jazz singer was a black woman with a huge voice, an American. Her voice hit the womb and opened love out into a three-dimensional flower of many shades and depths.

'What are you thinking?' asked a middle-aged poet who was next to her at the table.

'About love,' she said.

'Do you need love?' he asked her.

'Of course,' she said.

'Let me show you love tonight,' he said. 'Have you ever made love to a mature man like me?'

She was tempted, sorely tempted. There was something quite fascinating about his looks. He had penetrating grey eyes.

'Not tonight,' she said.

'When?' he asked.

'I'll let you know if I decide,' she said, and turned back to the music.

The days stalked by. The city grew crisp and chillier. The boxes belonging to Euska piled up in the big hallway of the apartment one by one.

Part of Oruela thought over the things that had happened since she'd come to Paris and resented Paul again for making her wait. She looked up the middle-aged poet and visited him.

It was a strange afternoon. He didn't leap on her. He sensed, perhaps, that she wasn't really looking for sex.

They smoked hashish together instead and talked about love. His views were not dissimilar to Euska's. Women, he said, know much more about the way people work – in general, he said. 'Some don't, of course, and some men do.' He drifted off into his own thoughts.

Oruela pulled out Baudelaire from the bookshelf and read poems that made her senses expand. 'Borrow it,' he told her. 'Bring it back another day.' She read it for days afterwards and then started writing herself. Her lines seemed childish to her and she threw them away.

It was raining on the day that Paul and Kim were due to arrive. She felt jumpy from the minute she got up. They were driving through the night to try to avoid Kim being spotted. At last, about ten, she saw a car draw up, the rain streaming off its flanks. She saw Paul get out and turn up the collar of his raincoat. She saw the familiar form of him, his hair, his shoulders. Her heart sang and her womb thudded.

Kim didn't wait for him to help her out of the car. She climbed out and stretched. She saw Paul place his hand on her back and guide her into the building. Something about the body language made a shaft of unease cross Oruela's mind.

Oruela flew into the bedroom and slipped on the dress. She looked stunning. It wasn't just the dress. Her skin glowed, her eyes were lively, her mouth was very kissable.

Ernesto opened the door and in they came. Kim ran to her and hugged her first and Paul kissed Euska on the cheek and shook Ernesto's hand. Then he walked into the living-room where she and Kim were. If Oruela had been in any doubt about what her true feelings were, she would have been relieved of it by the fact that the mere sight of him made her sex dance inside like some genie who needs a rub to get out.

He came over.

'Hello,' he said.

'Hello,' she said.

And they stood there for what seemed like an age,

just looking at each other. It wasn't an age. It was only a couple of seconds. The maid asked him for his coat and it broke the spell.

She was aware, as she moved about the apartment, showing him his room, ordering coffee and sitting on the couch with her legs curled under her, that he didn't take his eyes off her.

Euska noticed it too and made sure that either she or Ernesto or Kim were with them the whole time.

'What's going on?' said Ernesto quietly in the bedroom. 'Don't you want me to continue helping you with your packing?'

'This is more important,' said Euska, and she pushed him back towards the living-room.

That night when they were tucked up in bed, Oruela told Kim about her plan to stay and move into the little apartment with Paul. 'You can stay here as long as you like,' she said. 'Euska and Ernesto will be back in the spring next year.'

'Thanks,' said Kim. 'It'll give me some time. I don't think you'll have any trouble getting what you want. I really don't. He's really serious about you.'

'But it has to be right. I don't want to have to wait again like I did before. It has to be right this time. I want it my way.'

Kim grinned. 'Good for you,' she said.

It crossed Oruela's mind to ask Kim if anything had happened between the two of them. But she thought better of it.

Paul lay in his bed on the other side of the wall wondering. He might be in love but he wasn't stupid. He saw through Euska's manoeuvrings as clear as through a sheet of glass. He guessed it was some mild punishment for his silence for all those weeks. Every woman he knew thought he had been wrong and he knew they were right really, deep down. He considered the facts. If she was seriously displeased then she wouldn't have had him to stay, would she? Given that

265

he was sleeping in the very next room – the thought of it gave him an erection – he sensed it was a matter of waiting. He hoped it wouldn't be too long.

The next few days were an intense mixture of happiness and frustration for them both. There really was no chance to be alone in the apartment. There was the continual hustle and bustle of preparations. Once and once only they had some time alone and only because they met on the street. She had bought a table for the new apartment and had gone there to see it delivered. He had been to meet some film people.

'Come and have a drink with me,' he said. 'We've hardly had a chance to talk since I arrived. I like talking with you.'

They went to Le Dôme and drank beer. They talked about the misunderstandings and he promised never to be so stupid again. It was disarming.

'Have you made a decision about Rio?' he asked, when their second beer arrived.

She couldn't lie to him. 'I'm not going,' she said.

The smile that spread across his face was worth it. He beamed! She rested her elbow on the table and smiled back at him.

'Come here,' he said, and he kissed her lightly on the lips.

They walked back to the apartment together along the crowded, lively streets. 'The whole world is here,' he said. 'This is the place to be. I know it. If people like us are going to make a success of what we do, this is the time and place to do it.'

'I can take the entrance exam again if I want to,' she said.

'Do it,' he said. 'You've nothing to lose.'

That night they all went to a club. Kim was feeling brave and fed up of being inside when life was going by out in the city. So they chanced it. She didn't stand out. People from all over the world had gravitated to Paris and the excitement it offered.

If anything, Paul looked more hungry for Oruela. He watched her movements with his smoky green eyes as she and Kim were talking. Oruela caught him and when their eyes met he gave her a look that started her juices flowing.

The following day, though, it all stopped. Ernesto came across the article in the newspaper in the morning. In an American clock factory a group of women workers had been dreadfully poisoned and they had discovered the cause was the radium-based paint that they were using to paint the luminous clock faces. There were terrible predictions of deformed children, a slow death. The news provided an answer to the cause of Norbert Bruyere's death, but it also struck terror into their hearts.

Ernesto rang his doctor immediately and he told them he would meet Oruela at the Institute right away. Paul and Euska went with her and tests were done while they waited in the hall. The results would take three days. Ernesto and Euska put off their plans to spend a day or two in London before sailing. Everyone wondered if Euska would sail at all.

She continued packing. Everyone tried to act as normally as possible but it was difficult. There wasn't one of them that wasn't scared stiff.

They went back three days later. They all went. No one wanted to be left alone. Everything seemed fine, the doctor told them. The initial tests had all proved completely negative. They would monitor Oruela over the next few months but she seemed to have escaped harm because the doses she had been exposed to were so tiny.

It was the last day before Euska and Ernesto were due to sail and the rest of the afternoon belonged to Euska and Oruela. They both knew that it was right to say goodbye to each other, at least temporarily at this point. There would be time to reflect before they saw each other again. Having agreed this they spent a lovely afternoon together.

The same afternoon Kim had a revolution all on her own and went out and got a job in the chorus at Le Sphinx. Not only that, she met a black American trumpet player, a man as big as a house, she said. She was convinced he was the man of her dreams. She was to start that very night and she went off early to the club.

The other four decided to go to the club for Euska and Ernesto's farewell.

'And my return,' said Oruela. 'I feel like I've come back from the dead.'

Over cocktails the men went into a conspiratorial huddle. Euska had plenty of people to say goodbye to at La Coupole and everyone wished her *bon voyage* but Oruela wanted to know what was going on.

'We were talking about the idea of you and I flying to England with them to say goodbye,' said Paul.

'Oh yes!' said Oruela. 'I'd love to fly. Can we?'

'I don't see why not,' said Ernesto. 'I've hired our own plane.'

Kim looked delicious in her satin and feathers costume. She did little except bend and sway in the background with thirty other beauties. She joined them at their table after the show. But she wasn't staying. Things, it seemed, had progressed.

'I sort of ambushed him in the wings,' she told Oruela. 'The sparks were really flying and he's asked me out drinking. So don't expect me home . . .'

'We're going to England,' said Oruela.

'You and Paul?'

'Yes.'

'Marvellous,' said Kim. 'Have a good time.'

'You too,' said Oruela.

And then they both had the same thought at once. 'We'll give them one each for Marthe,' said Kim.

'I'll drink to that,' said Oruela.

Kim arrived home just after dawn, as the taxi that was coming to take them to the airfield was chugging up the street. She managed to let Oruela know in no uncertain terms that she was in love and wouldn't miss them a bit.

It was essential to wrap up well, even for the short hop over the water but even under her furs Oruela, sitting close by Paul in the plane, could feel a different tension. As soon as her mother was out of the way, things, she sensed, would warm up considerably.

They both enjoyed their first time flying and Oruela found herself thinking along very practical lines about how they had a lot in common as far as tastes went. Would they like each other in bed though? It was strange, for once, to be thinking so calmly about it but there was so much at stake. If they did like each other this could easily last a long, long time. It wasn't only air turbulence that gave her stomach little jolts.

The coastline of England appeared below, breaking the monotony of the grey sea and soon after, their descent began. Oruela gripped Paul's hands as the wheels of the tiny plane hit the tarmac and they sped along the ground at incredibly high speed. She opened her eyes to see him laughing at her. But there was no malice in it. She guessed he'd been a bit nervous too.

Having spent more time in Paris than planned, they were driving straight to the port. The liner was waiting in dock to sail on the afternoon tide. It was an American ship, the Atlantic Queen and it was 40,000 tons of pure luxury. They all went on board and made their way through the hustle and bustle of wealthy travellers, old and young, of porters, of stewards who were courteous to the passengers and barked at each other. Their uniforms, Oruela noted, were very dashing. But real wonder was reserved for the quarters that were to be Euska and Ernesto's home for the crossing. Everything was sumptuous. Floor to ceiling windows looked out on to the dockside where a band was assembling to play farewell. They ordered brandy to warm themselves up and peeled off their flying clothes for a tour of the ship.

The staterooms were magnificent, great high ceilings lavishly decorated with chandeliers, with filigree screens. The staircases were wrought iron. Elegant women glided up and down speaking in the American drawl that sounded so exotic to Oruela's ears. She noticed, too, how they looked hungrily at Paul and how he seemed completely oblivious to their attention.

The minutes ticked inexorably by and soon they had turned into an hour and the sailors were giving the call that all on board who were not sailing were to make their way ashore. Oruela and Paul were almost the last to leave. Euska and Oruela hugged for a long time.

'Be happy,' said Euska.

'You too,' said Oruela.

Then finally they were saying goodbye. Paul and Oruela walked down the gangplank on to the dock and waited in the chilly, damp air, huddled together as Euska and Ernesto did the same on deck.

The sailors threw ropes and as the ship began to move the band on the shore played a lucky song. There were tears and waving of hankerchiefs and the great floating hotel moved slowly out into the sea. Paul and Oruela stayed long after most people had left, watching the big white stern sail off. He held her close.

Eventually she turned around and looked up at him. He was hers now. She kissed his cold nose.

The car was waiting to take them back to the airport.

'It doesn't seem right,' she said as they settled in the back, 'to come to England for the first time and stay for only a few hours.'

'Would you like to stay, go to London perhaps?'

'Could we?'

'*Porquoi pas*?' he said. 'Why not?'

The city was misty when they arrived. It was after five and as they drove across Waterloo Bridge in the taxi crowds of bowler-hatted commuters streamed towards the railway station. The back of the cab had become cosy and warm. It felt like their world now, to do with as they wished.

'Have you got any ideas about where you'd like to stay?' said Paul.

'Ernesto stays at the Savoy when he's in London,' said Oruela. 'He has an account.'

'Do you want to stay there?' said Paul.

'No,' she said. 'I want to stay somewhere we've discovered ourselves. I want to get away from their influence. I don't want to follow in their footsteps any more.'

Paul smiled. 'I agree,' he said. 'What about Bloomsbury? I've heard about Bloomsbury.'

'Yes,' she said.

He was just about to tell the taxi-driver to go to Bloomsbury when he stopped.

'I've just realised something,' he said. 'You're not wearing a wedding ring.'

'Oh,' she said.

The taxi driver looked over his shoulder. 'Pardon me for eavesdropping, guv'nor,' he said, 'but there's a jewellers' in the Strand here. I happen to know because the wife and I bought her a wedding ring there, sir, and it brought me luck, I can tell you. She's as good a wife as any man could wish for.'

Oruela got the gist of this and began to giggle. They stopped at the place he suggested and paid him. He gave Paul directions to Bloomsbury and Oruela looked around her. The street seemed to be full of the sights she'd always associated with London: big red buses, men in caps selling newspapers to men in bowler hats, a theatre across the street had its lights on and its doors open waiting for the audience to arrive. She drank it all in. She had a delicious sense of being alone with Paul, a sense of adventure.

They went into the shop and spent ages choosing. It wasn't easy. How real was it? Would they ever really get married and, if so, would they keep this one? These were questions they couldn't even think of discussing.

Not there, not in the shop, with the obsequious shop assistant doing his best to please.

Eventually they saw one that they both liked. It was plain but it wasn't too cheap. The assistant put it in a box and Paul paid for it.

Outside in the glow of the doorway he took it out of its wrapping and took her left hand. 'I now pronounce you my wife,' he said. 'It's a bit of a risk really, I don't even know if you are any good in bed.'

Her mouth dropped open. 'You!' she said, and then she stopped and fixed him with a look. There was fire in her eyes. 'Heel,' she said, and pointed to her ankle.

For a moment he looked utterly perplexed and then a look of wonder spread across his face as he realised that she was putting him in his place. He reached out his hand, offering it to her. She took it and they walked out into the street.

The woman on the hotel desk was obviously suspicious but being foreign helped. They weren't questioned too closely. Paul's English was pretty good, although he had had most of his conversation practice with Daisy and so produced a fine cockney vowel or two which seemed to offend the woman's nose.

At last they closed the door of their room behind her and burst out laughing. The fire crackled in the grate. The room was cosy. There was a big iron bed with a lace cover and a window that looked out on to the street below. Outside the lamplights gleamed in the mist and the almost bare branches of the trees in the square below threw shadows across the pavement. It had grown quiet in the street in the hour before the city livened up again with nightlife.

Paul took off his coat and came close behind her as she stood by the window.

'Hungry?' he asked. 'Would you like to find somewhere to eat?'

'Not particularly,' she said, her voice was a little unsteady. She certainly wasn't going to say exactly what she did want.

He didn't need to ask. As he enclosed her in his arms her body became warm with life.

He helped her off with her coat and threw it on the chair with his own. She stood in her dress, the fine cashmere with its high neck. The soft material hugged her.

'That's a lovely dress,' he said. But he didn't mean that at all and she knew what he meant, because of the way he looked through the material and wanted what was underneath. His eye touched her, made her aware of her nipples becoming hard.

What was it about him that she liked so much, she asked herself silently. He took her by the small of her back and drew her close, bending his head down to meet and snare her eyes in a tender, rude question that could only be answered by an equal. She felt a smile curling on her lips, a faint smile shining in her eyes, its light betraying shadows of a deep feminine fear and desire. She drew her head back a little and looked at his lovely face, his lashes, his fine, straight nose with one or two freckles. This was all hers! This man, this soul, this person, wanting her as much as she wanted him.

Then she looked at his lips and she was captured. They were soft, sensual lips that kissed gently at first, tasting her, and then his hand slid up her back between her shoulder blades and drew her very, very close. She touched his neck, curled her fingers into the hair at the back and as his kiss became stronger, more urgent, she drank him in.

He drew away first and closed the curtains against the last of the outside world, then he took off his jacket and she watched his fine shoulders and his strong arms emerge in the shirt sleeves and touched the crisp fabric. Her fingers were so sensitive that the warm urgency of his body seemed to flow into her through their tips. She ran her hands up to his shoulders and round and down on to the silk back of his waistcoat. He touched the knot of his tie and she stopped him with her hands, taking the task away from him. She loosened the red knot and opened the collar. She pulled the tie apart as he unbuttoned his waistcoat and then she started on his shirt buttons.

Slowly she undid them to the waist and then she pulled out the shirt from his waistband and he gasped with the sensation of the fabric sliding across his skin. He slipped off his shirt and stood before her naked to the waist. The bulge in his trousers was evident.

He was really lovely and the sight made her wet between her thighs. He had a small amount of hair on his chest and the way his shoulders fanned out from his pectorals was fascinating, but Oruela didn't have that long to feast her eyes because he wanted her close and he took her body in his arms. He reached for the fastening at the back of her dress and slipped it undone and then he peeled the dress down from her shoulders. It dropped to the floor and, as if he were manoeuvring one of his models into a pose, he gently took her by the shoulders and sat her on the edge of the bed while he removed his trousers with one quick movement.

His arse was in perfect proportion with the rest of his body and his legs were long and Oruela almost purred out loud like a pussy-cat who has got her cream. But there wasn't long to look.

Quickly, he joined her on the bed and his strong hands enclosed her; strong, confident hands holding her ribs, feeling the curve of her waist as he shifted up her silky camisole, bringing his palm around to her belly and reaching upwards to the softness of her breasts where he paused . . . He stroked the outline with his fingers, mapping the unknown with the care of a renaissance painter, making her skin come alive with colour, light, electricity and sound.

Mouth. She wanted his mouth on them now. She wriggled herself out of the silk and lace and gave her breasts to his lips. He kissed and sucked their heaviness in his mouth, wetting the skin, licking the whole of one and then the whole of the other. She stretched her arms back lazily and gave herself up to the sensation of his lick, lick, lick, warm and wet. He took her nipples between his fingers and rolled them, he pulled a little, stretching the sensation out so that it became sharper, so that shocks crackled among her ribs and earthed in her hips, and then he massaged her breasts strongly, sending the blood tumbling in her skin and making her feel as if she'd never had her breasts loved till now. She rotated her shoulder and pushed one breast deep into his hungry mouth so that the white crescent squashed into his face and he snorkled. When he stopped momentarily to take some air the shock of the air left her skin bereaved.

He kissed her belly and she screamed with tenderness. She took his shoulder and pushed him on to his back. His hands encircled her waist as he fell into the softness of the big cotton- and lace-covered mattress. She stretched her torso and put her breasts again in his mouth each in turn and he sucked until she was satisfied and gave him her lips to kiss instead.

He rolled her on to her side and ran his hands down to the waistband of her knickers. He slipped his hand inside, on her hip, and pulled the fabric away. When she was bare he stroked the rounded softness of her arse.

'You're beautiful,' he said and she felt it. She kissed him, kissed his mouth, his chest.

His head was at her belly again, his mouth at her groin, first one side then the other, kissing her, eating her and then he kissed her hair there and pulled it gently with his teeth. His bite became stronger. He took the bulky, hair-covered flesh and squeezed it between his teeth until she screamed again because it was so strange the way it pulled the rest of her sex, the way it pulled the buried heart of her desire into the jaws of a certain and painless death.

Then he left her there, like that, open and dying while he divested himself of his underwear. She opened her eyes and glimpsed his cock standing straight and heavy in the curls of his body hair, but it was only a glimpse because he was with her again quickly, his body between her legs, his hands opening her thighs, stroking the soft skin at the top, moving to her sex and massaging round and around the heart of it, rolling the sensitive flesh in his fingers and sliding in. His thumb enticed her clitoris while another finger massaged inside until she was desperate to have his cock inside her and she raised one leg, spreading her sex wide so that he had no choice.

As he raised himself, she waited for the moment of truth with her whole body rigid inside, tense. There it was pushing, entering, the shiny pulsing sex of him, piercing the tenseness and making her love flow over him, bringing her the first peace. His whole body covered hers, she clung, burying her face in his neck and shoulders, pushing her hips to meet his and taking all his sex inside her.

The delight of having what she had been wanting for so long gave her an immediate charge, purely physical, that made her feel as if her body had jumped into a different existence. She was overwhelmed by a sense of being at one with him. He kissed her face, her ears, every bit of her that he could, and he whispered her name and held her tight.

She wanted to say his name but she couldn't form the word. Her spine was undulating, her belly touched his, her breasts slid against his chest. She kissed his waist with her inner thighs. She grasped her man by the shoulders and she printed herself on his pelvic bone.

And then the good stuff started. The heat and the sweat and the muscles working hard, the aquaplaning breasts and Queen cunt doing what she's best at, hot and heavy and lush. The first thud of her climax jumped at him like a tiger taking the plunge, its stripes rippling as it surprised its prey and rolled with it until it was conquered.

Who conquered? Who was defeated? She first, then him, filling her heart as he filled her sex and collapsed, spent.

They lay together for a long time, entwined, kissing, until they felt time ticking away in the room on the mantelpiece and looked at the clock.

'I'm starving,' she admitted and so they dressed, which was difficult because they couldn't stop kissing each other's skin as it was hiding itself from sight.

They found a chop-house that had stayed open late and ate lamb and peas and grilled tomatoes that tasted to Oruela as if they had just fallen from the plant that bore them. They had a discussion about the paying of the bill and decided that, because Paul wanted to, he should pay this time but they would share their expenses so that questions of money would never be an issue. They both knew that they were speaking about the future and that it was going to be their own personal struggle.

They each thought about it on the walk back to the hotel holding hands. Then Paul spotted a tavern and they went in and drank ale from big heavy glasses and studied the occupants of the room, who were few and absorbed by their beer or their books. The drink made them mellow and they left like spirits, without disturbing the timeless drinking of the men. As they walked lazily back to the hotel in the sweet darkness they talked about the future. He was excited about film-making, she about studying. But overall they were excited about each other. They didn't dare say so. Not yet.

As she lay beside him on the edge of sleep, she felt truly wonderful and she dreamed of great palatial doors opening and opening into infinity.

They both woke early, excited even subconsciously by each other's presence. She opened her legs and wrapped them around him and they made love in the chilly dawn. Afterwards he stroked her body as she drifted back into a half-sleep. Beneath his fingers her skin became known, became his as the minutes ticked by on the big old clock. At eight-fifteen exactly, when she was sleeping, purring softly, the clock ran out of spring. It stopped ticking and he lay listening to her breathing, to the faint sounds of the city going to work outside, imagining that they had stepped outside of time. He kissed her awake. He took her mouth and drank, he took her breasts and sucked, he kissed her belly and her hair and he buried his head, his lips in her salty cave, and she came awake at the point of no return.

She pushed him on his back and she straddled him. She enclosed him with a single slide and she rode him until her orgasm came like a horsewoman from the apocalypse. She fell off him and rolled and he rested back on the pillows, doomed. He knew it and he loved it. Briefly they lost consciousness of each other.

They were awoken by a knock on the door. A man's voice outside asked them did they want breakfast in bed and Paul, coming to first, covered Oruela's precious body with a sheet. He looked around the room. It was in complete turmoil. 'Yes,' he called. 'Hold on a moment.' He put on his shorts and went to the door. An ancient waiter, bent in the middle, stood there with a heavy tray. 'Let me take it,' said Paul.

'It's all right, sir,' he said. 'I'll bring it in.' And he did. He didn't bat an eyelid at the state of the room.

Oruela sat up, pulling up the coverlet, as he came back in and closed the door. She looked charming, all full of love and morning sex. He poured out two cups of tea and put one on the bedside table for her before climbing back into the warmth of the bed beside her. They sipped the hot brew.

Later they dressed and went to the British Museum where they marvelled at the Egyptian gods and goddesses in the quiet, still rooms, where they gazed at manuscripts written and drawn hundreds and hundreds of years before and where, on the staircase, when no one was looking, they kissed softly and quickly and held hands.

In the afternoon they went to a department store in

Oxford Street and bought underwear and a small suitcase. He sat a bit primly in the women's department, fiddling with his hat on his knees as the assistant showed her a selection. She brought him over a beautiful set of fine broderie anglaise underwear and asked if he liked it. He blushed crimson, making her laugh.

Then they went back to the hotel and he let her know who was boss.

After two days in London in a cocoon of love and sex they grew tired of tourist sites and made a crackly telephone call home to Daisy who squealed a lot and gave them her mum's address in the East End.

It was as they walked through the dark, narrow streets with the railway bridges overhead that Oruela became scared of something unknown. Paul held her close and told her that any murderous fiend had better watch out because she was his and he loved her and would let no one touch her.

It tripped off his tongue easily, the little phrase that meant so much. It had all seemed so natural and easy but now she knew she was scared. She became obsessed with doubts that it couldn't last. She kept quiet about it though and shook off the doubts in the parlour of Daisy's mum's little terraced house that was filled with family and furniture.

Later that night in bed, Paul sensed she was troubled but he didn't ask her what was wrong. He held her close, wrapping her skin in love and kissed away the phantoms. He held her close until she relaxed and turned to him and reached for his sex.

But the spell had been broken and she wanted to say goodbye to London and the little hotel where they had first made love and leave her doubts behind. He was good at sensing her moods. He agreed that they should go back to Paris. The day they left dawned bright and clear. The ferry boat was only half full of travellers. They sat wrapped up on deck and watched the white cliffs disappear.

On the train between Calais and Paris, as the twilight descended, he brought up a subject that had been on his mind since they left England

'I want you to live with me,' he said. 'I want to find somewhere where we can be together all the time.'

Oruela's whole body felt his words. She exulted. Her smile gave him the reply he wanted, even before she spoke. 'When we came back from the countryside I looked at a place that I liked,' she said.

'Let's see if it's still vacant then. Tomorrow,' he said.

They arrived back in time to go to dinner at the club where Kim worked and they told her the news. To Oruela's surprise Kim's reaction was understated, even a bit subdued. Oruela hustled her off to the powder-room.

'What's the matter?' Aren't you pleased for me?' she said.

'Yes,' said Kim. 'But I don't know about moving in with men. Every woman I know who has done it says they take you for granted in the end.'

'But that's a long way down the road,' said Oruela. 'Besides, I think I can keep him interested.' And she smiled a lewd smile. 'Anyway, what's made you so cynical? How's Earl?'

Kim grunted.

'What's the matter?' asked Oruela.

'He gives me the best loving I've ever had in my life and he's talking about marrying me and taking me off to America.'

'But that's lovely!' squealed Oruela.

'What do I want to marry the first man I've had since you-know-where for?' Kim wailed. 'I don't want to get wafted out of existence on some pink cloud of romance and I don't want to go to America.'

'You don't love him then?' asked Oruela.

'That's the problem. I think I might. I'm falling, I really am. Seriously. And I'll end up with kids and washing. I'm not doing it. I don't want to be anyone's slave and you'd better watch it too.'

The thought of laundry stirred Oruela up somewhat and two militants exited the powder-room.

'What do you think about housework?' said Oruela, when Kim had gone backstage.

'Housework?' said Paul. 'What do you mean?'

'Do you think women should do it?'

He smiled. 'I think we should get a maid,' he said.

Oruela had to go through some silly pretences in order to keep up the illusion that she hadn't yet rented the place. It meant telephoning no one, popping out to 'pick up the key' early while he was still in his pyjamas. But it was worth it. Knowing something he didn't made her feel more secure, more certain of her own strength.

He loved the apartment as much as she did and then she had to stop him wanting to sign the lease. 'I'll do it,' she said. 'It's my first home of my own. I want to.' And he accepted that without so much as a whisper.

They moved in. They put the bed next to the sloping glass roof. They filled up the cracks that let in the cold. They stored plenty of wood for the stove. They made the place sunny even when the sky was grey, with flowers and fabrics and lots and lots of love.

As they got to know each other better their fucking became deeper, closer to the bone, her orgasms became bigger, longer lasting. They made love in the bed under the stars, and against the sink with her arse squashed against the cold enamel. They went back to the bed and they spent whole days naked together with the stove blazing out heat to warm them.

Her body felt good all the time. People complimented her on her appearance. Often, if she happened to be alone, in a café, the men passing by would turn and look at her with hungry looks. She barely noticed.

* * *

281

Kim persuaded Earl to stay in Paris. It was the centre of things, she argued. Everyone was there. Everything was happening. She didn't want to go to America and have to sit in seperate bars from white people. There were no 'No Coloureds' signs in Paris to kill your spirits. The whole city was alive and exciting. He was convinced. He had plenty of work. The Parisians loved his music.

He took Kim and Oruela and Paul to a club where the musicians went to jam sometimes. The small, basement room was crowded with people from all over the world. Oruela and Kim talked quietly about the variety of men. All shapes and sizes, all colours, all shades of sexuality. The two women whispered their fantasies to each other. Nice though, they agreed, to have someone to go home with.

Paul was about as good as a man could be when it came to the domestic arrangements. But Oruela ended up barefoot and pregnant.

He took photographs of her as she swelled and they made love so that the infant would feel good. It wasn't all bliss. The labour was sheer pain but the newly born baby, all wet and slippery, mewling on her thighs. That was something.